Pulse racing, she crept back to the house and peered over a row of hedges. She paused, her blood suddenly surging with fresh adrenaline. The white station wagon was parked in the driveway.

All systems in her body sprang to life. But she would not make her move until she spent time observing, planning, thinking. In the light rain, she staked out a surveillance position behind a stand of evergreens that sheltered the ranch house opposite, and was relieved to find all its windows dark and no cars in the driveway.

The minutes ticked away, broken only by a passing train in the distance and her own heartbeat. To the far left, a few curtained windows flickered with the blue-white lights of after-midnight televisions. Would these insomniacs ever dream that something more terrible, more gripping than the movies they were perhaps watching, might be happening on their quiet street?

She glanced at her watch. 2:50. Had Katya been able to get any sleep, she wondered, and drew in a breath. Would she find Sam? Quickly, she turned on her flashlight to test it, when a clatter of metal spun her around.

"*Merde*," she muttered under her breath as a pair of masked faces froze in the beam of her flashlight.

ยฬ฿ ยฬ฿ ยฬ฿

Corners of the Heart

Leslie Grey

RISING
TIDE
PRESS

Rising Tide Press
5 Kivy Street
Huntington Station, NY 11746

Printed in the United States

The publishers wish to thank all of the friends who helped to make this book possible: Edna G., Adriane B., Pat G., Harriet E., Beth H., Bobbi B., Marian S.,and Evelyn R.

In Memoriam: Rising Tide Press dedicates this book to the memory of Marie Harrison, a former staff member, who devoted much of her good will, humor, time, and energy to the success of the Press. We will remember her with love.

Publisher's note:
All characters, places and situations in this book are fictitious and any resemblance to persons (living or dead) is purely coincidental.

First printing May, 1993
10 9 8 7 6 5 4 3 2 1

Edited by Alice Frier and Lee Boojamra
Book cover design and illustration by Evelyn Rysdyk

Grey, Leslie
        Corners of the Heart/ by Leslie Grey

ISBN 0-9628938-3-8

Library of Congress Catalog Card Number 92-062810

Acknowledgments

To Blinn:
Just for being yourself. You make living a gift; loving a privilege; writing an inspiration, and healing an art. One dose of your laughter every four hours, and I'd never have to call a doctor in the morning.

To *F*:
For keeping me real and in tune with my muse.

To *Lee Boojamra* and *Alice Frier* at Rising Tide Press:
For your gifted editing and never-ending patience, and for your compassion and encouragement.

To *Peg*: For helping me see the whole of the parts.

Corners of the Heart

I crave the last shuddering sigh
of your body poised on slumber's doorstep;
the first early yawn of morning's promise.
I ache to hear your healing laughter—
the thoughtful pause between your words.
I thirst to think the essence of your eyes—
To breathe the heady air
you breeze through
as I ride your wing-ed feet.
They seem to swallow up whole sidewalks.
I yearn to join our shadows,
and all the corners of our hearts.
I want to share the awesome journey
to the light.

Leslie Grey

❦ 1 ❦

*K*atya Michaels wanted her life in order. She wanted it predictable, like the carefully-placed pegs in her log cabin, not like the knots, ragged and random, that stared out at her. She shucked her wading boots, leaned her flyrod against the cedar porch, and relaxed, allowing her eyes to sweep across the wooded property that had become her haven.

Shivering, she rubbed a cold foot in its thermal sock, thought of her son, Sam, her only link to the outside world. If not for him, grieving would be a continuous wound of raw pain, rather than the dull, aching throb she had learned to live with.

"Hello?"

Katya hadn't heard anyone walk up the wood chip path, and turned, slightly annoyed, to the young woman standing a few feet away. Hadn't she seen the "No Trespassing" sign? It was the second time that week someone had trespassed.

"I did not mean to startle you." The voice held traces of a French accent; the vibrant light green eyes were unnerving as she glanced from Katya's face to the well-used trout flies Katya's father had embedded in his old fishing hat. "Beautiful workmanship. Any luck?"

Katya drew a controlled breath. "The trout are supposed to be running, but I guess they're running in the opposite direction."

The young woman smiled. "Then you must chase them, no?"

It's you I should chase away, Katya thought, but said, "If I was meant to swim upstream, I would have been born with fins." She glanced at the empty plastic milk jug in the young woman's hand.

"I am disturbing you," the intruder apologized.

A thread of guilt weaved through Katya. She was getting crusty, growing scales instead of fins. "Having trouble?"

"My radiator is very moody. I am afraid that it chose to have a temper tantrum in front of your house."

Despite herself, Katya smiled as she took the jug and filled it from a spigot under the porch. She couldn't keep herself from glancing back. The young woman's finely-chiseled features bore the mark of a sculptor who loved her work. It was the kind of face that drew stares, the kind that could handle such a short cropping of dark hair, spiked up in front like an errant crew cut.

"My manners are terrible," the young woman offered, wiping a well-shaped hand on grease-stained jeans before extending it to Katya. "I am Chris Benet."

Katya accepted the hand, not surprised by its warmth and strength. "Katya Michaels."

Chris glanced around the tree-studded front lawn. "I like what you have done with the Harrison property. I always thought it the most beautiful part of the stream. When I was a child, Mr. Harrison, our old postmaster, taught me how to flycast." She ambled over to the side of the house, took in the patch of woods out back where the stream gurgled over its rocky bed before her eyes came to rest on Sam's white bicycle.

"My seven year old's," Katya explained. "I had every intention of removing the training wheels before he got home from his grandparents...."

"But you and tools are a bad mix?" A half smile curved Chris's shapely mouth. "Some of the bolts look rusted. Has your husband tried?"

"My husband?" Katya averted her eyes. "He...he died recently."

"I am sorry," Chris replied, looking a little uncomfortable.

Katya expelled the breath she hadn't realized she'd been holding, gazed up into the pale blue sky and allowed her thoughts to drift with the clouds. Was it the young woman's curiosity that had forced the lie from her lips? Loren would have shaken her head, retorted: "You're out of the closet now, Katie, enjoy the air."

Why couldn't she keep the closet door shut behind her? Why did she keep slipping back inside?

"Perhaps I can help with the bike. Be right back." Chris Benet headed back down the wood chip path to the road, her wide shoulders erect. She reminded Katya of a healthy young aerobics instructor.

Though she jogged daily, and was in good shape at thirty-two, Katya often admired the muscles that young women cultivated today. A pang of frustration, tinged with envy, shot through her. She would never be a carefree twenty again. Life had been pulled out from under her startled feet.

A car door slammed and Chris returned with a small red knapsack. She leaned Sam's bike against the porch and opened the knapsack, spreading out on the grass, a collection of tools that had been neatly wrapped in plastic. In minutes, she had taken the training wheels off, oiled the gears, tested the brakes.

Katya felt, mixed in with her discomfort, a rush of pleasure that unnerved her. She swallowed hard. Loren had been handy with tools, too.

"I'm glad your car had a temper tantrum in front of my house," she managed, and absently pulled off her fishing cap, unprepared for Chris's double-take and blush, as a cascade of luxurious blonde hair tumbled down to her shoulders.

Katya stared into the light green eyes for a second, felt a flash of excitement, heard a warning bell resound inside her head.

"Good as new," Chris declared and cleared her throat. Her finely-honed cheekbones still held a flush. She made much out of gathering her tools and finally threw the knapsack over one shoulder as she prepared to go. "Thank you for the jug of water."

"I'm the one who should be thanking you. Can I offer you a glass of cold cider—some orange juice?"

Chris rubbed the dimple in her chin and left behind a smudge of grease. "My radiator should be cooled off by now and I am late as it is."

"Oh." Katya suppressed an urge to wipe the grease off Chris's chin, watched the young woman start back toward her car and disappear behind a row of tall ilex hedges bordering the front of her property.

She wondered if Chris Benet supported herself doing repairs, and mentally counted the disabled pipes and appliances that needed work inside the house. Other women handled these day-to-day problems. Why did they seem such a chore to her? She knew the answer and she also knew that one day soon she would have to grow up. Loren was not around any longer, as much as Katya wanted to believe otherwise.

It surprised her to notice that her hands were shaking. The last thing she needed was a distracting young intruder. If she was looking for a repair-person, the Yellow Pages were safer. Again, she gazed up at the sky, thought of Loren and the animal shapes she used to point out in cloud formations, delighting Sam.

Loren had been filled with life and its possibilities; had made her feel special, not in the grandiose manner her parents had, but special, nonetheless.

☾   ☾   ☾   ☾   ☾

"This may seem corny, but I'm sincere," Geoff Holden assured Katya, handing her a shiny yellow apple. "I never would have won that writing competition without your help." For a moment, he looked vulnerable, younger than his twenty-seven years, and Katya let her guard down.

"You deserved first place, Geoff." She gathered a pile of student manuscripts from her desk, and allowed Geoff to relieve her of the rest before they strolled out of the Fine Arts Building and across the sprawling Bear State campus toward the parking lot.

She drew in a breath of air, sweetened with the promise of a warm late spring. May was just around the corner and she wondered if it would be a hot summer.

Her eyes savored the budding April flower beds, the bright pink azaleas bordering the college's pathways and circling its magnificent, bronze, life-sized sculptures. She thought it ironic that a throng of male jocks clustered around a statue of Atlas shouldering the world. Clearly, unlike Atlas, they hadn't anything else on their minds but baseball, soccer, and girls.

Bees hummed. Several fat robins dotted the bright green lawn. A maintenance worker, on her knees in dirt, was weeding around a statue of Icarus. Katya didn't know if she shivered from the woman's obvious, bold appraisal, her macho posturing, or from the statue of Icarus itself. Tourists to the campus were often drawn to its winged beauty. As they walked past it, Katya turned to Geoff and voiced her feelings. "I don't know why Icarus is celebrated. What happened to him was a tragedy, a cross his father had to bear. Because Icarus had yearned to fly, his father, Daedalus, made him wings out of wax. And in his joy at flying, Icarus flew too near the sun, melting his wings, which caused his death. How could a father live with that?"

Geoff, who had looked distracted, became animated. "Don't forget that Daedalus saved his son from a demon. He made Icarus fly to escape the maze. I don't think it was so much that he *wanted* to fly."

Properly chastised by one of her most gifted students, Katya conceded with a slight smile, but still felt uncomfortable. "Daedalus was an architect; he built the Labyrinth. Surely he could have figured out its escape route."

When Geoff looked at her his eyes were rapt. "I'd love to fly. Even for a second. No matter what the consequences."

His overly-bright, intense brown eyes put Katya off. "If it had been me, I would rather have tackled the demon." She then realized why the statue frightened her—heights, loss of control.

"That *woman* gives me the creeps," Geoff remarked, gesturing back at the woman gardener they had just passed.

Katya tensed, sorry she had opened up a dialogue with him. She deliberately shifted her attention to the college grounds. She felt that she had made the right decision to move to upstate New York from Manhattan, accepting the Associate Professorship in Literature and Creative Writing. Here, she could lose herself in the beauty of nature, the abundance of forests...peace. Here, she could better grasp life through the eyes of the gifted students that were attracted to the university. And here, she didn't have to get personally involved.

At first, she had felt awkward around Geoff Holden and his obvious crush. Then she had learned to separate him from his talent, warding off his repeated invitations for a drink or dinner, keeping him at bay with the tired phrase: "You should be home writing." The only mistake she'd made was accidentally mentioning Sam to him, because he'd started offering to take the boy fishing and give her some time off.

Geoff wound up at the university after a tour in Kuwait during the Gulf War last year. Because he was so eager and because he had seen combat, she wanted to help him. It pleased her to observe his gradual change from a moody young man in army fatigues to a more relaxed student in acid-washed jeans.

"I hear the writer, Nicki Random, is going to lecture in one of your classes next semester," he said excitedly. "How did you get her? I know she lives up here, but has a reputation as a hermit."

"Well, it's not definite yet, but I'm working on it." Katya wondered how many people would also tag her with that label.

"Wish there were more teachers like you," he declared, helping her stack the manuscripts in the trunk of her pale blue Toyota. She closed the trunk and observed him shifting on his feet.

"Something on your mind, Geoff?"

"Yeah, I guess. I know that profs don't socialize with students, but I sort of hoped you'd help me celebrate the story getting published. You helped me whip it into shape...." He brushed an unruly lock of sandy hair off his smooth forehead and glanced down at his shoes. "Sort of a thank you...."

The size of his hands and feet had always struck her as humorously large, as if his tasseled loafers walked ahead of him.

Cocking his head to one side, Geoff regarded her mischievously. "Oh, my heart is like a yellow, yellow...apple."

She cut short his parody before he began to flirt seriously. "Plagiarism," she said lightly, "Is a no-no."

"Yes, ma'am." He saluted her, his ears reddening. The afternoon sun glinted off a silver chain she usually associated with dogtags, that circled his neck. The medallion was hidden under his striped oxford shirt.

"Is lunch a possibility?" He persisted.

"I'd like to, Geoff. But I play by the rules. As a military man, surely you can understand that."

A tic began a slow dance above his right eye. She had noticed it often when he was uncomfortable. Holding up the yellow apple he had given her, she assured him: "This is present enough. How did you know that I like yellow apples?"

He beamed. She had walked right into that one. He was staring at her so hard that she had trouble getting her car door open. Once inside, she cranked down the window for air, felt closed in, wishing he would just go away. Her thoughts raced. What harm would it do to have lunch with him, quickly dispose of his crush with a few well-chosen words?

If only his prize-winning story, "*Purple Hearts*," had not been so wonderfully crafted or based on the life of a brave young soldier. How much of it was true, how much wish fulfillment, she didn't know. She gathered that Geoff had only been overseas a month, under fire less than that, from the snippets he revealed.

"You going food shopping?" he asked, startling her. He stuck his hands in the pockets of his tan chinos, as if to assure her that his remark was casual enough.

But she felt annoyed. "Are you a mind reader, too?"

"I just thought that Tuesday was your day to shop," he said defensively. "I saw you at the supermarket outside town last week. You were arguing with a woman."

Oh, God. It had been so unlike her to make a scene. But behind her, in the check-out line, a frantic mother had slapped her child's face after he began grabbing at a stack of candy bars that had been carefully placed in the path of temptation. And, unable to control herself, Katya had lashed out at her.

"Before I could say hello," Geoff continued. "You were out of there."

Katya, a quick food shopper, hated making choices, and despised waiting in lines, listening to harassed parents taking their frustrations out on their children.

Releasing the emergency brake, she countered, "Have you started a new story?"

"It's outlined, and I made a first draft; ready for you to look at."

Ignoring his eagerness, she responded, "Of course. When you feel it's ready, just hand it in." She almost added, it's my job.

"So, how's Sam doing?" he inquired with an intimacy that made her cringe. She never should have used Sam as an excuse to avoid a private meeting with Geoff Holden.

He grinned. "Kids are cool."

"I really have to run, Geoff. We'll talk soon."

"Look, if you ever need anything...."

She turned the key in the ignition. The engine stalled. *Great timing*, she thought and began to perspire. Not the car. Not now.

"Pop the hood," Geoff offered.

The perspiration worked itself into a sweat. Engines were her Achilles heel. As in the past, it would be so easy to give in, and let someone help her, avoid the expense of a service station, or a repair-person whenever something broke down. But then she would feel indebted. It would be nice to be more like that confident young woman who had dropped by on Saturday. What was her name? Chris something, something French.

With a small prayer, she turned the key in the ignition again.

It sputtered then responded with a burst of enthusiasm. "The car's just temperamental, Geoff. Thanks anyway." Katya felt heady with relief. "See you tomorrow." Driving away, she wondered what he'd think if he knew that the woman he so admired had been in love with another woman for six years, had adopted Sam with that woman and bought a house with her.

At the parking lot exit, she glanced in the rear-view mirror and watched Geoff skirt a cluster of animated students engaged in light-hearted conversation. Tonight, she'd read their manuscripts and get a vicarious rush. Making a left turn out of the parking lot, she drove three blocks and idled at a stop sign. Gazing out her side window, she absorbed the cushion of dark green mountains, as comforting as breasts. They rose over the little town of Deer Falls, with Main Street nestled at the foot of the mountains. Turning right, away from them, she slowed down. Deer Falls never failed to draw her in with its pastel-hued storefronts, while the quaint homes reminded her of gingerbread houses.

To her delight, she learned that many of the businesses were women-owned. This had obviously been one of Loren's main selling points in coaxing her to move up here.

The Cow Jumped Over The Moon bookshop on the right beckoned with a colorful array of titles. Her foot pressed lightly on the brake pedal to prolong her journey down Main Street. One display in the bookshop window proudly featured the latest hardcover written by the woman Geoff had called a hermit, Nicki Random. Katya still bristled self-consciously at the mental comparison she herself made to her own sequestered existence. But she could well understand why, in this wooded, nature-blessed paradise, a woman would seek escape and seclusion.

She passed *Grassroots Press*, the home of *Women's Newsletter*, and as she drove by the *Herb and Spice Emporium*, she could almost smell the spicy aromas the health food store offered. *Molly's Sporting Goods*, as well as a few boutiques and watering holes for students and tourists spread their welcome awnings. A luncheonette for the regulars stood next to a modest library. Opposite these shops, a small post office and antique shop flanked the Women's Center, which was set back on a lawn dotted with benches. Deer Falls was touted as a future oasis of enlightened women, the cutting edge of feminist utopias. She wondered how the old-time residents felt about this particular population explosion.

Suddenly, a paunchy red-jowled man in a pressed beige uniform stormed out of *Grassroots Press*. Scowling, he slammed the door shut behind him, but not before a wave of angry voices drifted outside. Again, the door opened and a deputy joined the sheriff on the sidewalk, wiping sweat from the inside of his hat with a handkerchief.

So much for "Feminist Utopias," Katya mused, as she approached the railroad tracks. A clanging bell followed a flash of blinking colored lights, signalling the descent of a black and white striped wooden arm. Instead of impatience, Katya experienced the small thrill she always did when a train passed. She loved the sounds of train whistles and foghorns in the distance—the lure of faraway places she might someday get to see— especially when she was safely tucked into her comfortable bed at night.

Boxcars rumbled by. They seemed to repeat: "Come along, come along...."

Glancing in her rear view mirror, she was surprised to note how clear and bright her blue eyes appeared, how healthy the color tinging her high cheekbones. It hadn't been a bad week. She realized this with a start. Would she have to do penance for it?

No, it was time to celebrate the small victory of arising from her four-poster these past few mornings without the weight of depression that usually forced her back under the covers again. Suddenly, she remembered the French restaurant she had frequented with Loren. Maybe she'd take Sam. And maybe they'd explore some garage sales this weekend, visit the new *Railroad Junction* restaurant that boasted ice cream sundaes in chocolate dishes that looked like railroad cars. The promise of hot fudge might stir up his lethargic appetite.

What would it take to stir up her own?

 да   да   да

❦ 2 ❦

Le Provençal smelled like a saturated wine cork, sweetened with fresh herbs. Its soothing green and blue interior, white stucco walls and wicker chairs, the abundance of plants, and the lilting voices of French waitresses pleased Katya, as did the steaming trays of fragrant delicacies. To complement the ambiance, Gypsy violins spilled haunting refrains from hidden speakers.

As a hostess showed them to their table, Sam rushed over to gawk at a large fish tank separating the dining room from the semi-lit bar.

"Check out this fish tank, Mom," he called excitedly.

She strode over to fetch him, looked up and found herself staring into a pair of familiar light green eyes.

The young woman smiled. "Mrs. Michaels." She quickly dropped the brush in her hand into a jar of water resting on a green dropcloth. The cozy bar area where they stood was cluttered with paint cans.

Katya searched her mind for the name again.

"Chris Benet," the young woman supplied. She drew a paisley scarf from the back pocket of her paint-spattered jeans and wiped her hands.

"Of course," Katya responded, again felt the warmth of her handshake. Surprising herself, she took the handkerchief and removed a spot of wet paint from the fair forehead below the spiky black hair, delighted when Chris blushed.

"If it isn't grease, it's paint. Can't take you anywhere." Katya smiled, aware of Sam's look of curiosity.

She introduced them. "Sam, Chris fixed your bike Saturday." *It was Tuesday. Had only a few days passed? It seemed like much more.*

Pausing, he cocked his head. "Did she use Loren's tools?"

Katya flushed as she shook her head no.

Remembering his manners, Sam thanked Chris. "I rode it without the training wheels in the school playground today." His dimples blossomed.

It didn't take a genius to see that Chris was captivated by him. "Thank God for jogging," Katya confided, "Or he would have run me ragged."

"I didn't fall off. Not even once." Sam tugged at the collar of his new plaid shirt where Katya had powdered the tail end of a poison ivy rash.

"Except for the freckles and brown eyes, he looks like you," Chris remarked.

Katya had heard this comment before and it never failed to please her, for she and Loren had adopted Sam after his mother's tragic automobile accident. Battling chronic depression, and distraught over her husband's defiance of a restraining order, Meg DeLeon was desperate for help. She fled her San Diego home, dropping two-year-old Sam off at his grandparents. She had taken the treacherous coast road to Santa Barbara to consult with her lawyer, but never made it. Loren never recovered from her younger sister's death. First she blamed it on Meg's suicidal tendencies, and then on her vicious brother-in-law.

The accident, and their son-in-law's eventual trial and imprisonment for the possession and sale of firearms and drugs, had aged Loren's parents far beyond their sixty-some-odd-years. It had rendered them incapable of handling an active and curious toddler like Sam for more than short periods. Now they lived in Kingston, New York, spring and summers, so that they could enjoy a regular dose of Sam. Winters turned them into Florida snowbirds.

Pulling herself back up from a mire of painful memories, Katya gestured to a wall in the bar. "So this is what you're up to," she remarked as Chris led them inside.

Sam's eyes stayed glued to the half-completed mural. "Awesome!" It was a whimsical dance of aquatic sea creatures, some with tiny French berets, swimming between a myriad of plants, anemones and coral.

"You painted this?" Katya asked, impressed.

A slight, embarrassed nod was her answer.

Katya regarded the young woman as if seeing her for the first time. "Then you're a muralist. How unique." She noticed dried flecks of paint on Chris's long fingers, accentuating the perfect white crescents of her naturally pink nails. "And here I was assuming that you fixed bicycles for a living, or ran the only women's repair shop in Deer Falls...which would be admirable, too."

"You are kind. But my father is the one with the repair shop—still going at it in France. He always encouraged me to be self-reliant," she added with a laugh. "In place of dolls, I played with his tools." A mischievous gleam sparked her eyes. "Do you have something else broken?"

"Nothing a new dishwasher wouldn't fix. Maybe you can recommend someone reliable to take a look at the one I have before I start shopping around. I hate to shop." Katya had to stop herself from babbling.

"Would it please you to have me take a look at it?" Chris offered. "Perhaps I can save you some money."

"Oh, no. At least not without paying you. You've done enough already. Are you into community service, too?" She was teasing, but Chris's hurt expression stopped her.

Chris shrugged, grew silent.

Why did this young woman throw her so off balance? Why was it so hard for her to accept this offer of kindness? She was relieved when Sam yanked his collar again, distracting her.

"It still itches, Mom."

Bending down, Katya blew on the back of his neck. "Better?" When she glanced up, Chris was staring at her intently, and just as quickly pulled her eyes away.

"Neighbors should help each other out, no?" Chris offered. "Besides, would it not be a good idea for you to learn how to repair things yourself, Mrs. Michaels? There is nothing frightening about it."

You frighten me, Katya thought. Was she being lectured by this...self-confident *young* creature who could have been one of her students?

"I'd have to buy out the entire stock of Band-Aids in the supermarket first," Katya quipped.

"The Women's Center is starting a Car Repair course next month. Would you be interested?"

"I'd be more interested in a first aid course," Katya quickly rejoined.

No response. Didn't this distracting young woman have a sense of humor?

Chris absently fingered the cleft in her chin. "I could come by to look at your dishwasher this Friday and maybe show you how you can fix it yourself. Perhaps, 10:00 o'clock?"

"There's really no rush."

"I would not want you to get dishwasher hands."

Katya couldn't help smiling at the French interpretation of the familiar phrase. "Dishpan hands," she corrected. "Okay, but I must warn you...if you take me on as a student, you'll probably need a shrink afterwards."

"No sweat." Again, only the French could make American slang sound so charming.

"Check out the seahorses, Mom. Chris painted them just like the ones in the fish tank. They're unreal. Can I have a mural on my wall, too?"

"Hey, slow down, Cousteau."

"Please?" He waited eagerly.

Sam had asked for very little after Loren's death. His most plaintive wish had been to bring her back.

"I would love to paint a mural for you, Sam."

Sam's bright eyes flicked from Chris to Katya. "Just like this one?"

Though she felt trapped, the idea sank in and appealed to Katya. "How much would it cost?" She asked.

Chris stiffened for the second time. "Call it community service, if you like," she proposed with an edge to her voice. Her eyes locked with Katya's and it was Katya who looked away first.

"As soon as I complete this project for maman, I shall have a few weeks free." Chris spoke as if no tension had passed between them. "I have promised her this mural for *Le Provençal*." She smiled at Sam. "We can get together and talk about it, Sam, and you can have a special picture all your own if you wish."

"Neat!"

Katya felt left out and cornered at the same time. She changed the subject. "What part of France are you from?"

"Have you ever heard of a place called Paris?" Chris teased.

"So you do have a sense of humor. I was about to give up on you. Paris...." A sigh swept through her. "I thought you'd mention one of those quaint, provincial villages that seem so appealing in guidebooks."

"*Au contraire*. There is much to see in Paris that is quaint...not unlike your Greenwich Village, no?"

The remark unnerved Katya, as if she was supposed to be intimate with Greenwich Village. Was Chris fishing for something or was Katya paranoid and two steps back in the closet?

When Sam tugged her hand, she gratefully followed him back to their table after exchanging a quick good-bye with Chris. Once seated, she found it difficult not to glance her way, so she concentrated on Sam. It was good to see him excited about something. Perhaps his appetite would improve. His thinness and lack of focus during this difficult year had frightened her.

"Boy, am I hungry, Mom." A grin lit up his face.

The sound of the word "Mom," lit her up inside, too. It always did. Sam always referred to Katya as "Mom" and Loren as "Auntie." Loren had insisted on this in her desire to include Katya in the adoption of her little nephew. But Loren's concerns hadn't been necessary. After Katya got to know Sam, a dormant part of her had sprung to life. From the first moment they shared Oreo cookies and milk at bedtime, to the stories she read him at night, she had been hooked.

A chill suddenly shot through her at the realization that Loren had had another motive, too. She was dying. And she could only let go of life knowing that the people she loved were taken care of. Life insurance in the face of the inevitable. Her legacy to Katya and Sam.

"Can I have chocolate pudding, like they're eating over there?"

She studied his eager face. The cowlick she had plastered down with water and a dab of gel now stood up from his crown like a yellow flag. A cowlick, like his dimples, could break her heart. "It's called chocolate mousse, honey, and you have to eat something substantial first." She suggested onion soup and "cotelette d'agneau..."

He failed at pronouncing what she read off from the menu in her rustic high school French. "Grilled lamb chop," she explained. "And now that you know Chris, maybe you can learn some French. A lot of French people emigrated up here when they landed in America."

"Cause they had an earthquake like in California? Or something else bad?"

Katya laughed. "No, honey. Nothing that drastic. The French people must have liked it so much that they probably wrote their friends and relatives about it, and so they began to come here, too. Many of them opened restaurants and inns for Americans to enjoy."

"But are they still French?" He propped his elbows on the blue tablecloth and rested his sun-reddened cheeks on them.

It felt good that someone hung on her every word.

"Yes, they are still very much French in their hearts, I should think."

"Do they make mint jelly in France? For my lamb chops? Can I have a chocolate milk, too?"

Her stomach gave a small lurch at the combination. "Think you can wait until dessert for the chocolate milk? It's so sweet."

"I like Coke, too."

She reached over and tweaked his freckled nose. "I know you like Coke, but it doesn't like you. They make delicious apple cider here."

Expecting a "yuck" and a sulk, she was delighted when he nodded.

"But I want it in a glass like yours," he concluded, pointing to her wine glass. "Mom? Is Chris really going to paint a mural on my bedroom wall? And can I watch?" His little face was expectant, prepared for another disappointment.

How he had survived her own stages of mourning while dealing with his own, she couldn't fathom; nor did she want to fool with what seemed his healthy coping mechanism. How dare that woman in the supermarket take her child so for granted that she could slap and humiliate him in front of people. They should require licenses for parenting. "We'll glance through your picture books when we get home and see if we can stir up some ideas for a mural," she suggested. "How's that?"

"All *right*!" He leaned back in his chair, happily, as the waitress arrived. Katya ordered a half carafe of Chardonnay, and an apple cider for Sam. Without even realizing she was doing it, she glanced into the bar and saw Chris with a paintbrush clamped between her white teeth, jaunty as a pirate. Their eyes met again and set off a surge of electricity through Katya.

Then the wine arrived and the waitress took the rest of their orders. Katya sipped the crisp wine slowly and tried to act casual, though her heart was beating uncomfortably fast inside her chest. She gazed around at the other diners, at the delectable arrangements on their fine china plates. The last time she had come here she hadn't been able to look around so casually. Her soul had been consumed by anxiety. She had sat opposite Loren as they tried not to mention the latest medical report. Just thinking about it now twisted her insides. The same cold dread that had frozen her when she had heard the word "metastases" shot through her now. Clutching the stem of her wine glass she remembered how Loren had tried to make light of it; just another hurdle they'd leap together. But no amount of lovemaking or attempts at laughter could silence the enemy making camp in her lover's ovaries, marching on to devour other positions.

A peal of laughter brought her back to the present. Next to their table, a party of women were busy enjoying each other. Katya noticed two of them touch discreetly under the table. Another woman offered her companion a bread basket only to jerk it playfully away. A rush of longing flooded Katya and she had to blink back tears.

The restaurant door opened with a jingle. "Bon jour!" the hostess cried, welcoming a throng of lively Frenchmen. They sparred with her verbally in their native language. She parried each flirtatious thrust with aplomb. "Salut, mes amies. Ça va comme çi, comme ça," the pretty dark-haired hostess purred in a throaty voice. Her likeness to Chris became apparent to Katya, who now realized that she was looking at the impressive Gabrielle Benet, the woman who had turned a small French cafe into a highly successful, four-star inn and restaurant. Glancing at Chris, Katya imagined how she might look in about twenty years from now, if she could be any more stunning than she already was, despite the fact that her workshirt and jeans sported more paint than the green dropcloth.

What would she look like? Would she still have her nose buried in student manuscripts, afraid to enjoy life?

A remark at the table of women riveted her:

"You must have heard about the assault on the librarian."

"Is she still in a coma?"

"What could she have been thinking about?" another woman added. "Jogging alone at eleven at night."

"Well, this isn't New York City. She probably thought it was safe."

"Famous last words. The minute a town like Deer Falls opens up to tourists, you can kiss peace and quiet good-bye."

"Here's another piece of good news—the woman who runs *Grassroots Press* said she received phone calls warning her to stop printing *The Women's Network.*"

"It's scary. The new Women's Center was trashed, on top of everything else."

"Know what was painted on the door?"

Katya found herself straining to hear as the speaker leaned across the table and whispered: "Death to dykes."

Katya gave an involuntary gasp, causing Sam to look up from the dried wax he was busy peeling off a candle-holder on the table.

"Gay-bashing up here? I don't believe it," another woman declared. "Everybody knows...accepts the fact that the librarian is living with Bev Dillon, the veterinarian."

"The librarian isn't the only victim. The sheriff's been trying to hush it up, but there were two murders in March...."

Katya couldn't hear the rest. She immediately thought of the crank phone call she had received that morning and panic coursed through her.

I moved up here to get away from all this.

Their orders arrived just then, but she wasn't hungry any more. She watched Sam's fork hover over a lamb chop, then the julienne potatoes, before plunging eagerly into a small, fluted dark brown foil cup of mint jelly, glistening like a cluster of emeralds.

Katya drew a deep breath and let it out slowly. The women's concerns seemed unreal to her. They were surely over-reacting. How could there be anything evil lurking in Deer Falls, hovering over her and Sam, the log cabin, her students; even this Tuesday night out? Determined not to let it spoil her dinner, she cut into her Beef Bourguignon. It dissolved deliciously in her mouth, melting her fears away.

Smiling at Sam, she said, "Food's good, isn't it?"

"Can I have more mint jelly?" He held up the empty, mangled dark foil cup.

She started to flag a waitress when Sam mumbled something.

"Don't talk with your mouth full."

"Cause I'll choke like you did?"

She should never have told him *that* story. A slow, mischievous grin spread across his face and she almost choked on a morsel of potato. Somehow, Sam had managed to stick a piece of dark brown foil on his top front teeth, masking them.

"Sam!" Despite herself, she burst into laughter, as she washed the potato down with wine.

"Got my teeth knocked out trying to take out a couple of bad dudes."

"You and who else, tough guy?" She wiped her teary eyes with her napkin.

"Me, the Terminator, and Robocop."

"When did you see *those* movies?" she demanded, peeved.

"With Grandpa, on his new VCR."

Making a mental note to speak to Loren's father about Sam's nightmares, she watched the waitress deliver Sam's chocolate mousse. He was in chocolate heaven, gulping down half his chocolate milk at once.

Exhausted by the time they finished their meal, she glanced in the bar but the strobe lamp was off and Chris nowhere to be seen. A twinge of disappointment passed through her, then anger at herself for feeling it.

Outside, on the way to the car, she sucked in a lung full of crisp night air, again smelled the hint of May in honeysuckle and budding lilac; the ripe scent of the stream in back of *Le Provençal.* The pole lamps in the parking lot flicked on.

A few feet away, leaning against a red Jeep, she spotted Chris Benet, sporting clean jeans and a pale blue workshirt.

Katya's heart leaped.

"Shall I drop by Friday morning at ten?" Chris inquired.

"Oh, yes, the dishwasher." Katya fumbled for the keys she had dropped in her leather shoulder bag. "Would you prefer cash or check?"

Chris stared at her. "I would not charge you just to look at your dishwasher."

Katya mentally calculated how much time she needed to drive Sam to school, jog, and run a few errands. Finally, she muttered, "See you Friday, then. Ten o'clock is fine."

Chris turned her back and climbed into the Jeep. The engine turned over with a purr and the dashboard lit up, then her headlights. Grabbing a purple baseball cap off the sun visor, she pulled it down low over her cropped dark hair, swiveling the bill backwards.

Katya noticed Chris's jaw muscle working. She could also make out a large brass circle, with a cross beneath, hanging from the rear-view mirror. It was the same women's symbol that Loren had worn as an earring. Often, Katya had felt frightened when Loren called attention to their private life. She felt uncomfortable now, gazing at the prominent symbol hanging over the dashboard, as if she were Hawthorne's Hester Prynne, bearing a scarlet letter. *Why doesn't she just advertise?*

"Good-bye, Sam," Chris called out in her lilting voice.

Katya noted the muscles rippling in the smooth tanned skin below Chris's rolled-up sleeve when she shifted the Jeep into reverse.

She's so quiet, Katya thought. *Was I too abrupt with her?*

"Au revoir," she tried, but didn't receive the grin she had been hoping for, just a half-hearted wave of the hand. Torn, she watched the Jeep pull away, tires spitting gravel as it swung around and paused under the exit light, leaving Katya feeling empty and confused.

She wondered why Chris's sexual politics should matter so much to her. And then she knew that Loren had been right. She still needed approval from the world, the world being the specter of her strait-laced mother. Anger flared up inside her. How dare her mother judge her. She had lived *her* life, had been protected and worshipped by Katya's gentle bear of a father. And then after his death, she carried the role of widow with dignity, finally marrying again into the wealth she had long coveted and felt was rightfully hers.

Katya didn't begrudge her mother's happiness, so why did her mother begrudge her only daughter's choices in life? It was not that Louise Michaels had disinherited her when Katya told her about Loren, then Sam. She had done worse, treating her daughter's declarations like ashes in the wind.

"I'm glad you have a new friend, dear.... You're adopting? Isn't that a little rash? You know how hard single parents have it. And this child...you really don't know much about his father's family.... I know you're taken with him, but it will pass.... Katya, dear, Lou and I are late for our golf game. Why don't I call you later? By the way, when are you coming down to Florida? I'd say you were neglecting your mother."

Standing under the exit light next to Sam, in Chris's wake, she shivered, wondered where Chris was heading, if there was someone waiting for her. A thought struck her—the reason for her lightened mood this week had just driven away. It was clear that when Chris Benet appeared on the path to her house, she not only strode past the "No Trespassing" sign, but walked right into her life.

ᑭᕤ   ᑭᕤ   ᑭᕤ

❧ 3 ❧

When Chris adjusted her rear-view mirror, the brass women's symbol given her by her brother Simon twirled, sending shards of reflected light against the black dashboard. In the mirror, the figures of Katya and Sam grew smaller and smaller, and Chris's heartbeat, in the safety of her Jeep, louder and louder.

You are out of your league, Benet. This woman wears designer clothes and talks about money all the time. She paints her nails. Then Chris pictured Katya Michaels' shell-pink nails and thought of the graceful, expressive hands they belonged to.

WASP princess. Then she tried *Straight* WASP *princess* out loud, but it did not place the distance she needed between Katya and herself. It was never easy for her to open up, especially to strangers. What did you get, but a kick in la lune? This woman had mocked all her offers to help. Did she not realize how the mention of money each time that help was offered was an insult?

Ooo la la. What is really happening here? Had she expected this Katya Michaels to swoon over her, to cry, "My hero"?

From the moment that she had first seen Katya, she had been lost in those big blue eyes, in the despair and struggle reflected there. She had daydreamed about rescuing Katya from the demons that plagued her, riding up on a white stallion, grabbing Katya by the waist, and galloping off into the horizon. Fini.

What a hopeless romantic you are, Benet.

The Jeep rumbled over a steel bridge on the road into Deer Falls. She flicked on her radio and classical music swept through the car.

She has a child, a boy child. And probably a male lover, too. The only screwdriver she has ever held is one with vodka and orange juice, and here I am offering to teach her home repairs. What an andouille, a fool, she must think I am.

Swinging onto Main Street, the Jeep bumped over the railroad tracks. A view of dark green mountains, rimmed by the last traces of golden dusk in the darkening blue sky, filled the window in front of her.

It would be easy to forget the woman if she wasn't so beautiful, so sexy and desirable. Like Katya's gesture of blowing on Sam's neck to cool off his poison ivy rash. Chris had almost swallowed her tongue.

Street lamps reflected on Main Street's pastel storefronts, reminding Chris of the tiny village outside of Paris where her grandmother and uncle owned a vineyard and winery. Her Uncle Paul had managed the place after Chris's grandpère passed away. Etienne, her rebel father, had declined every offer to share in an enterprise that left grape stains, and not engine grease, on his coveralls.

Le Provençal still imported most of its wines from the vineyard. It was Chris's retreat, a place she tried to visit every year to replenish herself with rich earth and neatly-planted rows of grape seedlings set off by white arbors.

For one magical moment, as her brass women's symbol caught the light from the sidewalk street lamps, Chris thought of the lights that had danced in Katya's shimmering blonde hair; streaming down to her shoulders like liquid gold when she took off her fishing hat on the first day they had met. Suddenly, she had to swerve to avoid an oncoming car.

Sacré Bleu.

She had not felt this distracted, this vulnerable and infatuated, in years, having turned her energies to her paintings. The pain that had split her family in half five years earlier, as she said good-bye to her teens, was only just now becoming manageable. But not the rage. That still burned inside her like an incandescent, relentless flame, as it had the year she turned twenty. The rage was more powerful than her sexual drive and she used and nurtured it as a defense against helplessness.

Never again.

When the fury built up to an alarming intensity, she went to the gym to burn it off with self-defense classes. She shed it on soaked pillows at night.

Hooking a swift U-turn, Chris parked the Jeep on the opposite side of the street, hopped out and locked the doors. Five years ago, she would not have dreamed of locking her car in a town like Deer Falls. Would not have thought of arranging her keys so that their silver tips pointed out between her long, slender fingers, anticipating a surprise attack.

Amused by her own caution, she smiled, a smile that soon faded when a trio of leather-jacketed toughs roared by on motorcycles, heading for the interstate. Girl groupies, long hair flying, clung to the bikers' waists.

The influx of bikers during tourist season was one reason why Chris had helped set up a Community Watch. The safety of the town was what the meeting they had called would address. Striding over to the glass door, she inserted a key in the brass lock, surprised to find the door open, its welcome bells coaxed to life. She would have to warn Molly again to lock the door. This was a time for caution.

The darkened room Chris entered enveloped her in the smells of leather and varnish. She side-stepped display cases filled with hand-tied flies, lures and reels. The scent of almonds from the Amaretto cordials Molly offered her students at the end of each flyfishing class sweetened the air.

By habit, her gaze climbed up the wall above a rack of fishing vests and camping gear, where her four framed outdoor canvasses hung. She strained her eyes to see them better, realized that now there were really only three. One was marked "Sold." It brought a smile to her face. Molly loved the paintings so much that she often distracted interested buyers with the latest in outdoor fashions and her own exquisitely-tied dry flies.

There was an unspoken agreement between them: as long as Chris's oils hung for Molly's enjoyment, Molly would keep Chris wader-high in flyrods and flies for fishing. As a result, Chris now had a collection—from March Browns to Molly's latest Blue-Winged Olives—which was the envy of any stream enthusiast.

A steady click-click sounded from the back room of the store. Chris drifted toward the blue-white light streaming from the slide projector and stood at the door. Remembering why she was here, she sucked in a breath. *Gay bashing* resounded in her head.

The room lights flicked on. Lifting a hand in greeting, Chris watched Molly Cheever conclude her slide presentation with the same enthusiasm she always gave her students: "Get ready to strut your stuff on the back lawn tomorrow and don't forget, gang, the flyrod, line and reel should be properly balanced. Everything acts as one unit so that when you cast, it's an extension of yourself, like Zen. Go with the flow. Remember that the forward cast doesn't require as much thrust as the back cast, and keep your wrist firm and steady. And remember, release as many trout to the stream as possible."

Calling for a clean-up, Molly shut off the projector and answered a few remaining questions. Then she turned to Chris and beamed a radiant smile at her. Chris, smiling in return, warmed by the welcome, graciously stepped aside to let the group of men and women out.

When the last straggler left, Molly demanded, "Get that cute ass over here, Benet."

"Molly!" Chris felt her face flame, but despite herself, her smile widened. She almost always smiled at Molly when they were not arguing with the same intensity.

The embroidered yellow flowers on the light blue cotton blouse and matching harem pants that Chris had bought Molly last Christmas brought out the blonde streaks in her soft brown afro, the lights in her warm brown eyes now trained on Chris with unabashed affection. Everything about Molly Cheever appeared wide and generous. A large-boned woman, radiating good health, she carried herself with the grace of a dancer. As she moved from the slide projector to one of the long aluminum tables set up in the room, she gathered up some empty plastic tumblers to place in the adjacent sink.

To see Molly cast was to watch a ballet. At five-eight, an inch taller than Chris, she accentuated her height with two-inch clog sandals, played up her shapely calves with culottes or gauzy pants that she tied below her knees. Pretty in an outdoorsy way, Molly was the best advertisement for her sporting goods shop.

Approaching Chris, she grabbed the collar of her workshirt. "Mmmm, you smell like freshly-cut grass. I like it much better than turpentine."

"Liar. Turpentine turns you on. And *you* smell like chicken chow mein," Chris countered, squirming in Molly's sudden hug.

"You're acting paranoid again," Molly accused laughingly. "Friends can hug and kiss in public without setting off fire alarms. Come on, stand still and deliver."

In the middle of a second squeeze, Chris half-heartedly patted Molly on the back, the signal she wanted out. In her friend's bearlike embrace, she often felt like a secure, if foolish child.

"Still can't figure you out." Molly shook her head. "You wear lavender, advertise that humongous women's sign in your Jeep, strut around like a peacock with a rod up its tail, then run like a mouse when little old me shows affection." She swiped at Chris's purple baseball cap as if that, too, was evidence of Chris's mixed messages.

"LITTLE old you?" Chris teased. "Tell me about it, mon amie."

"I'm going on a diet, starting next week."

Chris groaned. "You are not fat. I was just joking." She winced when Molly pinched her cheeks; suggested that she help herself to a bag of sunflower seeds and raisins, cold Perrier waiting for her in the small fridge near the sink to the left of the doorway.

"Ah, here come Toni and Sara," Molly declared happily.

Chris smiled at the two women. Sara tall, with beautiful coffee-colored skin, and Toni thin, pale and sharp featured, with wired energy pouring out of her slight frame.

Toni could not seem to stand still. Even her red hair seemed to be on fire. She made it a point to greet Molly effusively while only offering Chris the briefest of nods, as if granting her a favor.

Chris pondered this as she crossed the worn green and white linoleum to the refrigerator, but as she grabbed a bottle of Perrier, prying the cap loose with a can opener attached to an overhead cabinet, she quickly dismissed Toni.

Opening the plastic pouch of seeds and raisins, she bit into one black fruity kernel and closed her eyes, imagining the taste of the plump raisins produced at the family's vineyard in Vieux Ville. Again, she could feel the cool, loamy soil under her eager fingers, the sweat dripping down her face while she pruned the weaker vines to encourage only the strongest, sweetest grapes to grow under the hot sun.

"Earth to Chris." Sara Wenning stood before her with open arms.

The hug was mercifully brief. "Hallo, Sara. How is Margo doing?" Chris inquired, concerned about Sara's business partner at *Grassroots Press*. She noticed Sara's large, mocha-colored hands fidgeting with a cornrow of braids in her dark coarse hair, and noted that her friend's lovely smile had not yet reached her eyes. "Molly tells me that she was pretty badly hurt, but will recover. Is this true?" Chris added anxiously.

"The injuries were bad enough to make her more paranoid than she already is. Whoever attacked Margo did a real number on her. You know how flaky she is? Now she has the nurses checking under the bed every night to see if her attacker is hiding there. And she's convinced that one of the doctors is in disguise, waiting to finish her off. First Randi, now Margo. Who's next?" She gave a worried sigh.

"That is why we are here. I can understand it happening to Margo because she takes chances, Goddess love her, but Randi? She never lets anything get by her. Just ask the kids who try to sneak library books past her desk. Now tell me what happened." Despite her calm tone, Chris felt a hot spear of anger.

Sara ran her hands down her yellow sweatshirt and pants. "She never came back to run the press as usual on Monday nights when we have to get the newsletter out."

"How did you hear about the attack?"

"Sheriff Wendell called from the hospital."

They slowly ambled over to one of two aluminum tables lining the wall opposite the doorway. Chris pulled out a chair for Sara and swiveled a second one around, which she straddled. She placed the bag of nuts and raisins, the Perrier, on the table behind her. Pulling off her baseball cap, she twirled it on one finger as if to spin off excess energy and tossed it in the direction of Molly's antique hat stand, used to hang wet waders. It sailed through the air, finding its target. "I still do not understand what happened to Margo and Randi, or why," she confided to Sara, her anger intensifying. "We are trained to be prepared for violence."

"It's pretty hard to deliver a well-placed kick when you've been bashed on the head. Wendell thinks it was a gun butt," Sara stated flatly. "I'll fill you in when Bev gets here."

Fear mingled with rage coiled inside Chris's gut. She stared hard at her purple baseball cap as if it held some answers, then glanced at Toni, seated at the first table facing Molly. Her pale green blouse brought out the color in her shrewd hazel eyes. Tapping one, long, lacquered fingernail on the table, she pulled a clipboard and ballpoint pen out of her tote bag and laid them on the table—ready to get down to business. The gesture reminded Chris of the time she had discovered Toni behind her neat desk at the Women's Center in her role as social worker extraordinaire. Chris smiled at her, but Toni's thin face closed up like it was going in for winter storage.

Peeved, Chris tried to figure out why Toni did not like her, wondered if it had something to do with Molly's affections.

The last to arrive, Bev Dillon, Deer Falls' devoted veterinarian, trudged in. Her short brown hair was unkempt and the outdoor clothing that was her style was rumpled like L.L. Bean rejects. Pushing granny glasses up over her small, upturned nose, she greeted Molly. "Sorry for tracking up your nice clean floor, but I got tied up in a barn with a colicky horse."

Toni clicked and unclicked her ballpoint pen nervously.

"Damned fool palomino rained yellow all over my boots while I was cleaning out his bowel," Bev complained.

"Why, that's good luck," Molly quipped. "Though unsavory. Remind me not to order dessert when we go out for coffee later." Her wise brown eyes flicked to Chris. "Why are you sitting so far away, honey? Is there manure on Bev's boots, too?"

Chris hoped that Molly would let it rest. She needed the space to contain her mounting fury. Since her trauma, five years earlier, she felt cornered in groups and small spaces. A rush of heat suffused her face, leaving behind a sheen of sweat. The last thing she needed was an attack of claustrophobia in front of her friends.

"So how's Randi tonight?" Molly asked Bev, abruptly changing the subject. "They're really tight-lipped at the hospital."

"Sheriff Wendell's orders. Guess he's afraid of mass hysteria." Bev rubbed her cheek as if to remove what was bothering her. "I spoke to her doctor." A tired smile hung precariously on her pixie face as she slowly, carefully, removed her dirt-spattered glasses and cleaned them with the tail of her tan safari shirt. "At least she's out of the coma. At least that...."

"Oh, that's super. Just what we've been praying for." Molly smiled. "She'll be back home and working in no time, you'll see."

"That psycho is literally picking us off," Toni bristled.

"You'll all be getting a call from the sheriff—to calm you down and avoid more trouble for himself. I also think the attacker chooses only gay women," Bev said with a deep sigh and a wrinkling of her brow.

After the shock of those last words wore off, Chris blurted: "Our welfare was never a priority with him before. What makes you think it will be now?"

"Because...." Bev circled the table and sat down next to Toni. She leaned forward in her chair. "He believes there's a link...to the two murders that happened in March."

Chris froze. "The women that were thrown off the cliff at Eagle Point?"

It seemed as if the air had been sucked out of the room.

"Goddess help us," Molly breathed.

"Why would Wendell make a connection between Randi and Margo and those murdered women?" Sara asked, her chocolate brown eyes wide with alarm.

"Because of what Randi and Margo heard their assailant say before he got scared off. In Margo's case, it was by a passing car; and in Randi's case by the unexpected fight she put up," Bev explained.

The women focused their attention on Bev, eager to learn of the cryptic message, yet dreading its revelation.

Bev drew in a deep breath. "It was something like, 'I can put you out of your dyke misery and really liberate you—I can give you one precious moment of pure freedom and endless space.' It had the same intent as the note a deputy found at the murder site of the two other women."

"To fly over Eagle Point," Chris whispered, as if she were talking to herself. Nervously, she tossed a handful of sunflower seeds into her dry mouth.

"Wendell could be exaggerating to draw attention away from himself and his good ole boys. Who's to say *they're* not behind all this? They hate the fact that we've taken over so many businesses in Deer Falls," Toni contributed. She swallowed hard—paled noticeably. "If he really believes there's such a terrible menace out there he wouldn't waste precious time sitting on his fat butt."

Sara, anxiously fiddling with a gold chain around her neck, spoke up. "The sheriff and one of his deputies marched into the press office this afternoon and as much as ordered me to shut down the newsletter, said our pro-choice and feminist philosophy were causing the attacks. When I pressed him for proof, he stalked out."

"Did you say anything else to him?" Molly questioned.

Sara cut her eyes to each one of them, the spark and challenge shining again. "I reminded the s.o.b. that elections were coming up and our little community carries a large chunk of the vote. Nobody's gonna tell ole Sara how to run her business, or her life."

"Way to go, babe," Molly applauded.

Puzzled, Chris asked, "What is so controversial about *Women's Network* that he told you to close it down?" In her opinion it was not a radical, but informative newsletter. The core of rage inside her began to boil, burning her gut. "Perhaps we should seriously consider building up our Community Watch, and depend more on ourselves than on the law. And I think it would be wise to question Margo and Randi ourselves." Just as the words left her mouth she regretted them, for going to a hospital brought on a wave of anxiety.

"Let's calm down," Bev advised, fixing her dark gentle eyes, barely gentle now, on Chris. "And not cross Oliver Wendell. If the hets get scared of what's going on, *they* can light a fire under him."

"Then again, they just might ignore it like AIDS, right?" Toni countered with an edge of sarcasm. "Let's face it—we're on our own."

"I agree with Toni. We can't just sit around and do nothing," Sara interjected. "I think it's a good idea to talk to Randi and Margo."

Bev shook her head. "The doctors don't want them shaken up any more than they are now. Randi could slip back into a coma, and Margo? Well, she's unpredictable."

"You are right, Sara," Chris jumped in. "We cannot slink away with our tails between our legs, and just wait for another attack. Granted Wendell is an asshole, but I cannot see him behind the murders. There is someone dangerous out there. I am certain of it. It's time for us to act."

"There's nothing wrong with being prudent, Chris," Bev counseled. "If we cut the sheriff some slack, he might do his job, and it may be all we need."

"It also might be too late!" Chris fumed. "Time is a luxury we do not have—our lives and our community are at stake." She bolted out of her chair and tried to stave off a wave of shivers. "We must put a stop to this, now—show Wendell that we are not afraid."

Recalling the weakest vines she pruned at Vieux Ville every year, she stated emphatically, "Before this menace grows and hurls more of us over Eagle Point, we have to cut him down."

Bev groaned. "That sounds like a call to arms."

"Damned right!" Chris began to pace back and forth in front of her friends. She stopped in her tracks and faced Bev Dillon: "You talk of prudence and you sound like the *President*, not the woman who wrestled me to the mat last week in gym. N'est pas?"

Bev colored.

Chris pressed further. "I can understand that all of you are afraid for your businesses." Her hands went up in a gesture of helplessness. "I also understand that you do not want to create more friction. But we took an oath to defend our friends and community here. We have all worked so hard to establish ourselves in Deer Falls. Let us not let *the boys* undo it. Right, Molly?"

Molly averted her eyes. "We're just exploring alternatives."

"Shrink talk. You are copping out," Chris spat. "We should be buying berets and Kiyoga sticks, sharpening our wits, not wasting time and talking about prudence, while our sisters are being raped, battered and murdered."

"I don't believe what I'm hearing," Toni interjected. "Why not just purchase an entire arsenal and parade around like vigilantes? Personally, I prefer to do my fighting counseling women, empowering them with choices, healing their psychic wounds. Leave the criminals to the authorities."

Chris's eyes shot green daggers at her. "You find fault with the Guardian Angels?"

"Hey," Sara said, helping herself to a handful of sunflower seeds and raisins. "If I were white and straight, I could go for Curtis Sliwa myself," she quipped around a mouthful of nuts.

Toni gripped the ballpoint in her hand so tightly that her knuckles whitened. "Frankly, I can't picture a bunch of women in berets and *Community Watch* T-shirts patrolling Main Street. Sure, it would be great for visibility, but kiss business good-bye. Get real."

Molly's eyes twinkled. "Actually, I *can* see it. *Lavender Berets*. It has a certain flair, doesn't it? Chris?"

Returning to her seat, Chris just stared at Molly. "Are you making fun of me?" Her eyes narrowed.

"Oh, honey, of course not. Don't pout. Lighten up."

"I do *not* pout. That is for girlie girls."

They burst into laughter. Even Toni couldn't control her mirth.

Flushing, Chris stared at her moccasins before raising her eyes again to Molly's. The expression on her friend's face made everything all right. Her smile had Chris's name on it.

"Don't encourage her," Toni warned, with just a hint of her usual bite. "Chris is serious. And we aren't professional killers. This guy's a psycho. Why make it easier for him by becoming visible? *Lavender Berets*," she scoffed.

Then, with a simple statement, Bev shattered the room. "The killer is not a guy, Toni, it's a she.... When Margo calmed down she said her attacker was a *woman*."

The confusion and disbelief Chris felt was mirrored in the eyes of the others.

"That's crazy," Molly whispered. "What kind of woman would trash a sister like that, for God's sake?"

Toni counted off the possibilities on her be-ringed fingers: "Someone gay with internalized homophobia, a straight woman with externalized homophobia, maybe a closet case with psychotic tendencies who snapped. Shall I go on?" As the others looked at her, stunned, she continued. "If she *is* a lesbian, we have to face the fact that the hets don't have a franchise on mental illness." Focusing on Bev, she asked, "What made Margo believe her attacker was female? It was dark out."

"Not so dark that she couldn't see breasts," Bev filled in. "And her hair was in a ponytail. She wore a lot of rings and Margo said her voice was a breathy whisper...the kind of whisper that's menacing, creepy...."

"And how did Margo see all the little details like rings?" Toni persisted.

"When a car drove down the hill and surprised them. She saw the *details* in the headlights." Bev paused and considered her thoughts. "It was only for a second...then the attacker disappeared."

Still not satisfied, Toni added, "All the clues you mentioned could be put-ons, say, a man in drag."

"Can you picture Oliver Wendell in drag?" Sara blurted, guffawing despite the serious air.

"Or one of his good ole boys," Molly chimed in with a smile.

Bev shook her head. "You're impossible. What about the women on county payroll? Some of them would probably swallow nails to get us out of town."

That sobered them up.

"How did you come by all this information?" Toni eyed Bev with suspicion. "Wendell's not likely to leak things out during an investigation. He's not stupid, you know."

Chris snorted at that remark.

Bev had a difficult time looking up at Toni and answering the question. "One of Randi's private duty nurses...."

"That cute number with the pregnant cat?" Toni admonished playfully. "Tsk, tsk."

"This is no time for jokes," Chris warned, raking a hand through her short spiky hair. "Bev is having a difficult enough time as it is. The important question is how does this maniac know who is gay and who is not?"

"She cuts right to the heart of the matter," Toni admitted, tapping the top of her pen against her front teeth. "The big question." And she directed a rare smile of approval in Chris's direction.

"She could be someone we all know," Molly offered.

Chris shook her head. A cold chill of possibility gripped her, an unwelcome deja vu. Sweat broke out on her forehead and she had to struggle for breath, to get the words out before the serpent of rage and fear coiled within her snatched them back. "What if the victims had taken out personal ads in *Women's Network*—for a starter?"

A collective gasp greeted the possibility. Molly's eyes, intently fixed on Chris, forced her to look up. Their gazes locked and she knew what Molly was thinking by the fear in her eyes.

"That theory's good, Chris. Very, very good," Sara conceded. "Margo got kind of antsy and obsessive when we added the personals to the newsletter. She even joked about renting post office boxes out of our office."

"So she could get off on the replies, right?"

"And Margo would be the first to try something new, like placing an ad herself." Chris's tone sounded ominous. Her head spun at the possibilities, with what the outcome could be.

"Come to think of it, the ads were *her* idea," Sara realized, emphasizing the realization with a slap to her forehead. "I thought it was a good idea, too, you know, women screening women before they met. I went along with it. Oh, Goddess, I even encouraged her!" Sara looked stricken.

Chris reached over and patted Sara's hand. "It is not your fault that Margo is impulsive."

"What about the woman Margo was seeing? It sounded as if it was getting serious to me. Why would she want to place a personal ad?" Molly inquired with a baffled look.

Toni snickered. "Because she's horny and real relationships scare her."

Sara wailed, "You could be talking about all the women in this room!"

Chris hardly heard her. A buzzing noise inside her skull signalled an attack of nausea and claustrophobia, but most of all, of memory. "What goes around comes around," she murmured, horrified. Bolting up, she knocked over her chair in her rush to the bathroom. Retching and heaving into the toilet, she reached over and turned the sink faucets on full blast so as not be heard. Gasping, she gulped in air to ward off another convulsive heave. The doorknob jiggled. Molly called out to her. "Go away!" Chris cried, waiting until the rescue effort stopped. "Oh God, oh God!" After several more minutes, splashing cold water on her face, she returned to her chair on wobbly legs, keeping her eyes straight ahead.

"Maybe we shouldn't be talking about this, Chris. It hits too close to home." Molly's face, too, was pale as she looked at her friend.

All ears, Toni inquired: "What do you mean, too close to home?"

"Nothing, nothing," Molly mumbled.

Chris took a long sip of Perrier, then placed the cool bottle against her forehead. "Must be something I ate," she explained feebly, embarrassed by her display of emotion. Another sip of Perrier did not erase the sour taste of fear from her mouth. Her hands shook. Suddenly, she did not care. Let them see her. They were her friends, weren't they?

"It's okay, Chris," Molly soothed.

"So what to do about this psycho before he or she hurts us any more?" Sara wondered aloud, with a concerned glance at Chris.

Then Bev responded sounding miserable. "You know, Randi was fascinated by the personals, too."

"You two having problems?" Toni asked, a bit too interestedly.

Bev's face turned tomato red. "Look, it's been six years!" she snapped uncharacteristically. "We have our fights, okay? Maybe Randi wanted to make me jealous, put a little spark back into our relationship. I've been spending more time in the barn than the bedroom, lately." Bev's eyes filled with tears, but she felt the need to go on. "Could be she was bored and the anonymity of the personals appealed to her. *If* she placed an ad. But I don't think she'd actually go out and meet somebody." Her voice lowering and her speech barely audible, she explained, "Randi would just correspond for the novelty of it, I think. Oh, Christ, it's my fault. I should have taken her seriously." Bev buried her face in her hands.

Molly, eyes glistening, stood up and circled the table to stand behind Bev. She began to massage her friend's back, her words matching the soothing circles her hands made: "Do you really think you could have stopped her? Are you that powerful?" With that, she directed a glance at Chris as if hammering the point in her direction too.

"Sara, just in case, maybe you should cool the ads for a while," Toni said thoughtfully.

Chris shook her head vehemently. "No, Sara, please place an ad for me in the *Network*. And do it before the sheriff figures this out for himself and makes a mess of it."

Sara agreed with a nod. "We're not sure that the personals are a link to the stalker." She fiddled with her gold necklace. "I can't just close the column down. Subscribers have paid for months of ads," she reasoned, glancing in Toni's direction before resting her thoughtful brown eyes on Chris. "Just make sure you know what you're doing, Benet."

"Trust me," Chris urged.

Molly walked back to her chair and pushed up the sleeves of her pale blue blouse. "Chris?" she started, "You're out of your mind."

"Perhaps." Shoulders erect, fighting for control, Chris strode over to the slide projector, tore a sheet of paper from a legal pad and grabbed a pen. Turning, her green eyes bored into Molly's.

"I know what's going on in that crazy head of yours," Molly challenged. "And it won't bring him back."

Toni was all ears again. "Bring who back?"

As far as Chris was concerned, the meeting was over and so she drifted away from the others. But Sara followed her. "Just want you to know, I'm with you, Chris. I'm sure Toni and Bev will come around, too," she added softly.

Toni's voice interrupted Chris's grateful reply. "My tired brain's begging for a cup of coffee and a jelly donut," Toni called out, placing her belongings in her tote bag as they all stood up and gathered around Molly at the door. "You coming?" she said to Molly, her face expectant.

"I'll meet you at the cafe after I tie up some loose ends here." Gesturing in Chris's direction, she urged, "Let's set up another meeting for next week."

They agreed on Tuesday night again and Bev waved at Chris, who said her good-byes distractedly. As they trooped out the door, Chris sat down and hunched over the yellow piece of paper on the table in front of her. Slowly, controlling the anguish and fury the task wrought on her senses, she let her pen do the talking while her dead brother's ghost whispered in her ear.

ℱ℈ ℱ℈ ℱ℈

❦ 4 ❧

*F*or the second time, Chris re-read the personal ad she had written under the name of "Lavender Woman," each word choking her, adding fuel to the slow fire of outrage burning inside her. The light whisk of Molly's broom could be heard as she crossed out a word, realizing how seductive writing personal ads was, how it stroked the ego. You merely put yourself in the best possible light to hook your quarry.

Adding another word, she pictured her brother, Simon, composing such an ad five years earlier. She recalled how excited he had been by one man who responded, and, as a result of that first meeting, how he was unmercifully stabbed and thrown six floors down an elevator shaft. In that small space, his life's blood had drained out of him. All because of money.

The man had thought Simon was well-heeled by the way he presented himself. Back in Simon's modest apartment, though, he discovered otherwise. It had come out at the trial that Simon, spooked by the abrupt change in the man's attitude, from seductive to demanding, had ordered him out of the apartment. A fight ensued, a knife was pulled, and Simon became tragic history. As a result, Chris had lost, not only a younger brother she adored, and was supposed to protect, but her own healthy sexual appetite.

Folding the ad, she stood up. Molly swept dirt off the floor and into a dustpan with deliberate movements, slowly placing the broom back in its corner, her face thoughtful, as if deliberating how to break the silence. A flush of repressed anger still tinged her cheeks.

Finally, she spoke. "Simon wouldn't want you to put yourself in jeopardy, Chris."

Chris weighed her friend's words. "There are bastards out there who prey on us. Now there is one in Deer Falls. Man or woman, the fight is mine." She pulled on her purple baseball cap and headed for the door, then half-turned. "I am very sorry if I worry you, Molly, but this must be happening for a reason. Perhaps now I have a chance to make things right."

"Why you?"

"To clean the slate. For retribution. I must...." Chris's voice broke. "Make sure that it does not happen again. I should have tried harder to stop my brother. But I was too involved with myself to see what he was doing was dangerous." She did not say that Simon was as flaky as Margo.

Molly didn't buy it. "You heard what I told Bev before. None of us is powerful enough to play Goddess. There was no way you could have stopped Simon, just as there was no way Bev could stop Randi, or Sara, Margo. The ads were placed and that's that. You talk about making things right." She paused, her brown eyes blazing. "It wasn't the way that Simon died that turned you off to sex or took the life out of you, at least not completely."

Chris froze. "What do you mean?"

Molly let out a long sigh. "The person who came to my house the night her brother died, looking for solace, trying to forget...well, she got scared off, remember? *That's* what made you celibate, Chris."

"You are surely crazy, Molly," Chris retorted. But she could not halt the image of Molly's soft, warm arms opening to her that night, how she had panicked, pushing her friend away as soon as she felt the terrifying melting inside herself.

She had always been the initiator of sex, the one in control. To discover that her body could respond with such abandon, like a *woman's*, to yield under Molly's eager, pliant flesh, had scared the hell out of her.

She noticed tears in Molly's eyes and suddenly, all the fight went out of her. "It had nothing to do with you," she whispered. "It was *me*."

But Molly's anger could not be smoothed away. "You don't care how *I* feel seeing you like this, knowing you could get hurt. Chris, as much as you'd like to believe otherwise, you're not the best or strongest of men."

Chris wheeled around and stormed out, welcoming the escape the anger gave her. A cool drizzle misted her burning face. How dare Molly! Clenching her teeth, she dropped the personal ad in the *Grassroots Press* mail slot and circled the parked cars at the curb.

Country music streamed out of the cafe across the street; headlights of passing cars reflected on the wet asphalt. Suddenly, the air fizzed out of her like a punctured tire. "Oh, shit!" A slick of lavender paint ran down her Jeep's red hood, partially covering the left fender, pooling around the front tire. She kicked it fiercely. "Merde!" She loved this car. Like a punch in the gut, it hit her full force now, the threat they had skirted in the back room of Molly's, deflecting it with laughter. Shaken, she leaned against the driver's side and rode out a wave of paralyzing fear, followed by the shattering image of Simon's broken, bleeding body in that small elevator shaft. Now another nightmare scenario was beginning to take shape.

Bitterly, she thought, *Sheriff Wendell will probably say the paint tossed on my Jeep was a prank by local kids. Kids who knew that lavender would make me see red*!

A few more cars whooshed down the rain-slicked street, headlights marking their trail. Frustrated, she climbed into the Jeep and turned the ignition. She had to calm down. Popping a relaxation tape into the deck, she slowly gave herself up to the sound of surf on a beach.

By the time she reached the first steel bridge on the road back to her cottage behind *Le Provençal*, her mood had mellowed somewhat. She was a child splashing in the surf, at her first American beach, Jones Beach, laughing at Simon's fear of the waves. She had been frightened, too, but would never have showed it in front of maman.

Chris was eleven when they arrived in America and had accepted the role of her beautiful mother's hero and little Simon's protector. She had welcomed the false sense of power and invincibility maman had bestowed on her. Though she was lonely, she never cried. Though she felt alienated from the American girls who were her classmates, she never showed hurt. Instead of breasts, she developed biceps. *Feel then, maman. See how strong I am.*

Her windshield wipers kept time with her thoughts as she headed home.

By fourteen, she was still maman's little tomboy trying to disguise her budding breasts with layers of flannel shirts. If anyone presented her with lipstick, perfume, or dolls as gifts, she showed her poor manners. Tools and toy guns were all she craved. They helped her hide her feelings and pretend she was not afraid.

What were her losses in this strong fantasy world? Molly's last words echoed inside her head. "Your rage is not all for Simon. As much as you'd like to think otherwise, you are not the best or strongest of men."

Did she really want to be a man? **No.** As she grew older, surprising choices opened up. She met enlightened women who taught her to make those choices and walk the avenues of empowerment paved by her sisters before her.

But in the process, she had sacrificed something precious that she managed to capture in her art: vulnerability. She gripped the steering wheel tighter. Molly saw right through her. That Molly still loved her did not matter. It made her squirm when someone got close enough to see what a fraud she was.

Once, Molly had commented: "You walk around like you wear armor instead of skin." Digesting the meaning behind those words, Chris recalled the incident that had welded the final sheet of metal in place. When maman divorced Andre, her second husband, Chris had been overjoyed. No one could replace papa but her, and she and her father were allies, both hungry for maman's affections. So, in America, Chris took over what papa had claimed in France. But in America, Andre came along, and though he was eventually rejected, too, things were never the same again. Men seemed to have some kind of powerful, seductive key to maman's heart. Something that Chris could not comprehend. Maman was lost to her.

She shifted gears with the thought: *I shall paint my Jeep lavender and flaunt it.* Her anger was palpable now, her thirst for revenge, real.

Without figuring out why, she stopped in front of Katya Michaels' property. To ward off the chill that the rain had brought, she grabbed the black slicker she always kept in her Jeep, put it on. Hopping out, she stood at the foot of the wood chip path. Searching for something, not sure what, she listened to her heartbeat; her eyes lingering on the log cabin, climbing up the river rock chimney, following the smoke curling upward and disappearing into the midnight blue sky. It was a slice of rich, dark velvet heaven, slightly misty, and she could have been gazing at it from her own cottage window. It felt comforting, like a child's favorite blanket, made even more comforting because she shared with Katya Michaels, the same constellations beyond the velvet curtain, the same hazy moon.

A shadowy figure passed in front of one lit window. Chris's heart leaped. She waited for it to re-appear, and when it did not, imagined Katya sitting in an armchair in front of a fire kindled for just such a cool late April night as this. Perhaps Katya held a book in her hands. Perhaps she was reading a story to Sam in his bedroom after a nightmare awakened him.

She pictured Katya brushing her hair. *Even if Katya Michaels is brewing a cup of tea, even if she is just paying bills like the rest of us, all is right with the world.*

Wiping mist off her face, Chris bent down and plucked two medium-sized white stones from the edge of the path. She rubbed their cool, moist surfaces all the way back to her Jeep before dropping them in the pocket of her slicker.

She would be seeing Katya Friday. Just three more days that seemed like a lifetime.

℘ℓ   ℘ℓ   ℘ℓ

5

*K*atya straightened the quilted patchwork comforter on her brass four-poster bed. She then tossed an assortment of pink, white and mauve throw-pillows her mother had carefully stitched onto the bed. Every morning they fell into a different pattern—sharp contrast to what she considered the sameness of her life.

Her bare legs felt chilled as she perched on the edge of the bed looking around with pleasure. She was almost through decorating, she realized, a luxury she never thought she'd be able to afford. But two instructional books she had written on creative writing had been published and sold remarkably well, to schools and libraries. Then there was the money her father had divided between her and her mother in his will, which came to her after his stroke. She would much rather he had lived, she thought, and sighed. But as a result, she was no longer a struggling college professor. Loren had also provided for her and Sam, leaving, besides the log cabin they had commuted to on week-ends, a stock portfolio that would come in handy for Sam's future college education, and Katya's eventual retirement.

The muted colors that surrounded her brought her again to thoughts of Loren. Too busy with her dental practice, she had left the decorating to Katya with one stipulation—that in the large picture windows of the master bedroom and bath she would have stained glass inserts celebrating the Goddess.

Katya had thrown herself into the renovations as if to ward off the unbelievable reality that Loren was dying of cancer. Manically keeping that dream of moving up to Deer Falls alive, Katya made sure that their rustic retreat became the home of their dreams.

A place to heal.

They would share space with fertile plants and enjoy wonderful aromas from their country kitchen. The pattern of log walls and gleaming hardwood floors would be softened with pastel drapes and lush earth-toned carpeting that invited bare feet.

They would entertain in celebration of their home, their future. Make love afterwards in their cozy bedroom, which was tucked, like Sam's, into the upstairs loft.

As she dressed, Katya felt how alone she was and glanced around the bedroom. Two oak rockers with Early American needlepoint cushions flanked her Queen Anne desk. Overhead shelves held a multitude of literary voices. But the bedroom was silent.

The phone rang, jarring her thoughts. She walked over to the night table, picked up the receiver and cradled it between her shoulder and ear, pulling one Nike sneaker over her foot. Heavy breathing answered her hello.

"Who is this?" Annoyance darkened her brow, then turned into fear when she remembered the ominous whisperings of the women at the table next to her in *Le Provençal*, two nights ago.

She challenged the caller again. Nothing. It was the second crank call that week and a knot of terror formed in her stomach. "Who is this? What do you want?"

"You," said a breathy, strained whisper that made her think of someone recovering from, or feigning pharyngitis. "I want *you*. But if I can't have you, I'll take that little blonde boy." A sinister laugh ended the call.

Katya's mouth opened for an indignant retort, but the phone went dead.

Heart hammering, she dialed Sam's elementary school. And not until she was assured by the secretary that Sam was safely engrossed in music hour did she remember to breathe. Her hand trembled as she phoned the sheriff's office and reported the incident to a laconic deputy chewing gum in her ear.

"Not much we can do, ma'am. But if it keeps happening, I'd advise changing your number."

"My seven-year-old could have told me that. Are you going to wait until he's kidnapped?" Realizing she sounded hysterical, Katya modified her voice. He seemed to pick up on her underlying panic and softened his response. *Or was he just humoring her?*

"Lots of teen-agers got nothing better to do than stuff double chocolate chip cones down their throats at the ice cream shop, and get their kicks freaking people out on the phone. Don't take it seriously." He paused. "Your house been broken into? Anything else to report?"

"I am reporting a threat to me and my son," she metered out slowly, as if she was dealing with a half-wit. "It didn't sound like a teen-ager. My son was threatened...my little boy." Her voice cracked.

"Was the voice male or female?"

Her mouth opened when she realized that she didn't really know. "I couldn't tell."

He chuckled. "These kid callers can do all sorts of things with their voices. They just wrap a handkerchief or piece of Saran Wrap around the receiver...I, uh, understand your concern, ma'am, but we've gotta have something more concrete."

"Concrete like in a block of cement attached to a body in the river?" She hung up on his further attempts to mollify her and suddenly felt abandoned. Realizing that this was just exactly what the crank caller had wanted, she paused, drew a breath, and tried to think clearly. But her palms were wet and her heart was pounding. It left an ache in her chest. *Maybe the deputy was right*, she rationalized. *Still, there'd be no harm in picking Sam up from school today...but what about every other day this week?*

She alone was responsible for Sam. She was all he had. It would be counter-productive to worry his emotionally frail grandparents.

She couldn't help thinking about Sam's father, imprisoned in California, and how one day she'd have to tell her son the truth about him. Pacing back and forth, too worked up to correct manuscripts, she grabbed a T-shirt and shorts, and decided to go jogging before she started working. The hell with the crank caller. Whoever it was had played on her 'Big Apple' mentality. She was living in Deer Falls now, not New York City. This couldn't be happening here.

Still, she found herself pushing aside some sweaters in her bottom dresser drawer—staring down at the .38 revolver Loren had originally stashed away in her dental office after two robberies in her building. Over Katya's objections, Loren had extracted the promise that the gun be kept in the cabin for protection. She shivered. Closing the drawer, she completed her outfit with an ankle wallet. Then with a small brass watering can, she moistened the Asparagus and Dallas ferns hanging with an assortment of Philodendrons from the beamed, stuccoed ceiling. She liked the way the sturdy log walls yielded to them. Finally, she poked a finger in the soil of the Coleus. Ficus and Norfolk Island Pines dotted the polished hardwood floor that bordered the oatmeal rug. They were still moist.

Reaching into her bag for a set of keys, she hurried down the spiral oak staircase. It curved to the left and spilled out into the great room. To the right, below two curtained windows, sat a long free-form indoor rock garden filled with tropical plants and sculptures. The wall opposite the staircase was part river-rock and housed the fireplace. To its left, a bookcase and wall unit hugged the log walls, and opened into the dining area which was partitioned off with a Japanese screen and led out to the deck.

Katya veered right into the vestibule and flicked off the large Tiffany cut-glass fixture she always left burning through the night. The last sound she heard after locking the carved oak door behind her was the chime of her grandfather clock, before her feet hit the three-mile stretch of road into Deer Falls. The steady slap of jogging shoes against asphalt, the rush of cool air sweeping through her lungs restored her, as did the heady scent of the stream, the canopy of trees marking the woods that lined both sides of the main road.

As if they, too, sensed that May was just a few days away, a chorus of birds twittered from their perches on tangled branches above, celebrating the season. A brush of morning sunlight painted Katya's face, then a gust of air off the stream threw it into cool relief.

Katya noticed the same discarded comb, a few more teeth missing, that had survived winter. And wildflower buds dotted the grassy shoulders of the road. Churning below on both sides of her, the stream surged, as she crossed the first steel bridge into town. Where the land started in earnest, the stream bowed to it, with a sweeping gesture, and forked behind a line of cottages in front of her. She began mentally counting signs on her left: two for "Firewood" and "Topsoil" and one for "Fresh Honey." On her right, a crooked, old weathered plank on the weedy front lawn of a dilapidated wooden shack, announced "Antiques." Most of the items strewn about on the front lawn appeared rusty. *Dogpatch, U.S.A.,* she thought, half-expecting to see Daisy Mae chasing Li'l Abner.

A truck roared by spewing hot exhaust fumes in her face. She held her breath and with the first intake of air, caught the pungent odor of a dead animal. The cottages thinned out up ahead where the road separated a farmhouse, on her right, from its unplowed field, to her left.

This was the only point in her daily jog where she could not hear the steadfast sound of the stream, where she became uncomfortably aware of her heartbeat.

Suddenly, two German Shepherds leaped out at her, breaking the silence with menacing barks. She froze.

"Back off, boys," she said soothingly, trying not to panic.

A pair of sharp canine teeth were bared at her. Maintaining eye contact, she slowly crossed to the other side of the road when one of the dogs snarled and bounded toward her. A mind-flash of a neighbor who had been bitten while jogging in Washington Square Park in Manhattan rose to her mind.

In panic, her eyes searched the shoulder and found a stick. She quickly picked it up. Heart slamming against her ribcage, she faced the angry dog. Just then, a woman's voice rang out, and reluctantly, the animals trotted away and retreated behind a hedge of forsythia.

Outraged that their owner would allow them carte-blanche use of the road, Katya steadied her breathing, crossing back to the other side and loped forward on legs that felt boneless.

A raccoon lay sprawled in her path, victim of a careless driver. The odor assaulted her nostrils. Its paws, drawn up in rigor mortis, seemed to be praying. She stifled an urge to give last rites, noting how clean the carcass was except for a patch of matted blood. Shivering, she hesitated to step forward, half-expecting it to rise up and bite her. The hungry caws of waiting crows overhead made her think of her own mortality and Sam's fate if she should die.

Straight ahead, a white station wagon approached in the oncoming lane. It seemed to pause before passing her, as if the driver wanted directions. Through the tinted windshield she could make out the outline of a smiling face, with dark hair pulled back in a ponytail.

A chill climbed up her spine, but the station wagon had already passed her. She continued her pace alongside the sparse traffic in her lane, barely paying attention to the occasional vehicle motoring by in the opposite direction on the narrow road. Jogging to the second steel bridge, she became aware, with a surge of relief, that the stream had stopped playing hide and seek with the land and had branched off into three narrow tributaries. They wove in front and back of roadside cottages, and beneath her, gurgling contentedly, beckoning her to follow before the watery arteries finally joined the heart of their mother river beyond Deer Falls proper.

When she was halfway over the steel bridge, she heard an engine purr behind her. Swiveling her head, she saw the same white station wagon. Warning bells went off. She remembered the two crank calls that week and the librarian who had been attacked while jogging.

Just as her legs seemed about to give out, the station wagon swerved around her. She thought she heard a laugh, compared it to the laugh that had filled her ears on the phone. The vehicle clattered over the wooden slats of the bridge and sped away. Though she was only a mile from town, she considered turning back, then chided herself. What could happen in broad daylight?

Okay, she was spooked, but then she sighted the familiar flagpole in front of the low-slung brick facade of Sam's school. She heard a bell ring and was somewhat assured by its normalcy.

The bell triggered thoughts of the first time she and Loren had seen Sam off on a school bus to nursery school. He had cried, parting from them, and Katya had felt a keening wail in response. Sam was on his own for the first time, and it wouldn't be long before he went off on longer and longer trips. When the bus disappeared down Fifth Avenue, Loren had clasped her hand and kissed it, and everything had seemed all right. Together, the gesture implied, they'd see Sam through all the childhood diseases visited on the young; through football and soccer injuries when he reached high school age. And finally, Katya's overactive brain had projected, they'd be welcoming him home, the warrior-scholar on holidays from college.

Aching for Loren, Katya was catapulted into the dizzying memory of the events that had irrevocably changed her life.

ぞð　　ぞð　　ぞð

🌿 6 🌿

*K*atya had been lunching at a New York restaurant with her publisher. He was rambling on about royalties, foreign rights, library acquisitions. Tired and distracted, Katya had looked up from her plate and was jolted awake by the deep hazel eyes of the woman staring at her from the next table. She was sitting with an attractive redhead. Katya watched, fascinated, while the tanned face that owned those deep hazel eyes, that sensual mouth, laughed easily, spoke and ate with an animation that charged the air around her. Wearing an expensive beige linen suit, her long brown hair streaked with blonde highlights, the woman lifted a glass of white wine with her large, capable unadorned hand. Again, she stared at Katya; her glass arrested in mid-air. Her eyes held a questioning amusement, and Katya felt something turn over inside her.

Confused, captivated, heady, but not from her wine, Katya was so unnerved that she almost knocked over her own glass of burgundy.

For the next half hour, as they ate and discussed the terms of the contract, Katya had one ear cocked to the next table, waiting to hear that softly-modulated voice. When the woman stood up, Katya felt she would somehow die. *Was she leaving*? There wasn't a damned thing Katya could do about it.

So distracted was she, that she swallowed a piece of steak before chewing it thoroughly, and the next thing she knew she was choking. Her publisher panicked, slapping her too hard on the back, which only lodged the meat further down Katya's windpipe.

She didn't recall blacking out, remembered only a pair of strong arms encircling her from behind, a fist centered just below her sternum, driving upward.

The hands supporting her head while she gasped for air were gentle, the voice patient and calm. And when Katya looked up, the woman's eyes so close to her own were filled with concern and relief. Just as quickly, she was gone, leaving Katya not only embarrassed by her childish awkwardness, but wondering if she had imagined the whole affair.

From her publisher, Katya discovered that a reporter at one of the tables had witnessed the rescue and tried to interview Loren. Instead, Loren had escaped to the rest room when the paramedics arrived, emerging only when her luncheon companion fetched her.

Before they left, Katya had managed to get the Good Samaritan's name from the Maitre d': Dr. Loren Hollander, an endodontist on Madison Avenue.

The flowers they sent each other crossed paths the next day. It wasn't enough for Katya. She waited for the phone to ring, wondered how Loren Hollander had obtained her address, blessing the angel who had provided it. *What to do now*? She had never experienced these feelings before. Infatuated with a *woman*?

Two days later, her prayers were answered. She broke a tooth clear down to the gum-line and required root canal work. To this day, she didn't know if she had bitten down on that chicken bone on purpose.

(((((

Katya smiled at the memory as she continued jogging. Her thoughts had taken over so completely that she was amazed to find herself in front of *Sprinkles*, the new ice cream and frozen yogurt shop on Main Street. Bracing her foot against a fire hydrant, she stretched her legs, then headed down the street toward *Molly's Sporting Goods* for some dry flies that would match the mayflies she had seen hatching over the stream earlier that week.

A bell above the door tinkled and Molly Cheever, dressed in a soft plaid flannel shirt tied at the waist of her jeans, glanced up from the Chinese take-out carton she was stirring with a pair of chopsticks. Opposite her, two attractive women sat on stools, chatting amiably over several cartons of food on the glass counter. The aromas made Katya's mouth water.

"Hello, Katya, nice to see you again," Molly greeted her and wiped her mouth with a napkin. Katya thought her hair was pretty, the blonde streaks weaving in and out of her light brown curls more the result of sun than a bleach job.

"Hi, Molly," she said, and returned the greeting of the two other women as well, who now began to clean up after Molly made some introductions.

"I have a client coming in ten minutes," Toni Cabrera announced, glancing at her designer watch. "Next time, lunch is my treat, okay?"

Sara Wenning stretched languorously. "I feel so good, I'm tempted to close down the press today." She flashed a brilliant smile at Katya before heading for the back room with the remains of their lunch.

Feeling a bit uncomfortable—she had broken up their little party—Katya browsed through some display cases of lures and hand-tied flies, before her gaze was drawn upward to three oil paintings above a rack of fishing vests and camping gear. It seemed as if the canvasses were beckoning to her. One took her breath away, evoking a poignant sense of well-being. The technique somehow seemed familiar.

Bathed in a golden glow, a woman and little girl, both blonde, knelt by the edge of a stream. The woods surrounding them were alive with spring growth and seemed to vibrate. The goldleaf frame complemented the colors—and, for a moment, Katya reflected on the photos her father had taken, when she was a little girl, standing by a stream with her mother. She could almost hear him explaining the life cycles of nature in his Biology Professor's voice.

The other paintings, depicting nature in fall and winter, were captivating, too, but she just had to have *this* landscape. Turning to Molly behind the counter, she opened her mouth to speak.

"Breathtaking isn't it? I was thinking of buying the spring scene myself," Molly said quickly.

"Oh." Katya faltered on the edge of disappointment.

"There *were* four of them," Molly explained, as the redhead listened intently. "I just sold the summer landscape to a writer who lives near the river. It feels like a part of me is missing."

Katya, confused by Molly's possessive tone, asked: "Are you the artist?"

The redhead barked a laugh and Molly shot Toni a withering look. She ran a hand through her hair and set off the silver bangle bracelets on her wrists.

"She wishes," Toni chimed in. "Chris Benet is our local artist."

"Chris?" Katya asked.

Molly looked taken aback. "You know her?"

Katya wondered if Molly had seen her excitement and a flush of heat suffused the back of her neck. "I don't really *know* her. I've been to *Le Provençal* and she was painting a mural there. In fact, my son, Sam...."

Molly seemed to instantly relax the moment Katya mentioned that she had a son, and Katya stopped herself from blurting out anything else she might be sorry for.

"Toni," Molly said, in what Katya thought was an attempt at a conspiratorial tone. "Those boots you wanted are in the other room."

Toni didn't seem like a woman who would tolerate being shunted aside, but she slipped off her stool obligingly, though peeved.

Eyeing Katya carefully, Molly said, "Chris and I go back a long way."

Katya couldn't decide if Molly was possessive or protective of Chris, and it struck her, with a pang of jealousy, that they might be lovers. "Are those paintings for sale?" Katya inquired of Molly. "I'm interested in the one with the mother and child."

"I hand-tied some more Light Cahills for you...."

"How much does she want for the painting?" Katya persisted, trying to keep the annoyance out of her voice.

Molly shrugged. "Chris leaves that up to me."

Katya moved closer to see the painting. "I can picture it hanging above my fireplace."

"I can, too," echoed a male voice from the door. Half-turning, Katya saw Geoff Holden, her writing student, close the door behind him, his brown eyes eager at the sight of her. "Even though I've never had the privilege of seeing your fireplace." He wore a gray sweatband around his sandy colored hair. "How're you doing, Professor Michaels?" And when she nodded, he looked up at the painting, too. "The blonde woman looks like you, except you have a son." About to add something else, his attention was diverted by the tall woman in a caftan who strode back into the room just then and was regarding him intently.

Under her gaze, he seemed to squirm.

Sara looked at Katya with a raised eyebrow.

Unnerved, Katya responded to Geoff's remark with abruptness. "The likeness is coincidental." Masking her discomfort, she looked at the painting again. Was Sara's raised eyebrow a sign that she thought something was going on between her and Geoff? And why should she care about what this woman thought?

But Sara was distracted now, even humming.

The woman in Chris's spring scene called to her once more—the way she leaned expectantly toward the child. "I just have to have this painting," she said, almost to herself.

After scrutinizing both Katya and Geoff, Molly seemed to relax. Maybe Katya posed no threat to her and Chris. "I guess it's okay—for the right price."

"I've never seen you smile like that before," Geoff said to Katya. "You must think it's some terrific painting."

The nervous tic above his right eye danced. Damn, he was jealous! Annoyed, she couldn't be bothered with him and resented the false sense of intimacy he was implying.

Then a smile passed between her and Sara, and Katya instinctively knew that this was a woman she could like.

She chose three Light Cahill dry flies, making sure to compliment Molly on their workmanship. "What did you get for the other painting you sold?"

Molly, who seemed to have softened after Katya openly admired her work, hesitated, but only for a moment. "Six-hundred and twenty-five dollars. But the prices vary."

I bet your commission doesn't, Katya mused as the redhead returned to the front of the store with a pair of hiking boots. And then she felt unkind. It was obvious that Molly Cheever didn't want to sell Chris's paintings. She couldn't blame her. Obviously, she wasn't motivated by money. "I'll leave a deposit," she said, smiling at Molly. "And thanks. I would hate to part with her work, too."

Molly's face opened up like the sun breaking through clouds. Katya bent down and unwound the velcro wallet from her ankle, uncomfortably aware of Geoff's gaze. Leaning on the glass countertop, she wrote out a check. "Two hundred okay? I can pick it up later on this week and give you the balance."

Molly nodded, all smiles.

"Do me a favor, though," Katya requested. "Mark it 'Sold,' and don't tell Chris. You know how generous she is. I'm afraid that she'd find out and leave it gift-wrapped on my doorstep, anxious to make sure that her new neighbor was properly welcomed."

Molly sighed. "That's Chris." Generously, she gestured at the painting. "You know, there *is* a resemblance between you and the subject. But I'd know if Chris had used a model...."

Sensing that Molly was fishing, Katya chuckled. "I didn't pose for her. I'm just a patron of the arts." She took the bag with her purchases and faced the tall woman standing in front of her.

"Any friend of that brush-wielding rebel, Chris Benet, is a friend of mine," Sara offered, extending a hand.

A burst of warmth suffused Katya's body as she returned the handshake.

"I run the women's press down the street. You're probably on our mailing list."

"And if you're new to the area," Toni Cabrera chimed in. "I'd be glad to take you on a tour of our new Women's Center. You never know when we might be of service...." Her sharp, hazel eyes penetrated Katya's.

Outside, a scream startled them.

"Goddess, not again," Molly cried. "This time, I'm going to nail that bastard for good. Watch the register, Toni." She ran past a startled Katya and pouting Geoff, flung open the door and disappeared outside.

One by one, they all followed, Sara gently nudging Katya back against the safety of the store front, threatening Geoff with a look that would kill if he interfered.

A scraggly, scowling wiry man, fists raised, wearing a soiled grey uniform with his shirt-tails hanging out, was chasing a teen-aged girl around a dented pick-up truck across the street.

"Leave her alone, you piece of garbage," Molly shouted, red-faced, as she stood in the middle of the street facing him, her hands poised for combat. He stood there wobbling, obviously drunk, flicking his bloodshot eyes from the young girl to Molly, measuring her before he lunged. Molly tripped him and grabbed him by the hair, yanking his head up. When he flailed out to hit her, she used the edge of her palm in a swift chopping motion against the bridge of his nose. Blood gushed out and he screamed in pain.

The long-haired teen-ager clasped her hands to her mouth and paled.

"I'll take care of this," Geoff Holden declared, but Sara grabbed him by the collar. "Stay put, macho man, you're not needed."

Stunned, Geoff stared at Sara, then backed down. Katya almost felt sorry for him, but she felt even sorrier for the scared teen-ager. Without thinking, she ran across the street, grabbed the frightened girl and pulled her away from the scene, hugging her gently to calm her.

"That's my father," she cried raggedly. "He's really gonna kill me now."

"Hush. Nobody's going to kill you." But Katya could believe it. The girl's left eye was badly bruised and swollen half-shut and her cheek was red and scraped. For a second, Katya thought of the toddler she had seen slapped in the supermarket. It didn't matter what age kids were, she thought, they could always be victims of parental abuse. She was also surprised that not one person in the throng of onlookers now dispersing had done anything to help. But then again, Molly and Sara hadn't seemed to need help; and she was used to indifference from living in Manhattan.

"It'll be all right," Katya soothed. "Calm down."

Sara helped Molly drag the whining man back to the sidewalk and propped him against the storefront.

"I called the sheriff," Toni said from the doorway, looking totally disgusted.

"You threaten that girl again, asshole, I'll break this off," Molly snapped, swiping at the nose he had covered with his hands. Both she and Sara were splattered with blood.

Deflated, he wailed. "Goddammit, she's a whore! I can do anything I want with her. She's mine! You hear me?" He yelled across the street: "You're mine, you tramp!" A second later he broke down. "She never comes home...never calls."

"Look at yourself," Sara barked. "And you'll see why." Looking up at Toni, she added, "Can you call off your one-thirty appointment? That girl needs counseling now."

Toni nodded and retreated back into the store.

Sara crossed the street, heading back to Katya and the trembling teen-ager, and as she did, one of the remaining stragglers gave her the thumbs-up sign.

"This is maybe the fourth time he's come after her," Sara explained to Katya. "But she won't report him." Shifting her gaze to the teen-ager, Sara placed a gentle finger on her quivering chin and held up her face for scrutiny. "Lord, girl. You both need help. Next time it might be a gun instead of fists."

The girl nodded, sobbing dramatically, more for sympathy, it seemed now.

"Katya? I'll stay with her until the sheriff picks up that pile of trash in front of Molly's. A sorry display for sporting goods, you might say. And thanks for helping, you didn't have to get involved."

Katya smiled. "I'm just a meddler at heart." In the face of Sara's puzzled expression, she added: "I beat up on abusive mothers in supermarkets."

Sara howled with laughter. "Well, I'll be damned." And then she shocked Katya with a quick, impulsive hug. "What's your hat size, babe?"

It was Katya's turn to look puzzled.

"Chris and I are going to be handing out some lavender berets pretty soon," Sara explained.

"Lavender berets?"

"Private joke, honey. You okay? Can I give you a lift home?"

Katya studied Sara's finely-planed face and felt good, stronger somehow. "I'm fine," she assured the other woman as Geoff headed in their direction, concern on his sheepish face.

Sucking in a breath, Katya announced, "Well, I'm ready to jog off." And she left the teen-ager in Sara's able care after saying good-bye, aware of Geoff trailing her.

Tentatively, he stopped her with a hand on her arm. "Let me take you home. You could've gotten hurt with those...lezzies." His face tightened sourly and she wanted to reprimand him, but controlled herself. Instead she made certain that he took note of her scrutinizing his freshly-shaven face, too-clean sweatband—his unrumpled jogging suit. And he smelled of aftershave, not sweat.

"I thought you jogged into town, Geoff," she said suspiciously, sensing that he had wanted her to think that, too. Irritation flared up inside her.

"Well...I sort of...had planned to jog home with you," he admitted. "I know you take a run into town every Thursday and stop off for errands."

"You know too much." Katya's mind instantly flew to the white station wagon, the dead raccoon and vicious dogs who wanted to make dinner out of her. Now she had Geoff Holden to contend with. Somehow, the eagerness in his eyes seemed more troublesome than all the rest.

"I can pick my car up later," he coaxed, gesturing at an old black Volkswagen bug they were about to pass.

A group of teen-agers poured out of *Sprinkles* across the street as she halted in front of Geoff's car. "Look, I'm a bit shaken up. Maybe another day. The run back will give me time to let off steam."

"Sure, I can understand you need some space," he responded, but the tic above his eye belied his words.

She ran across the street. Threading through the cluster of teens gobbling their ice cream cones, laughing and horsing around, she thought of her conversation with the deputy on the phone earlier that morning.

Staring at hungry mouths devouring melting mounds of double chocolate chip and vanilla cones, his words echoed in her head: "Lots of teen-agers got nothing better to do than stuff double chocolate chip cones down their throats at the local ice cream shop, and get their kicks freaking people out on the phone."

Observing their faces, she sensed no menace. Shrill girlish squeals and giggles, and boys posturing and preening like peacocks were not the mark of sickos. What had happened outside of Molly's a little while ago, on the other hand, *would* give a person pause.

Give it a rest, she commanded her brain and jogged around the corner.

Tomorrow was Friday. The day that Chris was coming to look at her dishwasher. Chris. Those beautiful paintings. A tingling feeling swept through her.

How should she act? She wanted to ask her about the women's symbol in her Jeep, confess that she lied about being married and widowed. The tingles lumped into a ball of apprehension, weighing her stomach. Maybe tomorrow wasn't such a good idea, after all. Why look for trouble? She wasn't prepared for any more heartache.

Sam would say, 'Go with the flow, Mom.' Even if he didn't quite know what it meant, his timing was usually flawless.

ॐ   ॐ   ॐ

❦ 7 ❧

*E*xhaling a slow, sensual sigh, Katya sank back into a froth of herbal-scented suds that filled her white claw foot bathtub. Overhead speakers spilled a Rampal flute melody into the long, narrow, plant-filled retreat where she did her ablutions. Mist from the tub mingled with the slightly vinegary aroma of the freshly-chinked log walls; the scent of pine and tar released into the air by the heat.

She gathered soap over her breasts, and with a lazy lift of her head, gazed at the stained glass design in the center of a large window overlooking the back woods. A tiny, raven-haired Goddess, draped in a simple white tunic, was surrounded by nubile young women paying homage to her by tossing flowers all about. The stained glass seemed framed, as if intentionally, by the trees and bushes surrounding it. Looking through the window, Katya saw the rising sun dancing through the treetops.

Her stomach fluttered with a multitude of imaginary butterflies. All week, they seemed to have taken permanent residence there. She had little over an hour before Chris Benet's arrival. A few times that morning she'd considered calling it off, opting instead for the safe anonymity of a Sears repair-person. Especially since Loren was coming to her in dreams. Last night it was so erotic and explicit, so unexpected, that she had masturbated twice in order to fall back to sleep. It was the first release she had permitted herself since her lover's death thirteen months ago, as if orgasm, even by her own hand, was cheating.

In spite of the year of abstinence, she hadn't gotten rusty, still found the rhythm, the right pressure in the right places that evoked the most pleasure. But she had felt empty afterwards.

With the memory of last night guiding her, she submerged her hand into the hot water and trailed her fingertips along the soft, downy outer lips cushioning her throbbing clitoris.

Her head fell back on the vinyl tub pillow and several strands of hair escaped the clips holding them up. She pictured the very first touch of Loren's fingers on her as her own fingers explored, reliving her first orgasm.

It had been after the chicken bone fractured her tooth, after the root canal, that the concerts and trips to the beach began, both of them reaching out shyly. Katya was still denying her attraction to a woman, though she had come to the realization that she had been drawn to the gentleness of women most of her life. Loren's hesitation was anchored in a sense of responsibility. She did not want to be Katya's first, and used the doctor/patient relationship as an obstacle to further intimacy.

One fateful night's snowstorm changed everything. They had been forced to stay overnight in a bed and breakfast inn run by two of Loren's friends. The bedroom they were given faced Main Street in a Christmas-lit and tinseled, greeting-card small town.

Centered in the village square reigned a Christmas tree which was framed in their bay window. Katya had stood gazing out at a flurry of snowflakes swirling down from the midnight blue sky, turning the rooftops of the quaint storefronts white. She could hear, as she stood there trembling, the Christmas party still going strong downstairs. The aromas of wine and potpourri filled the warm, cozy room. From the nearby Hudson River, a foghorn sounded. Inside her, a yearning, poignant and nearly painful overcame her. She wanted to live in or near a town such as this.

Just then, Loren emerged from the bathroom. The green satin nightshirt she wore was backlit and illuminated every curve, every elegant line of her long, slender body.

Katya, in a white silk nightgown she had brought in case the threatened snowstorm materialized, could not swallow. Only her heart wasn't paralyzed. It felt like it would burst out of her chest.

Slipping behind her, Loren placed large gentle hands on Katya's forearms. "Are you sure?"

Katya's flesh prickled. All she could manage was a slight nod.

"You're shivering, Katie. Come away from the window."

"My goosebumps are not from the cold," Katya said hoarsely. She groaned as she turned and slipped into Loren's arms, felt the delicious pressure of soft breasts against hers, the flatness of belly; and below, the incredible white-hot heat of their sexual desire. Answering Katya's groan, Loren reached a long arm behind her, cupped her buttocks, and pressed them upwards to join their burning centers.

Katya's knees buckled. Moaning, Loren guided her to the bed and Katya sank down—her mouth hungrily, blindly seeking Loren's. Underlip yielded to moist underlip, slid into hot wetness, then the incredible thrill of Loren's tongue. Katya responded in kind. Tongues searched, gentle first, then insistent, matching the primitive rhythms deep inside them.

For one agonizing moment, Loren pulled back and gazed into Katya's eyes. "I love you," she whispered. "Let me show you how much." With tantalizing deliberation, she peeled off Katya's nightgown and lowered her smooth, satin body to Katya's bare, fiery flesh. Surrendering herself to the light nipping of lips, the fluttering tongue on her neck and throat, Katya arched her back.

"Let me love you, Katie," Loren murmured.

Katya's nipples instantly hardened under the expert tongue-tip circling them; her stomach muscles tightened with excruciating bliss as Loren's tongue swirled downward, teasing her.

"God!" Katya cried out when she felt Loren's hot breath at the juncture of her thighs.

"God has nothing to do with it."

Katya shut her eyes to a whirl of neon lights exploding in the darkness, felt the most sensitive core of her smoothly sucked in, lovingly stroked and worshipped by Loren's hot, knowing mouth. She cried out, clutching the coverlet to keep from flying into space. It was that frightening. And so quick, so thunderous, that she shivered violently. Just as she was about to explode, Loren stopped again, kissed her throbbing flesh, swirling her tongue around and around.

Katya rocketed higher and higher like a kite spiraling up from a pocket of air. But there was more, unbelievably more, and no relief, as a more exquisite climb grew beyond that—endless widening circles, endless orgasmic peaks. Animal sounds escaped her throat. Her body thrashed and twisted on the bed, as Loren stayed with her.

"Please don't stop," Katya begged. "Don't ever stop."

"Never, never...."

"I'm dying!"

"Not from this, love." Loren's hand caressed the back of her knee, her shin, worked down and slid over her bare feet, between her toes.

Arching her body up to Loren's demanding mouth, Katya grabbed a handful of long, brown hair. She felt those soft lips enclose the tight, pulsating core of her again. Loren's fingers weaved through

Katya's sensitive toes. Then there was nothing but sensation. She was one, huge, throbbing organism out of control, needy, at the mercy of Loren's tongue.

Her heart stopped. "Oh, no...no!"

"Yes...."

"I'm burning!" Her body soared, reaching heights she never dreamed existed. Loren's tongue thrust deeper. Katya cried out, cried out again and again as her body touched the first precipice, no turning back, reaching the next plateau; shooting up again....

"Aaahhh!" She cried out from the bathtub as her own fingers claimed her body in an ecstatic burst of release. Her head lolled back against the pillow. Pulsating, coming down, drained; she floated, half-smiling, allowing her fingers to drift on the warm water. Rampal's flute melody accompanied her descent.

She expelled a long sigh and shut her eyes. When the music stopped, she reluctantly climbed out of the tub, reached past a row of seashell-filled apothecary jars, and grabbed a fluffy pink bath towel. Wiping mist off a corner of the mirror over the double sink, she stared at her languid blue eyes. Her pink cheeks glowed back at her.

"You were a quick study," Loren had remarked that night, hazel eyes playful and bright from the orgasm Katya had eagerly given her. That night there had been no fear of surrender, just surrender itself; no emptiness, just her greedy body coming and coming again; her willing fingers and mouth learning this new and wonderful kind of loving.

I look ready for another round, Katya thought, with a wistful glance at the draining bathtub. *Anybody can see it on my face. Chris Benet will notice*, she thought with a jolt. Not about to feel any more awkward with her than she already did, Katya reached into the pink-tiled shower and turned the brass faucets on cold. Stepping in, she gasped as the spray hit her.

Toweling off, she brushed her hair up and fastened it with tortoise shell combs.

Time to dress quickly. Time to move on. Slipping into a mauve silk blouse tied at her throat with a bow, and tailored taupe slacks, she chose a pair of low-heeled pumps that matched the slacks, and topped the outfit off with the gold seashell earrings that had been her father's last gift. Everywhere she turned there were memories.

Checking herself in the full-length mirror in the cedar closet, she noted, with a frown, that the blouse clung to her curves with more than a suggestion, and contemplated changing. But that would mean she was overly-concerned about the appearance she was presenting. What was she afraid of?

Once down the spiral staircase, she crossed the great room, skirted the brown velour couch, glass coffee table and arm chairs in front of the fireplace, and stood by the cold hearth glancing at her watch. It was nine forty-five. Her heart slipped from first to third gear. To distract herself, she picked up the *Women's Newsletter* she had tossed on a glass end table yesterday and recalled the struggle outside of Molly's store. Though she had been jarred by their militancy, Katya had to admit that she had also been impressed with Sara and Molly. Especially Sara, so feminine, yet so obviously unconcerned about what people thought of her. *She isn't trying to win her mother's approval*, Katya mused with a sigh.

Collapsing on the couch, she leafed through the newsletter when a headline caught her eye: WOMEN'S CENTER BATTLING AUTHORITIES OVER LATEST ATTACKS ON LOCAL WOMEN. The article mentioned that Toni Cabrera, the center's coordinator, suggested an open forum to discuss the threat to the community. Apparently this was meeting resistance from the sheriff who insisted that his job was to keep things quiet and orderly, avoid panic, and prevent the victims from additional danger while their assailant was on the loose.

Frowning, Katya flipped some pages and froze; her eyes zeroed in on a personal ad in boldface: "Lavender Woman: Artistic, sensitive, open. Looking for soul-mate. If you enjoy good French wine, truffles and pâté, and meaningful conversation write: P.O.B. 18, Deer Falls, N.Y. Am also addicted to popcorn and old movies."

It was a simple ad, intriguing, too. Would she dare answer such an invitation? Katya's imagination took flight. She visualized herself walking into a restaurant to meet a phantom soul-mate dressed in lavender, only to discover that the mysterious woman was Chris Benet.

She smiled at her fantasy. Gazing up the multi-colored rocks set into her fireplace, Katya's eyes stopped above the oak mantle. She visualized Chris's painting there, its warm, golden spring glazes illuminated by tongues of fire from the burning hearth. Her heart took flight.

Sam, too, wanted Chris's artwork in his room.

Slowly, this young woman was taking over her house. With that thought, she heard the doorbell chime, got up and strode into the vestibule to answer it.

❦ 8 ❦

"Voila! Benet Repairs at your service, madame." Chris removed her purple baseball cap with a flourish and bowed, drawing a chuckle from Katya.

"My, but you're chipper this morning." Katya wondered if Chris's show of ebullience was her way of dealing with the same butterflies that were still fluttering around inside her own stomach.

Chris peeked into the vestibule and let out a slow whistle. "Ooo la la. Foxy place."

Katya took in the faded Levi's and matching workshirt, the scent of fresh air and licorice drifting her way as Chris brushed by on her way into the house. As she tucked her baseball cap into the red knapsack, her light green eyes lit up like a child's, and like a child, she caressed the varnished log walls with her hand, admired the perfectly-joined tongue and groove corners. "C'est magnifique."

Katya had to stop herself from staring too hard into those unnerving eyes. She might as well have tried to stop her own heartbeat.

"Norwegian Pine?" Chris guessed. Katya nodded, caught up in her enthusiasm. She led her into the great room, where the young woman's gaze was immediately drawn up to the beamed cathedral ceiling and the upstairs loft that housed the bedrooms.

"I thought I would feel claustrophobic in a log cabin, but this— it makes one want to fly." Chris's attention then went to the fireplace and she smiled approvingly. "River rock. How appropriate." Her smile included Katya. "This home you have made. Well, it almost breathes the name, Katya Michaels."

The simplicity of the compliment opened Katya's heart. "Thank you. It *is* a refuge for me."

"Well, it certainly does not breathe old Mrs. Harrison's name," Chris added with a mischievous gleam in her eye. "My mural for Sam will have to be worthy of all this." Her arm swept the great room and dining area.

Without realizing it, Katya had moved closer, drawn by the playfulness in those magnetic green eyes.

They stood silently gazing at each other for a heartbeat before Katya cleared her throat and nervously fiddled with the bow at the neck of her blouse. Just as she dropped her hand, Chris impulsively reached out and trapped one silken ribbon between two fingers and straightened it.

Katya jumped as if burned.

"It was crooked," Chris explained, a blush creeping up her face, but the spark still in her eyes. "Surely you are not afraid of *me*. Not after what Molly and Sara told me about *you*."

Horrified, Katya asked, "What?"

"Oh, that you have a very cool head. That instead of running away from an uncomfortable situation, like most of the people in this town would do, you stuck by them and helped that young girl out yesterday. They were very impressed."

"I think you've got it wrong. *I* was the one impressed." Katya wondered what else they had told her. "The dishwasher...," she began, trying to find a diplomatic way of removing herself from Chris's unnerving proximity. But Chris had already moved close to the fireplace and ran a slender hand over the cool rocks.

Katya felt that hand like a caress.

"When I was a child I was fascinated with your American pioneers and their log cabins," Chris volunteered. "Even though Mr. Harrison taught me flycasting, I was never invited into their cabin." She let her gaze sweep the room. "It can hardly be called a cabin any longer."

"Well, it's hardly an estate," Katya rejoined, self-consciously. Then, becoming playful, "If I wrote fiction, the cabin itself could be a character in a novel: *Log cabin swallows villain when he tries to murder heroine, then swallows heroine when she messes with its plumbing.*

"And let that be a lesson to you, Ms. Benet Repairs *at your service.*"

Chris laughed, a delicious musical sound. "I grant you that this place has character. Worthy of a Hemingway or Woolf. A setting that lives, no? Like in Stephen King books as well. Is your Norwegian Pine refuge a bad or good guy?"

It was a question that Sam might ask. "Depends on the point of view...or what appliance breaks down."

Another charming laugh delighted Katya's ears.

"I have heard of cardboard characters, but not ones of metal and wood," Chris pronounced, obviously willing to go as far as she could with their banter.

Katya was finding it disturbingly sexual. "Are you trying to get a rise out of me?" she challenged.

Resuming her tour of the room, Chris admitted: "But of course." She stopped and admired an arrangement of pen and ink ballet drawings next to an extensive wall unit and bookcase which lined the long fireplace wall into the dining room. "Mmmm. Nice." Her back was to Katya now as she studied some books, casually slipping a box of licorice candy from the back pocket of her jeans. She half-turned and offered one to Katya with a slight lift of one eyebrow.

Katya graciously declined before turning mock-serious. "They're not good for you."

"Ah yes. So many things are not good for you. But these...well, they are for quick energy when I do not have sunflower seeds and raisins to eat." She popped a few black candies into her mouth and chewed thoughtfully, running a tongue-tip over her lips.

The gesture was extremely seductive to Katya who began to wonder if *she* was turning into a sex maniac. "Any other weaknesses?"

Stop it! A voice in her head warned. *You're flirting shamelessly.*

Chris opened her mouth to reply, blushed again, and then considered the question.

"Let me see.... Popcorn?" she said suddenly, throwing Katya a curve, reminding her of the personal ad in *Women's Network*. But a young woman like Chris with so much going for her, would not have to place such an ad.

"Do *you* have any weaknesses?" Chris countered.

After stumbling on her words, Katya managed: "Strawberry ice cream at melting point and...I like popcorn, too."

"We are compatible, then. I shall buy out the entire stock in the *Ice Cream Shoppe* for you," Chris promised. "Even if I must melt the ice cream myself."

Katya shivered at the seductive image and a long moment of tension filled the space between them before Chris turned back to the books. It was an opportunity for her to admire the width of Chris's shoulders, the back of her finely shaped head, her hair cropped close and ending in a V curl. Her sensitive hands brushed over book spines.

"You wrote these?" Chris pointed to two texts on creative writing: *The Writer Within* and *Becoming Your Characters*, and when Katya nodded, gave another low whistle. "I have never known a real writer before."

Making light of it, Katya offered: "It pays the bills, but my real work is teaching Creative Writing at Bear State. I love helping young writers reach their goals, seeing their work immortalized in print, even if it's just college journals." *Liar*, she thought. *You'd love to have a best-seller.*

"An English teacher once told me that writing can't be taught," Chris remarked. "What is *your* secret?"

Katya had heard the criticism before and felt peeved. "I teach it indirectly." And when Chris looked at her perplexed, explained: "You open up a student's senses, have him or her become actors to get inside a character's mind. I use certain exercises that work—playacting, actually. You'd laugh if you walked into one of my classrooms and saw how these sophisticated college students turn themselves into mad doctors, swooning women—even Indian chiefs. It's great fun." Katya chuckled and became aware of the open admiration on Chris's face. "Enough about me."

"No, please. When you speak of your work, your whole face...well, it lights up.... I should like to paint you that way."

"Oh."

"I have embarrassed you, yes?"

"Actually, I'm flattered."

"Mmmmm. That is a start." Chris cocked her head to one side and studied Katya. "You remind me of a dream I once had. A woman who lived near a stream. Blonde like you with a blonde daughter; not a son like Sam. In this dream, well, they took care of the stream together, and as they did it turned golden. More golden every day." She smiled, remembering. "This image stuck in my mind." With a look to see if Katya understood, she added, "I had to paint it to free myself...."

"And it became a landscape. A beautiful spring day in the woods that's hanging in *Molly's Sporting Goods*," Katya said softly.

Chris looked startled. "You have seen it?"

"Yes. And it took my breath away." It was on the tip of her tongue, but she didn't add: *Soon it'll be hanging right above my fireplace mantle.*

"Ooo la la. From the first moment I saw you...it was," and Chris drew in a breath. "Like you stepped out of that dream."

Katya's face heated up. She held up a hand to restrain the image. "Hey, it's just a coincidence. My feet are made of clay."

A slight Gallic shrug of the shoulders, an unreadable smile was Chris's response. "But if you pose for me. If I can capture you the way you were before, talking about your students.... Why, then..."

Katya waited.

A quicksilver grin greeted her. "I will not have to rely on dreams any longer."

"Flattery is *one* way to lure a model," Katya pointed out. "But you might find me more of a nightmare. I can't sit still for long. And I'll bite your head off if you tell me not to move."

"Hmmm. You do not scare me, Katya Michaels." Chris licked the last remnants of licorice from her teeth with a cat-like tongue. *But you scare me.*

Chris continued to examine Katya's books and paused at *Portrait Of The Artist As A Young Man.* "Ah, Joyce. This is one of my favorite classics. Stephen Daedalus had such a long, hard journey into himself before he became a writer. Why must artists suffer so?" Her brow knitted. "But there is also the supreme joy." Facing Katya, she asked, "Do you see this paradox with any of your gifted students? I would imagine that a good teacher would view her students as so many hot-house orchids."

"Yes. It's just like that," Katya marveled.

"I was very fortunate to have a dedicated teacher like you. An art teacher. She is the reason I am painting today."

"In France?"

"Oh, no." Inching her way along the wall unit, Chris admired the Hopi kachinas and Native American masks that had been a gift from Katya's mother when she first moved into her own apartment. To her mother, Katya's was a temporary situation to be humored—a step before marriage—a way to get her daughter's restlessness out of her system.

"Where did you go to college?" Katya asked.

"N.Y.U."

"And decided to stay in the states?"

"Oh, I was not an exchange student." A cloud passed momentarily over Chris's face. "We, that is, maman, my brother Simon, and I settled here when I turned eleven." She plucked Joyce's classic from its place on the shelf and absently rubbed its plastic spine. "My mother married a third-generation Frenchman a year after she divorced papa and settled in America. She bought *Le Provençal* from him. Actually, bought him out. He had the gambling sickness."

"Why are you smiling?" Katya asked.

"You bring out the words in me."

Touched, Katya returned the smile. "Your mother has done well with *Le Provençal*."

"Oui. But not so well with her life. Men come and go at her whim. Her only real passions are work and literature. In fact, you two would have much in common. She reads Sartre and DeBouvier, your Faulkner and Joyce Carol Oates, but," and Chris smiled indulgently. "You cannot tear her away from the Sunday comics."

"I'm addicted to Garfield myself," Katya admitted. "You mentioned a brother. Simon?"

Chris's body stiffened. "My little brother was a true American tragedy. He...was murdered in New York City."

"Oh, no, Chris. I'm sorry." The flash of rage in Chris's eyes took her aback.

"Simon...," Chris murmured. "Perhaps I could have prevented what happened to Simon."

Katya sighed. How many times had she questioned herself the very same way about Loren's death? If only she had done this, not done that. She waited for Chris to elaborate, but the young woman fell silent.

To break the mood, Katya walked into the dining area, parted the curtains, and revealed, in a wash of sunlight, her oak deck. Craving air, she unlatched the sliding glass door and stepped outside, drawing deep breaths, glancing quickly at the plants, bird feeders, and picnic table. She glanced up at the wooden staircase that wound up to the small deck she had added outside her bedroom. She looked at her things as if searching for happiness.

She could hear the stream running in the background. A flurry of birds broke the silence and a saucy bluejay chased two crows away from its perch on a Catalpa tree. She was reluctant to walk back into the sadness.

Facing Chris at the bookcase again, she chose her words carefully. "I know about grief and anger. It can play nasty tricks on the mind."

"All I know is hate," Chris burst out, but what Katya saw in her eyes was pain.

"Hate can eat one alive, Chris," Katya said softly.

"Then we must turn it outward. People who have seen loved ones murdered; abused women, are learning how to turn their feelings of guilt and fear around. They can act on their rage—make the world theirs."

Katya digested the words and shivered.

Just as quickly as she had tensed, Chris relaxed and allowed herself a long look at Katya. "When we met? The first thing I noticed was the hurt in *your* eyes. I wanted to...well, slay the dragons that had wounded you so. Some would call that arrogant, no?"

Surprised, Katya smiled. "My knight in shining armor? If only it were so easy. The only one who can slay my dragons is me."

"You must miss your husband. And Sam still mourns his father. You look so unhappy, mon amie."

Katya sighed. If only she could say, There is no husband. Never was. I'm lonely and scared. Terrified of someone getting close to me. Of *feeling* again. Instead, she blurted: "Sam's father is the kind of man who ignores kids until they're old enough to share a beer with—a jealous man who resented his wife's pregnancy; who had a fit when Sam cried and she went to comfort him."

What she was waiting to add was that Marty DeLeon was the kind of person who demanded monthly checks from Loren's parents to keep him out of their lives; a man who sold guns and drugs to teen-agers. Was not only homophobic, but hated Blacks, Jews, in fact, any minority.

Taking courage in hand, she continued. "I was never married, Chris. I lied to you because I was afraid. You were a stranger so I just let you think what you wanted."

"I do not understand," Chris responded. "What about Sam?"

"I was in love with a very special woman for a very long time, Sam's Aunt Loren. We adopted Sam when Loren's younger sister died in a horrible car crash. I only met Sam's father, Marty DeLeon, twice. Once, at Meg's funeral, and once at his trial for possession and sale of firearms and narcotics. He was so hungry for money that he signed a paper giving up all rights to see Sam if Loren paid all his legal fees. Now he's doing time in a California prison."

"Goddess," Chris breathed. "He made a devil's pact."

"You've got that part right. But I know more about the devil than I do about Marty DeLeon."

"Was he an abuser? Did he beat Sam's mother?"

"Not physically, just the insidious kind of beating. Emotional abuse."

"So he would not harm you or Sam," Chris said with concern.

"I don't think he'd do anything to jeopardize his monthly checks from Loren's parents. They're very wealthy." Katya grew silent, remembering something. How Marty had cried at Meg's funeral. Hopefully, that part of him, and not the rest, was in Sam's genes.

Hesitantly, Chris reached out and touched her arm. "Please do not feel guilty for lying to me. I understand."

An unexpected rush of tears burned Katya's throat. She swallowed hard before they could spill over into her eyes.

"How do you tell a child that his father abandoned him?" she asked, her voice cracking. Someday, maybe soon, her son would start asking longer and more probing questions about his father.

"You will know the answer when the time comes," Chris promised. "Now, perhaps it is time to tackle your dishwasher." She said it in a voice so tender that Katya almost hugged her.

"You're right. Time for the dishwasher," Katya agreed, more than happy to move on to the kitchen. She smiled at the younger woman, would have to find the words to tell her that she felt surprisingly lighter than she had in what seemed a lifetime.

9

*K*atya turned the radio dial to one of her favorite stations and was rewarded with Gershwin's "Rhapsody In Blue." In the small red and white country kitchen, she heated up the pot of chicken soup she had started that morning on the renovated cast iron stove. Varnished pine cabinets lined the log walls and ended where a strip of molding divided wood from red and white flowered wallpaper. The kitchen was partitioned off by a butcher block work-table into a cooking and eating area. To one side, a round, white marble table rested on wrought iron legs and the polyurethaned hardwood floor was shiny enough to reflect Katya's favorite brass flowerpots.

While Chris was down in the basement shutting off the water, Katya grabbed a copper-bottomed pot from a ceiling rack over the butcher block partition and set two eggs inside to boil later. Sam loved well-cooked chunks of eggs in his chicken soup.

With affection, she glanced at his drawings on the coppertone refrigerator.

"You have a budding artist there," Chris observed when she returned to the kitchen, settling herself on the shiny floor in front of the dishwasher and sink. Setting her tools out carefully on a ragged but clean towel, she reminded Katya of a doctor preparing a patient for examination, especially in the series of questions she fired at Katya about the Kenmore patient.

"It doesn't drain properly," Katya responded. "And the dishes, to quote Sam, come out all 'yucky.' But, if it's a big job, forget it. I really don't need a dishwasher for just the two of us."

"Your appliances are not new," Chris observed, surprised.

"Mrs. Harrison was so proud of the way she'd kept them up, I didn't have the heart to throw them out. She swore there was a lot more mileage in them, and she tossed them in for nothing. How could I resist?"

The answer seemed to please Chris. Nodding, she lifted the chrome top off the air gap and unscrewed the gap cover, inserting a wire inside to free what was lodged beneath. As she worked, she described parts and their functions in a matter-of-fact voice, certainly not like the one she had used earlier to confide such personal things to Katya. Katya was just as surprised at her own opening up, for she wasn't given to intimate revelations either. It seemed as if they had known each other much longer than six days.

Katya found herself involved in how Chris was fixing the dishwasher, and this also surprised her. In the past, anything mechanical would instantly have turned her off. What really interested her, though, were Chris's competent hands—fine hands. She would have associated them with an artist, not a laborer. Loren, too, had been handy around the house, but hadn't seemed as confident around breakdowns as Chris seemed to be.

"See the air gap, here? It prevents waste from backing up into the sink drain," Chris explained, her words framed by strains of Beethoven's Fifth, now on the radio. Crouched beside her, Katya still smelled the licorice, and a trace of soap. As Chris took things apart, the odor of grease, decayed food and sweat joined the heady mix, and Katya felt herself getting turned on again. "Smells like the patient's dying."

"Ooo la la. I must work quickly then. Save any life left in the old girl." If she was aware of how close Katya was to her, the only indication Chris gave was to drop a screwdriver.

But Katya was aware enough for both of them, aware of Chris's long, jean-clad legs, and strong arms; biceps working under the sleeves she had rolled up. Feeling somewhat helpless, Katya asked, "Is there anything you can't do?"

"I am terrible at math and English. I would rather tackle a brown bear than conjugate a verb." She lifted a shoulder and pressed her arm against the sheen of sweat on her forehead.

Katya stifled the urge to rest her hand, just momentarily, on one of those wide shoulders. She remembered their earlier conversation and thought of the pain that Chris had experienced in her young life. Though carefully avoiding any further talk about her brother, it was evident that the anguish, in some way, directed her energies.

"How old are you, Chris?"

"Twenty-five."

"You could be one of my students, you know," she said and for some reason thought of Geoff Holden. An involuntary shudder went through her.

Chris swiveled around to look directly into her eyes. "And how old are you, madame?" she challenged.

Those cat's eyes made Katya hot all over. "Let's just say I've got seven years on you."

With exaggeration, Chris began counting on her fingers before throwing up her hands in mock exasperation. "Much too old. Too ancient for someone who is so terrible in math to figure out."

Katya used the opportunity to pinch Chris's cheek, which, as she expected, turned scarlet. "Don't get wise with me, young woman," she chuckled. "How about something cold to drink?" She was hoping that Chris would stay for lunch. Though she had no classes ahead of her, Friday had been re-scheduled as a conference day and she felt she wouldn't be missed. "Juice?"

"Do you have Perrier?"

"Mmmm. Nope, but I can let the bubbles out of some club soda." She made a mental note to stock up on Perrier, just in case. You never knew when another appliance might break down. Or, if she found the courage, she could invite this fascinating woman for dinner.

When she handed Chris a tall glass of White Rock garnished with a slice of lime, their fingers brushed and Katya felt as if she'd been hit by a live wire.

Chris's eyes widened. She shivered once, gazed up at Katya helplessly, and seemed to be waiting for an explanation.

Katya, in confiding about Loren earlier, had as much as admitted that she was gay. Now she felt exposed, a little frightened, and strangely excited.

With a sigh, Chris turned back to her work. Katya watched a slow blush creep up the back of her neck, which set off another electrical charge inside her. She almost touched Chris's skin just to experience a third rush. The sense of power that came over her was new and exhilarating, as if she had captured and had control of something dangerous. With this inscrutable woman, she felt heady.

In their relationship, Loren had been the more assertive one. Katya the captive, caught in a helpless passion that she often was at a loss to express until Loren made the first move. It wasn't until Loren became ill that Katya had tentatively started to initiate sex. At the best of times it had been thrilling, but never before had she so wanted to uncover the mystery of a person with her hands, her mouth. Her mind. This new awareness brought with it a sense of responsibility. What could she really gain but momentary pleasure, from teasing such a young person? It would be cruel.

"I have tightened the drain hose." Chris pointed to the larger of two pipes leading down from the air gap. "And will clean the debris from the strainer bucket on the bottom of your dishwasher. Would you like to watch and learn how to do it yourself?"

"Do I have a choice?" Katya joked.

"Perhaps, someday, you will feel comfortable with tools." As she completed each step, she again explained it like a surgeon lecturing students in an operating theatre, so that Katya started to question just who was the teacher and who the student in that kitchen. Chris Benet seemed perfectly capable of handling her own life, including what gave her pleasure.

Reaching under the sink, she opened the trap and cleaned it out. "I noticed downstairs that the water temperature of your boiler was set at one-hundred and forty degrees. I raised it. That should also help, especially with the 'yucky' stuff Sam finds so hateful on his plate." Lithe as a cat, she rose to her feet.

Katya saw a smudge of grease on her cheek. There always seemed to be some mark of Chris's work branding her. She pointed it out, offering Chris a paper towel. At that moment, she was so scared of her feelings she didn't dare make any suggestive moves. Her body was burning.

Chris took the towel and swiped at her face. "Thank you." She cleared her throat and stared at Katya. Again a small shudder, a sigh passed through her until she composed herself. Holding up a finger, she said, "One moment. I will be right back."

Katya heard noises down in the basement and they were strangely comforting. Just the opposite of what she felt at night, alone in her bed. Maybe she *should* take that Home Repair program at the Women's Center that Chris had mentioned. But as soon as she started on a positive course, the demon of insecurity took a bite out of her. How could she ever handle this house alone?

Chris, who had returned to the kitchen, seemed to be reading her mind. "I am leaving you my telephone number. If you have any problems, please call me." She cocked her beautiful head to one side and raised an eyebrow. Katya found the effect charming.

Smiling, Chris added, "Together, we will make a Ms. Fix-it out of you." And her hand swept the kitchen. "These are machines, not monsters." She adjusted the timer on the dishwasher and turned it on. The welcome sound of healthy spray hissed through the kitchen.

They both smiled.

When she bent down to collect her tools, Katya could not resist the urge to touch her this time. The back of Chris's neck did not seem as dangerous as her face, with those penetrating eyes. Katya's own eyes drank in the natural line of short dark hair converging to an irresistible center curl. It was slightly longer than the rest of the hair on the back of her neck.

Katya's hand had a life of its own. Almost without her volition, it reached out and at just that moment, Chris turned to face her. She sucked in a startled breath. Katya slowly withdrew her hand. "Your hair was messed," she explained feeling foolish. How could such short hair get messed?

Chris studied her soberly. She tentatively extended her own hand, brushing Katya's cheek so lightly that it might never have happened at all, except that those fingertips had left Katya tingling. The gesture was so tender it almost broke her heart. She caught Chris's hand, was about to press it to her still burning cheek when the phone rang.

Saved by the bell, she thought. Her legs were trembling when she went to answer it, heard the school nurse describe Sam's symptoms. Her gut clenched as it always did when he took ill.

She hung up and looked helplessly at Chris. "Sam's just thrown up all over a classmate's lunch. The nurse thinks it's a virus. I'm afraid I have to pick him up at school. Will you wait for me? I thought we'd have lunch together." To her dismay, Chris looked at her watch, but then she smiled.

"I have plenty of time, which is the way I planned it," Chris admitted without a trace of guile or flirtation. "If there is anything else you would like me to look at while I am here...like your sink? I noticed the faucet dripping."

"Chris, please. I know you feel awkward about this, but I want to pay you in some way. Please don't take it as an insult."

"There is no need. We are neighbors. Perhaps someday you will teach me how to write."

"Don't move," Katya ordered and rushed into the livingroom, opened a drawer in the bookcase, drew out two extra copies of her creative writing texts and brought them back into the kitchen. "These are for you."

"Ooo la la." Chris brightened, turning the books over in her hand. "Will you autograph them for me?" she requested shyly.

Grabbing a pen, Katya was suddenly at a loss for words.

" 'To Chris Benet from Katya Michaels,' would be perfect," Chris encouraged.

Katya scribbled the inscription, adding: "For a memorable morning," and was rewarded with a grin.

Riffling through her bag, Katya found her car keys. She hesitated for a moment, then stirred the chicken soup which had begun to scent the kitchen. "Don't disappear on me," she warned.

"Go, go...before your Sam decides to, as you Americans like to put it: 'Gross out the entire cafeteria.' "

"I must say, Chris, you give American slang a bit of flair," Katya admitted. "I won't be long."

"And I will be waiting."

Slipping out the kitchen door, Katya bridged the distance from lawn to gravel driveway, which ran opposite the wood chip path. The house was separate from the garage, a smaller replica of her log cabin enclosed within a thick stand of fir trees. Chris's last statement echoed sweetly in her head: "I will be waiting."

When was the last time she had heard those reassuring words?

As she drove past the farm and caught a glimpse of the two German Shepherds, barking and chasing cars, she realized how fortunate she had been yesterday. Unwittingly, she had done everything to provoke them, from staring them in the eye, to raising a stick. They could have torn her to pieces.

She'd be prepared for attack next time she jogged with a homemade spray of spicy hot, crushed Jalapeno peppers.

It wasn't until she had driven approximately a mile that she noticed, with disbelief, the same white station wagon in her rear-view mirror, that had followed her yesterday.

Hot peppers? she thought, furiously. _I'll get my gun._

Cursing inwardly, she screeched to a stop and tore out of her Toyota with every intent of hurling a piece of her mind at the driver. The wagon seemed to hover there, as if challenging her. The short hairs prickled on the back of Katya's neck. Then, just as she drew closer, it backed up, made a swift, tire-peeling U-turn on the weeded shoulder bordering the field opposite the farmhouse. Exhaust fumes and dirt blew in her face. She clenched her fists, and watched it disappear back where it came from, with one of the German Shepherds in its wake. The other dog glared at her from the side of the road.

"Damn you," she said to the dog and slipped back into her car.

This time she had seen more of the driver—still the outline of dark, frizzy hair pulled back in what could have been a braid or ponytail, and the glint of rings on the steering wheel. But through the tinted glass there had been something else glinting as well. Jewelry or buttons, the kind of brass buttons that decorated military shirts. This shirt was light-colored and covering what seemed to be an ample chest. A woman? Why would a woman be following her?

Back behind the wheel of her Toyota, she drove down to Sam's school, part of her relieved that bellyache or not, he would now be safely home with her; the other part disappointed that there wouldn't be much time alone with Chris. If Sam was sick, he might lie down for a nap. Then she could get to know Chris better, discover what made her tick.

Unless Chris had other ideas about getting to know each other.

That was something she wasn't prepared to think about.

ℱℑ   ℱℑ

❦ 10 ❧

*T*he cuckoo bird popped out of the Swiss clock above the sink, startling Chris, who nearly dropped a faucet washer down the drain. Already on edge from the conflicting emotions battling inside her, she drew deep breaths and tried to calm herself. In the silence of the kitchen, Katya's presence was palpable: the simmering chicken soup, the trace of herbal shampoo she used, the soft strains of a Brahms violin concerto from the radio.

Mon dieu. What am I doing? I am supposed to be celibate, not hungry to get my hands on this woman.

She glanced at her watch, at the entrance to the alcove that spelled freedom, but could not get her legs to obey. Instead, she inserted a new washer with a sigh of resignation; tightened the faucet with her tape-wrapped wrench; finally succumbed to the image of Katya hanging on her every word in the living room. *Was this love she was feeling? Could Katya love another woman again? Or was her relationship with this Loren a once-in-a-lifetime thing?*

Wiping sweaty palms on her jeans, she leafed through the book Katya had signed, ran an index finger over the inscription as if she could absorb Katya through her neat, slanted handwriting.

She wondered how she could have thought that this enigmatic woman was a WASP princess when here she was trying to get the most mileage out of Mrs. Harrison's old appliances. Just because the house was elegant did not mean that Katya was spoiled and wealthy, Chris rationalized. If that were so, she would not have been so willing to wash dishes by hand when a new dishwasher could be purchased.

Chris recalled the shameless way she had flirted with Katya. *Goddess. Thank Goddess she had stopped pulling at the bow on Katya's blouse in time. Thank Goddess she had not made a complete idiot of herself. This was not a woman one toyed with, but opening the bow at*

*that lovely neck had been so very irresistible. Had Katya thought her far
too bold?* The sense of power she had felt at Katya's hot reaction had
quickly dissolved into a burst of embarrassment, for Katya had jumped
back, not leaned forward.

It occurred to Chris that she would have to learn a new set of
rules. Katya could not be thought of as a conquest—Chris could not act
like an enamored student flirting with a teacher.

But Katya had toyed with her, too. Of this she was certain. She
recalled her excitement when Katya had knelt so close at the dishwasher;
her warm, inviting breath drifting Chris's way.

"Remember your oath of celibacy," she said under her breath
while another little voice nagged: "Has it brought Simon back?"

No matter, she would be cool, keep her defenses up just as she
had the night Simon was murdered so violently; the night she had sought
comfort in Molly's willing arms.

She stood in front of the coppertone refrigerator like a voyeur
and pored over Sam's drawings—potato head figures sprouting stick
arms and legs—the usual artwork of children his age. At his age, she
had been uncannily aware of perspective and shading, though she had
to admit that Sam had an eye for color and detail. The windows on his
square houses displayed curtains; the lawn flowers, rocks, even mailboxes.
In the background of one picture, rose a devil over a rooftop; a skull
glared from a top window. The demons of a child. At least Katya
allowed him to express his fears; and there had to be many from the story
she had told.

In the face of demons and skulls, maman would have recoiled.

There are no such things, only sunshine, mon petit oiseau.
There is only the good side. Be happy, little bird. Life is short. In the
wastebasket go the morbid pictures.

With a sigh, Chris opened Katya's refrigerator. It was spotless
except for one splotch of dried ketchup. Neatly-arranged bottles of
juices, milk, buttermilk and cider lined the bottom doorshelf. Whole-
wheat bread, relish, mayonnaise on the middle rack with spices. Inside
the vegetable bin lay crisp heads of Boston and iceberg lettuce, bright
orange carrots, radishes, leeks and mushrooms. No signs of green
fungus or wilted vegetables as in her own small fridge. A bottle of
Chardonnay lay on its side on one shelf, and Chris smiled at the bowl
of bean-sprouts soaking in water.

Opening the freezer, she was greeted with a white mist of frigid air, as if a genie had been liberated from its bottle. She realized that what she really was searching for were signs of another person in Katya's life.

A noise to her right had her quickly closing the freezer; like a thief caught in a robbery. A key turned in the door in the alcove off the kitchen and Sam burst in, all dimples and bright brown eyes. It struck Chris then, what a beautiful child he was, the only sign of illness in his overly-red cheeks, the patch of dried vomit decorating the bib of his overalls. "Bon jour!" He rocked back and forth on sneakered feet, pleased, his eyes darting around the kitchen with excitement. "Can I help you fix things? Do you have a ladder? Can I climb it? Have you got wrenches and stuff?" When he noticed just the red knapsack, he frowned as if he had been the last to arrive at a party and all the gifts had been opened. "Loren has lots of tools in the garage," he offered.

Chris flinched involuntarily at the mention of Katya's former lover. Then Katya rushed in carrying Sam's schoolbooks, flushed and smiling. A few wisps of blonde hair had escaped the neat pile on top of her head.

Chris imagined herself slowly pulling out each hairpin, watching the soft drapes of golden hair spill out. It made her ache.

"Mom, Chris is gonna let me help her. Right Chris?"

"Whoa. It's break-time. Let's get you washed up and changed. You smell like a bleu cheese factory." Katya rolled her eyes at Chris. "He doesn't act like he's sick, does he? He couldn't wait to see you." She pressed her hand to Sam's forehead.

"Fever?" Chris inquired, concerned, recalling how good it had felt when maman had pressed soft lips to her fevered forehead. Worth getting sick for.

"He's a little warm. A nap should take care of that."

"No way, Mom. You promised I could sit at the table with you and Chris. Can I show her the pictures we picked for my mural?"

"Chris has been working hard all morning. We'll talk about the mural the next time she comes."

The next time she comes, Chris thought with a thrill. "I can take a look at Sam's pictures," she offered, feeling the generosity that happiness can bring, "before we sit down to lunch."

"Look here," Katya warned with mock severity. "I'm the boss in this kitchen. And I say it's time to fill that grumbling stomach of yours."

Horrified, Chris protested. "My stomach does not grumble!"

"Oh, right. Superwoman is above stomach grumbles. Even *she* ate lunch between rescues."

"Stomach noises are undignified," Chris retorted.

"Biting your toenails at the table is undignified."

"Then I will keep my sneakers on."

"An obliging guest." Katya pulled a chair out from the table and motioned Chris over.

I will not only keep my sneakers on, but just ask me, and I will fly to the moon with you.

Katya fetched a fresh shirt and pants from the alcove's laundry room, then bathed Sam's face and neck at the sink, answering his barrage of questions affectionately.

What a lucky child, Chris thought, and a swell of longing swept through her.

After his mother's gentle ministrations, Sam plunked himself down at the table opposite Chris and began to make sputtering noises with his mouth, accompanying the motion of the phantom toy truck he held in his hands. His blonde hair was slicked back and an errant cowlick popped up, making him all the more irresistible. His face was that of a child waiting for something wonderful to happen.

"Thanks for fixing the sink," Katya mentioned. "The washer, too. Your father did a fine job teaching you." She ladled steaming soup into two earthenware bowls and placed one in front of Chris.

Salivating, Chris studied the plump carrots and parsnips; the chunks of chicken and bean curd. If Katya only knew that she had just taken inventory of her refrigerator. A warm loaf of French bread appeared with two tall glasses of apple cider. Sam was disappointed with his meager cup of tea and two slices of dry toast.

"Why can't I have soup and hard-boiled egg?"

"If you keep this down you can have it. There's plenty left for dinner."

"I promise not to barf on you," he coaxed and would only settle down after she spread newspaper on his place mat and laid out a pad, crayons and three containers of Play-Doh. He pushed one can in Chris's direction, the other at his mother's bowl, before another barrage of questions rolled out: "Why did all the French people move to America?"

"Hardly all the French people moved here, Sam." Katya sat down on Chris's right. "He asked me the same question at *Le Provençal*. I guess it's still on his mind. To tell the truth, I don't know the reason either. I thought it might be because our countryside resembles certain French provinces."

Chris nodded her agreement. "This county is reminiscent of the Rhine River Valley, but that is only one reason." She tasted the soup. It was delicious and she told Katya so. "Some think a Frenchman emigrated to the United States after World War II and fell in love with this area. He built an inn and invited all his friends. Soon more inns and restaurants went up and the French people that lived in New York City relocated. Families arrived from all over France." Chris speculated.

"Say something French," Sam demanded.

"French mustard?" Chris teased just to hear him giggle. Then she pointed to the lace-curtained window where a shaft of sunlight filtered in, pooling on the butcher block countertop. "Le printemps est ma saison favorite. Et tu?"

"The window's dirty?" Sam guessed.

Chris laughed. "Not quite. It means: "Spring is my favorite season. What is yours?"

"Winter! I'm getting a new sled, maybe skis, too."

"Then l'hiver is the French word for winter. Can you say: winter is my favorite season?"

His shoulders hunched up in an exaggerated shrug. Filled with energy, he placed his hands over his cheeks, sucked in a mouthful of air, ballooning his cheeks and slapped them. A small explosion popped out. "You say it first."

"L'hiver est ma saison favorite."

Sam fractured the words as he tried to repeat them.

"Can you say, Ooo la la, instead?"

"That's cool. Ooo la la." He looked at his mother with satisfaction.

"A real Frenchman, no?" Chris leaned over and patted his hand. "What are you drawing?" she asked, aware of Katya's eyes on her, making her senses excruciatingly sharp.

"A man." His eyes lit up with an idea. Taking a black crayon, he drew the amoebic shape of a beret on the figure's potato-shaped head. "Now he's a Frenchman."

"Come. Bring it here to me."

Chris showed him how to draw a neck and shoulders and urged him to try another figure. When he leaned closer, she smelled the soap that Katya had just used to wash him, and a not unpleasant odor she associated with overactive boys. His blonde head smelled sweetly of shampoo, and while he attempted the figure, his tongue peeked out of the corner of his mouth. He caught on quickly, delighting Katya and Chris with the results. When he returned to his chair for more crayons, Chris's thoughts drifted to Molly, Bev and Sara. They would laugh at her playing nanny.

When I should be using the time to track down the Deer Falls Attacker.

Katya Michaels had directed her thoughts from hate to love in one morning. The personal ad she had placed had been printed on Wednesday, the day after their meeting in back of Molly's store—and circulated yesterday, Thursday. It should be netting responses soon. She hoped to be meeting some women next week. The thought made her foot itch with anticipation.

Although there had been several openings for her to warn Katya about the attack, she'd held back. Perhaps part of the reason was that she assumed that whoever had been preying on her community of friends would never guess Katya to be a lesbian. The assumption annoyed her. Under normal circumstances, she'd give anything to hear Katya announce her emergence from the closet.

Sam handed over a brown crayon and asked her to draw some animals. Her father had taught her to draw objects from geometric shapes. Guided by the instruction he had given her as a child, she sketched a triangle and small half-circle and showed him how to transform it into an owl. Half an oval became a turtle's shell, delighting him.

Throughout their interaction, she felt the heat of Katya's gaze. Chris glanced up and caught an unguarded flicker of desire in Katya's blue eyes; it sent a shiver through her. But just as quickly, it disappeared, as if a shutter had been closed on a window, leaving Chris's heart pounding.

Struggling to open his red can of Play-Doh, Sam finally asked for help.

"I will help you if you give me a kiss," Chris blurted, shocking herself. Shyly, he ambled over, handed her the can, and planted a quick, noisy kiss on her cheek. His lips were as warm as Katya's smile.

Satisfied, he returned to his seat and was soon absorbed with clay.

Katya's voice electrified the silence. "Can you open this for me?"

Chris wondered if she heard right. Her heart thundered.

Katya held up the yellow can with a question in her eyes.

Chris forgot to breathe; and when she could get the words past the blockage in her throat, repeated, like a robot: "I will, if you give me a kiss."

She had heard right. Katya crooked her finger.

Slowly, like a dazed sleepwalker, Chris stood up and moved toward her, until she was inches from Katya's upturned face. And, just as slowly, she bent down and paused above Katya's inviting mouth.

It was the lightest touch of lips, yet it sent a hot current sizzling through Chris. The aftershock was mirrored on Katya's startled face. Like a magnet, Chris was drawn down again and kissed Katya fully. A shudder of desire rocked her. She felt as if she were drowning, sinking into Katya's hot, sweet mouth.

Katya gasped and wrenched her lips free. Her eyes glazed and wild. "Sam...," her voice tremulous; a pulse throbbing in her throat.

How Chris found her seat without falling or bumping into anything, she would not be able to say later. What she did know was that she would never forget the incredible chemistry of that kiss, or the heart-shattering moment when time stood still for her.

₰ ₰ ₰

❦ **11** ❧

hris had spiked her hair up with gel, dressed in a black
turtleneck jersey, tight black pants and boots. A small hoop earring,
once Simon's, reflected the lights in the parking lot as she crossed it and
stood before the door of *Ruby's*. She had not faced the bar scene since
her brother's ill-fated death.

Holding a breath, she pulled the door open. A rush of beer,
smoke, and loud country rock assaulted her senses. After paying the
bouncer, she walked in, injecting just enough saunter into her stride to
draw stares.

Shooting a quick, restless glance around the dimly-lit room, she
approached the bar and Ruby. "I am expecting a Vera Hudson." She
pointed to an empty table as far away from the half-filled dance floor as
possible.

Ruby's dark eyes flickered with recognition at the name, but
she quickly masked it with a shrug and wiped down the bartop. Her dark
good looks were accented with heavy jewelry and a low-cut red sweater
that hugged her ample breasts. Her eyes were suspicious.

Once seated, Chris became uncomfortably aware of curious
stares in her direction, some blatantly bold with invitation. Had her own
eyes been that hungry when she cruised women's bars in her late teens?
She wondered.

The bar could have been plucked out of a western movie. In one
corner, a solidly-built redhead, sporting mirrored sunglasses and black
leather, stared at her. Something about her struck a familiar chord in
Chris, who rarely forgot a face she had drawn. This one she had once
seen on the steps of the Deer Falls courthouse, but instead of black
leather, the redhead had been wearing the brown and beige uniform of
a deputy, and conversing with a male colleague. Her body language was
familiar too, nervously tapping her black boot against the bar stool, as

she had on the concrete courthouse step. The same large birthmark stood out on her cheek. Chris had pulled out her small sketch pad that day while waiting for an order of Chinese take-out to share with Molly. Bored, she rendered a quick sketch.

Either the female deputy was cruising after hours, Chris mused, or Sheriff Wendell had finally staked surveillance teams at the only women's bar in Deer Falls in response to the attacks. It was just a matter of time, she figured, before he discovered the possible link between the Deer Falls Attacker and the personals. The undercover female cop was bait, a role Chris felt was rightfully hers.

Her first "date" resulting from the personals had taken place on Wednesday. Today, Friday, she was celebrating the arrival of May, as she played the role of Ms. James Bond again.

Had it only been a week since she last saw Katya? She'd been praying and hoping for another appliance to break down—for her phone to ring with a call for help. She wondered if Katya missed her too—was waiting for Chris to make the next move. There had been times, all week, that she literally had to pull her hand away from the phone so as not to seem too anxious. Playing games as she had in the past; waiting for the surge of power that never came.

Heart aching, walking around in a fog, her vows of celibacy were rapidly slipping away. She didn't want to be in this bar feeling sexually vulnerable. What she wanted was to be with Katya.

As she sipped her glass of wine, Chris's mind jumped ahead to Vera Hudson, one of the responses she had culled from a stack of letters smacking of loneliness, hunger and just plain kinkiness. Vera Hudson seemed to fit into the second and third categories. Only one other letter had sounded promising, and that was from "Mystery Woman," who was paranoid about her anonymity, and a control freak to boot. Following her initial reply to Chris's ad, she concocted a strange game plan for communicating. Chris had no way of getting in touch with her except by following explicit instructions and placing subsequent ads stating: "Lavender Woman is interested and asks 'Mystery Woman' to write again. When can we meet? Pick up a pen and talk to me." Unlike tonight's assignation with Vera Hudson, the strange 'Mystery Woman' had carved out her space and dared Chris to enter it by any other rules than her own. Immediately, Chris's antennae shot up. Could she be the menace stalking Deer Falls? But that question would have to be answered another time. Tonight she had to deal with an impatient Vera.

She opened Vera Hudson's letter and spread it out beside a lit candle on the red formica tabletop.

> *Dear Lavender Woman:*
> *If you'd like to spice up your wine and popcorn with some heavy excitement, then I'm the woman for you. I can show you the ropes (or chains), if you want to make the personals more personal. Your ad says you're artistic. I'm creative myself, in ways you'd never imagine. I've seen and done it all.*
> *Maybe you can fill up some empty spaces in my life. I'll bet that an artist like you would be sensitive to my needs, so if you want to live life on the edge, and have an unforgettable experience, let's put our pens aside and meet.*
> *Yours in intrigue,*
> *Vera Hudson*

The promise of quick thrills, S/M, and a one-night-stand made Chris suspicious of Vera, too. Maybe she knew something. She certainly seemed knowledgeable about the current bar scene—perhaps visited *Ruby's* for a frequent fix. From the scant information leaked out of the hospital, it was apparently the place that both Randi and Margo had set up liaisons for their deadly blind dates.

Folding Vera's letter and returning it to her pocket, Chris thought about her theory. After her two hospitalized friends provided a sketchy description of their assailant, she figured that whoever had set them up, male or female, never showed their face when Randi and Margo arrived. Instead, the stalker tagged the two women at *Ruby's*, followed them out into the parking lot, tailed them home and attacked when they were least prepared.

"Like to dance?" a deep woman's voice asked. Glancing up, Chris recognized the good-looking brunette who had been eyeing her from the next table. Dark, shoulder-length hair brushed the shoulders of her red cape.

Uncertain, Chris shifted her attention to the door, then back to the brunette. Smiling, she tilted the glass of house wine Ruby had sent over. It was almost tasteless compared to the full-bodied burgundies produced by her family's vineyard, but suitable enough for a toast. Deliberately, she allowed her eyes to roam up and down on the woman's shapely, if over-packed figure. In a weak moment, she granted that it was the kind of body one could get lost in. And forget the outside world during the journey.

As she offered the brunette a proper French greeting, she tested the strength of her celibacy. A reflexive wave of tingles washed over her in response to the clear invitation in the woman's seductive, dark eyes. "I would love to dance," she sighed, employing the slight gallic shrug she had perfected. It had come so naturally at Katya's last Friday. "But I am waiting for someone, une bonne femme, like yourself, who, I am afraid, is very, very jealous. Perhaps you come here often? Perhaps I can take a raincheck, no?" Spreading her French accent like peanut butter on warm French toast, she watched the woman take the bait, hoping it would reel in some information.

With a knowing smile, the brunette placed a hand on the back of Chris's chair and leaned toward her. She gave off the scent of spicy cologne and revealed a good dose of cleavage which swelled against the bodice beneath her cape.

"If *I* was your date, Frenchie, I'd be jealous, too."

Chris flashed her most winning smile and engaged in some light banter—a prelude to her next move—nonchalantly slipping two photographs from the back pocket of her black jeans. "You look like a woman who does not let anything get by her." She lowered her voice conspiratorially. "I have been trying to find someone who might have seen these two women in here." She showed the pictures of Margo and Randi and held her breath—some confirmation that her friends had been seen at least once in here.

The woman pulled away abruptly, startling Chris. "You a cop?"

Chris's mouth formed a protest before she composed herself. "But of course not. Sacre bleu! I am just trying to track down the sister of a French Canadian friend. These photos have been updated by computer. You see...," and Chris lowered her voice again. "My friend's sister ran away from a convent with this other girl. They have not been seen since...and there is a question of inheritance..." She let that sink in, hoping the story she made up would work. "Do you recognize either of them?"

Still suspicious, the brunette flicked another glance at the photos, then back at Chris. "Never seen them in here, and I'm a regular. What makes you so sure they're living in the county?"

"Good question, mon amie. This French Canadian friend has saved every Christmas card she received from her sister. They were that close." Allowing herself a sigh, Chris continued. "I am afraid that something has happened to the sister, as last year's card never arrived and the cards were all postmarked from different towns in the county." She studied the other woman's face, surprised that she did not recognize Randi as the town librarian, but then, perhaps she read paperbacks, and didn't use the library.

The brunette shook her head. "Sorry, can't help you." She placed a hand on Chris's shoulder. "Do yourself a favor, Frenchie and don't ask questions in here. *Ruby's* is the only place a lot of women feel safe."

Pondering this, Chris nodded. She re-pocketed the photos and knew she had made her first mistake. Too anxious, too obvious. Disappointed, she watched the brunette turn on her heel, red cape swirling, and stride back to her table. She then said something to her trio of companions, who in turn measured Chris with wary eyes.

Checking her watch, Chris wondered if Vera Hudson was going to stand her up. It could mean that she had gotten an attack of cold feet, or, from somewhere in the bar, she was watching and weighing Chris, prepared to attack later. The ball of her foot began to itch. Nerves.

Impatient now, she took out a ballpoint pen and began to sketch rapidly on a napkin, capturing the gestures of women gyrating to the loud rock rhythms of the all-woman band dressed in cowboy hats and fringed vests.

With a few skillful, economical lines, she rendered patrons at tables—a sprinkle of women at the bar, and soon, the white paper napkin was filled with figures and faces.

Something made her look up as a honey-blonde walked in, paid the bouncer and waved at a couple on the dance floor; at a young woman with: 'Dyke Power,' emblazoned across her T-shirt at the bar. The blonde then ran a boldly manicured hand over her light blue jumpsuit. Overly-bright, prominent blue eyes dominated her heart-shaped face.

That is what Vera said she would be wearing, Chris thought nervously.

The blonde whispered something to Ruby, still behind the bar. Ruby put down her martini shaker and pointed in Chris's direction. She poured out a martini and lifted one eyebrow as the saucy blonde confiscated it.

Sashaying across the room, Vera nodded at patrons along the way as if she owned the place.

Chris braced herself in the face of those sinuous hips approaching.

"If I knew you were such a knock-out I'd a been here earlier."
Vera Hudson's eyes glittered ravenously. She had a high-pitched voice
and nasal twang Chris found disconcerting. She associated it with the
speech patterns of city-bred women, like those she had attended classes
with at N.Y.U. Somehow, it didn't fit the package Vera presented.

Settling in the chair next to Chris, she exuded a nervous energy
as strong as her flowery perfume.

Shifting her attention from Vera's martini to her own glass of
insipid burgundy, Chris wondered if one drink of hard liquor would
hurt. But she remembered long ago vodka hangovers—waking up in
strange beds with strange women. Then her thoughts touched on Randi
and Margo in the hospital, with serious head wounds, and she decided
to keep her wits about her. Vera Hudson hardly looked like a killer,
except maybe in bed, but Chris wasn't taking any chances with her life
or fragile libido.

As if tapping into her thoughts, Vera gestured at Chris's glass
of wine. "Where's the popcorn, hon? To round out the picture? You *are*
French, aren't you?" Her pink tongue circled her red lips as she studied
Chris. "I've seen you before."

"I was just thinking the same thing," Chris admitted, but before
she could say anything else, Vera snapped her fingers.

"Got it." Vera smiled. A nice smile that softened the intensity
of eyes that were more cold-gray than blue, up close. "The Chrysler
dealer in town. Know how I remember? Had to close my real estate
office that day to check out some Jeep Cherokees. Oh boy. When I saw
you in the service area talking to that mechanic...." She rolled her eyes.
"Almost bought a car on the spot." She chuckled. "My lover had a fit
when she saw me giving you the once-over. Almost punched you out....
I saved those nice white front teeth of yours." She smiled wickedly. "So
I guess you owe me one."

"Perhaps." Chris mumbled, also recalling the tall, hefty woman
at Vera's side. Rough trade. A woman with unkempt, brown hair
carelessly tied at the nape of her neck with a rawhide thong. Wearing an
assortment of heavy rings on roughened, stained hands. Drab, olive
green army fatigues.... The only soft thing about her: generous breasts
that even a loose-fitting army shirt could not hide.

Alarms went off in her head as she remembered Margo's
description of the attacker she had seen momentarily in a flash of
headlights. Or was this just a coincidence?

Go slowly. Do not turn her off the way you just did the brunette.

"Your lover, *est formidable*—difficult to forget, no? Has she punched out any of *your* front teeth?"

"Nah. Bobbi Jean's harmless. And it's *ex*-lover." Though she said it lightly, Vera shot an anxious glance around the room and began to fidget. She opened her bag and fished out a cigarette, touched the flame of a silver lighter to it with a flourish. "Mind if I smoke?" Without waiting for Chris's reply, she blew smoke in the opposite direction. "We're still an item, Bobbi and me. But...."

"You are looking for someone to fill up your empty spaces," Chris supplied.

A crafty look stole into Vera's eyes. "Bingo." She leaned forward. "Last fling you could say. Bobbi's gonna support me while I raise a kid." Her face softened. "Boy, do I want a kid. Enough to retire and sell my real estate office. Hate it anyway. Took it over from my pop. Inflation's eating it alive."

Somehow, Chris couldn't picture Vera in the smooth role of real estate broker. *Perhaps a manicurist or waitress?* She could not see her as a mother either. "You are thinking of adopting a baby?"

"More. The whole bit. *Having* one. But it's gotta be artificial insemination or Bobbi won't buy it. And she'd do anything for me."

"Why do you jeopardize your relationship by answering personal ads?" Chris inquired.

Vera blew a smoke ring, her gaze drifting up with it. Then she shrugged. "Why not?"

Chris' mind raced. With jealousy as a motive, Bobbi Jean could very well be picking off women who placed ads. Ads that her lover, Vera, might be tempted to answer. "What does this Bobbi Jean do for a living?" Chris pressed, excited now.

Vera's eyebrows arched. "Maintenance and garden work at the college. She gets to wear a uniform. All those keys on her belt. Real macho." Drawing another drag on her cigarette, she stared into space. A small smile lifted one corner of her mouth.

"Was she in the service?"

"Only in her head. It's her fantasy. The great hero," Vera chuckled, her voice heavy with sarcasm.

Chris flinched, picturing her own fantasy of rescuing Katya on a white steed.

"Yeah, she fantasizes about those women professors, too. Says that when she's down in the dirt planting, she looks up their skirts.... What a flake."

A thread of anger wove through Chris. She imagined Katya strolling by and being ogled by Bobbi Jean.

"They think they're smarter than she is. Better, too. So she looks up their skirts. The bottom line is simple, she's a little nuts. Know what I mean." But Vera was still smiling.

Chris thought they both needed a shrink. She watched the other woman down half her martini.

"Sometimes she can be a real bitch." Vera yawned and stretched flirtatiously with a side-long glance at Chris.

"But you stay with her. Why?"

"Why?" Vera asked slyly. "She's got a tongue like a serpent." Deliberately, she slid her own tongue out of her mouth and demonstrated. At Chris's gasp, she smoothed the collar of her pale blue jumpsuit and smiled with satisfaction.

Chris was starting to feel hot around the collar herself, but it was more a feeling of being closed in—claustrophobic. To make things worse, a private ballet began orchestrating itself under the table as Vera's shoe started a slow, sinuous dance up her leg.

Chris tried to move away, but her chair was wedged in. "Have you answered the personals before?" Her voice cracked.

"Sure. You're looking at a pro. New experiences are a turn-on, don't you think?" Again the self-satisfied smile.

With a shrug, Chris replied. "One must be cautious, no? Especially if that one is a novice like I am."

"Oh, poor baby." Vera's foot became more insistent, climbing up to her thigh. "You *are* a surprise. Most women exaggerate their looks in personal ads, but not you," she said, as her foot continued its journey. "You sure are one gorgeous babe."

It was Chris's turn to chuckle as she tried to ignore the gathering of heat that had started to radiate from the spot between her legs where Vera's foot seemed to be aiming. She shifted her weight. At the worst possible moment the band switched to slow dance music.

"Dance?" Vera suggested. "Then go back to your place. Be alone." Her eyes hungrily devoured Chris, who had crossed one leg over the other and out of temptation's way.

"Playing hard to get?" Vera insinuated. "I don't mind. Don't mind working for my pleasures."

"Look, Vera, I do not want to mislead you. But I am seeing someone, too...." Glancing purposefully at her watch, Chris added, "And I promised her I would call."

"No problem," Vera replied quickly, her eyes glinting. "We can always do a threesome. The more, the merrier."

Chris almost swallowed her tongue, shot a glance in the direction of the phones near the restroom...a growing hunger to hear Katya's sane voice...to be assured that what they had experienced in the kitchen had not been a dream....

"How about it?" Vera challenged. "Your place?"

"What about your lover, Bobbi Jean?" Chris tried to buy time.

"She'll never find out. Relax, huh? Boy, you're uptight."

Again, Chris made a show of checking her watch. "We have only been acquainted for twenty-five minutes. Are you aware of the assaults on Deer Falls...."

The hand holding Vera's martini stopped mid-air. "What're you saying?" she asked nervously, her body rigid, as if to stop any more disturbing questions, an attitude that Chris had seen before in women who refused to face reality.

Softening her approach, Chris offered: "I would not want anything to happen to you," she said sincerely, and wished it was five years earlier with Simon sitting next to her. More knowledgeable and mature now, she might not have been so preoccupied, so filled with herself; she would have cooled his enthusiasm over the personals. Guilt weighed her down as she pictured her younger brother trapped in that elevator shaft.

"You sure ask a lot of questions." Vera frowned. "Who do you think you are, Kate Delafield, P.I.?"

Laughing, Chris put Vera at ease. "Mon dieu, I am just a struggling artist."

"Then show me. You sell your stuff? Thought you might be snowing me in the ad. If it's a bummer making money in real estate, it must be worse for an artist. If you're really an artist."

To prove it, though she felt awkward showing off, Chris slid the napkin filled with drawings over. Vera was wide-eyed, then delighted as she pointed to the portrait of the brunette in the red cape who had asked Chris to dance.

"Amazing. Looks just like Bonnie Pearl." Her eyes appraised Chris in a new way. "A real artist. A real French artist...can I model for you?"

Parrying the suggestion, the suggestive tone with a wave of her hand, Chris explained, "I paint mostly from memory." She tapped her forehead. "Landscapes, murals. The models are in my head."

"Invite me over anyway," Vera persisted.

Suddenly, Chris realized what it felt like to be treated like a piece of meat. She smiled without feeling it. "Your place or mine?" she bantered. It was the wrong thing to suggest, and she could not help herself when she added: "Venez voir mes estampes japonaises—you desire to come up and see my etchings, yes?"

Encouraged, Vera captured Chris's hand. The other woman's was damp. And hot like her eyes. As soon as Vera circled her palm with a suggestive fingertip, Chris pulled her hand away.

Angry now, because she herself had treated women like objects in the past, Chris said hotly. "I have nothing to show you. *Molly's Sporting Goods* in Deer Falls exhibits my work. They are on consignment if you wish to buy a painting. In any case, you can see them anytime you desire. At Molly's."

But you will not see me again, Chris fumed. *You will not be able to brag to your friends how you turned a struggling French artist into a conquest.*

Looking startled, then confused, Vera confiscated the napkin full of drawings and placed it in her bag, settling for that instead of Chris as a trophy. But she was angry. "You're crazy," she hurled at Chris.

To impart more weight to what she had to say, Chris leaned forward. "I did not want to mislead you. But I placed the ad for friendship."

Vera's jaw dropped. "Bitch. Leading me on like that. People like you got no right to place personal ads." She deliberately re-lit the cigarette that had gone out in her ashtray and blew smoke in Chris's face.

"Stop that. You are acting childish."

"Like hell I will. You need a shrink."

With an exasperated sigh, Chris slowly rose to her feet and stared down the other woman, shuddering inwardly when she recognized the bird of prey she had once been. She, too, had encouraged desirable women to run after her. A daily high at that point in her life. "I am certain that you can have any woman in this room that you want, but I am not available for one night stands. I do not intend to fill the empty spaces your lover cannot fill, Vera, because you will always have empty spaces if you cannot fill them yourself. You should stop game-playing. Believe me, it can get you killed," she said self-righteously, instantly regretting it.

Furious, Vera countered with, "At least Bobbi Jean has *feelings*. You're a cold bitch."

Disgusted, Chris fished the photos of Margo and Randi out of her pocket and slammed them on the table. "*They* almost got killed. It could happen to *you*, if you are not careful." She paused, ignoring Vera's defiant face, and felt suddenly old. "Have you ever seen these women at *Ruby's?*" she asked, her French temper gone cold.

Huffily, Vera shot a quick, condescending glance at them, but Chris could tell she was scared, and so was disappointed when she shot up and showed Chris her back. Chris's eyes shifted from her retreating form to the photos on the table. She pocketed them. *Merde, I certainly screwed that one up*, she thought. *C' est la vie*, and headed for the phones to call Katya. Even though she had blown it, anticipation restored some bounce to her walk.

Maybe she was not cut out to be Detective Delafield or V.I. Warshowski. Too much rage. Quickly, she dialed Katya's number, which she had memorized, then found herself at a loss for words. *Sorry I have not called before, but I was playing hard to get?...I think that you are the best thing that ever happened to me?*

By the third ring, Chris realized she was clutching the receiver with a clammy hand; that she had been afraid to call Katya all along.

When Katya finally picked up, Chris's vocal chords froze. Swallowing hard, she tried for the levity she had used last Friday when she went to Katya's cabin to fix her dishwasher. "Bon jour, madame," she greeted in a strained voice. Her heart drummed a staccato beat inside her chest.

There was a long pause, then Katya's rich voice. "Chris? Is that you?"

A thrill shot through Chris. *She has been waiting for my call!*

Another pause, and when Katya spoke again, Chris realized, with dismay, that she had been crying.

"What is wrong?" she asked with concern.

"I...just can't talk right now."

Dread wormed a slow trail up her gut. "I...thought I might drop by to pick up Sam's pictures...for the mural...for an idea of what he wants. Do some preliminary sketches.... Maman's mural is nearly complete."

"Please," Katya explained. "I can't handle it right now." To Chris's ear, Katya was saying. *I cannot handle you.* The desperate and final tone on the other end left Chris shaken.

It occurred to her that Katya might be angry she hadn't called sooner. She cursed herself for playing games. Clearly, this woman lived by different standards. Her body ached when she pictured their kiss in the kitchen. Had it frightened Katya away? "Should I call back later?" she asked hopefully, steeling herself for the answer.

The prolonged silence was just as bad as a no would have been, and she heard Katya blow her nose into a tissue. "Please, tell me. What is the matter? Perhaps I can help," Chris implored, sinking fast, hating herself for it. When Katya still did not respond, Chris masked her anguish with cool abruptness. "I will try some other time. Au revoir." Pain twisted her insides and she wanted to strike back. She felt like a canoe abandoned in the rapids.

Katya interrupted before she could hang up. "Chris...what took place in the kitchen...Well, I never expected...never thought.... I...it was my fault."

"Your *fault?*" Chris exclaimed, fresh anger consuming her. She had felt more in that kiss than in making love with anyone. Her body sang during that kiss. And she *knew* that Katya had felt the same way.

It did not make any sense. Was Katya basically straight at heart—bi-sexual? The possibility brought her thoughts to Sam. She realized that he might be her only link to Katya. What irony. Her love life dependent on a young male. The idea of losing what she had just found, what they *both* had found, seemed impossible. She could not, would not, fathom it.

Katya's voice broke in on her, "I've hurt you," Katya said in a shaky voice. "I'm...sorry."

I will not grant you absolution and I do not need your charity, Chris said to herself, anger and disappointment hardening her heart. "I must go now. My friends are waiting." She hung up on Katya's: "Wait, let me explain..." and strode over to the bar. The bottle of Smirnoff's Ruby was holding beckoned to her shattered ego. She wanted that drink now. Why shouldn't she have it?

Anger saved her. She would not give Katya the satisfaction of hurting her, and abruptly headed for the door. With one last glance over her shoulder, she noticed Vera clinging to the brunette on the dance floor.

Arranging her keys between her fingers, almost hoping for a fight, Chris stormed out. She crossed the parking lot with chaos in her heart. She would not let her guard down again. Not for Katya, not for anyone.

❦ 12 ❧

*W*atching Sam collect rocks along the stream's bank trig-gered memories of her own childhood summer vacations. Katya poured the last drops of broccoli carrot juice from her thermos and drained the cup.

It was the second Saturday in May, unseasonably warm. A cloud of mayflies burst out of their nymph casings and emerged over the stream. Katya recalled how she had relished those healing hours on the stream with her father at the Catskill bungalow colony where they vacationed. She could still smell the musty odor of rooms that were boarded up all winter; hear the morning wake-up call of roosters from a nearby farm—the serenade of katydids and crickets at night when she and her parents played scrabble on the screened-in back porch; moths slapping against the porch screens, drawn to the light.

Those summers had been a source of joy for all of them, even met the needs of her fussy mother, an art historian who had dragged Katya to local historical landmarks, museums, suburban theatre groups. Her father, on leave from teaching biology at a Brooklyn high school, reveled in the enormous lakes and flowing streams, passing his love of nature on to his daughter.

But she was a child then and things shifted when she reached adolescence. It seemed that as she grew breasts and matured, her father grew distant. And when she displayed the natural athletic abilities that had been encouraged in her as a little girl—fishing, climbing trees, softball—suddenly her tomboy ways offended her mother's sensibilities. To win back their approval, her place in the sun with them, Katya had conformed and become ladylike, and she had learned to do it so well that the adventurous little girl inside her, curled up into a tiny ball and found a hiding place deep in her heart. With the fear of her parents abandoning her, she never knocked on that bad little girl's door.

Until Loren and then Sam came along, coaxing that little girl back into the light.

Katya tied a Quill Gordon fake fly to the tippet end of her leader with the blood knot her father had taught her. Even then, he seemed a study in contrasts: oversized hands that were capable of the most delicate work.

"Ouch!" The tiny hook pierced her thumb. A bubble of blood inflated like a tiny red balloon. She had even begun to welcome the spankings, she mused, for they were the only time her mother touched her.

From her mother, Katya had learned the art of worrying. Constantly on the alert for natural disasters, she hoped to ward off illnesses that plagued the unprepared. Her mother kept herself busy, almost manically, to ward off nasty surprises. Doing and worrying was life insurance. Without it, fate could slip in, slap you with a zinger, and render you helpless.

The hot sun beat down on the short-sleeved pink blouse and white shorts she had thrown on instead of heavy stream gear. The heat felt good on her skin. Anticipating the relief of dipping her bare toes into the cold, bracing current, she stood happily on the lip of the rock-studded stream bank. She gazed languidly across an abutment of boulders, swirling riffles and still pools. Time to cast away unpleasant memories of growing up. Time to rest her eyes on the dark green shoreline opposite her property. A trio of eager birds swooped down and stole mayflies from the mouths of rainbow and brook trout, reminding her that *she* was the intruder here.

She glanced back at Sam and was reassured to see him still busy with his rocks and smooth river stones. Dipping one foot in the water, she shivered with bliss, recalled how numb her toes had felt in the shallows of country ponds those long-ago summers, how sunfish and huge carp nipped at them.

She cast her thick orange flyline out over the stream, again courtesy of her father's patient instruction. Casting and reeling in, she teased the trout with her tiny Quill Gordon.

Katya was certain her father would have appreciated this stream, her log cabin, the collegiate ambiance of Deer Falls; if not her chosen life-style—the life-style her mother refused to accept.

Abandoning her.

Perhaps, if her parents had been born of a different generation, they would have appreciated Loren, allowed themselves to go crazy over Sam.

What a waste, she thought bitterly.

Finally, Sam picked up the inner tube he had tried out earlier in the week. She had carefully fastened it by rope, to the trunk of a sturdy swamp maple with the strongest knot her father had taught her. Sometimes she worried that she was overprotecting Sam. But she didn't feel bad about insisting he wear a life jacket as double insurance. The tube was tethered by a long enough expanse of rope to keep him both safe from the current, and allow him the freedom to ride the riffles and cross-currents in the still pool he loved best.

She restrained herself from checking his corded lifeline wrapped in countless loops around the tree. She had checked it only three days before, and even her overactive imagination could not imagine such a sturdy rope breaking. Lately, she had been trying very hard not to surrender to nerve-wracking, unreasonable caution, afraid that it would rub off on Sam. Katya drove Katya crazy. She didn't want to drive her son crazy, too. That was a legacy she was determined not to perpetuate.

Besides, a thicket of prickly vines had started growing up the swamp maple, and she didn't relish picking its thorns out of her fingers.

He waded into the water and choked back a gasp.

Probably afraid she'd change her mind and ground him. She smiled at him and he drew in a deep, shivery breath.

"Only for a little while now, darling."

He sucked his lips in tightly, gumming them up and down, teasing her.

"So I won't be able to see them turn blue?"

Even his nod was happy. With caution, he waded up to his thighs, bent over, holding the tube at his side, and studied a school of hovering trout. Satisfied, he took another step and placed his tube in the still pool. With a deft flip, he hoisted himself up on the rubber donut and paddled contentedly; the swiftly flowing current swirling around his tranquil watery oasis. Ripples banged the tube from boulder to boulder like an aquatic bumper car and he squealed with laughter.

Suddenly, she saw a terrifying image in her mind's eye—Sam being carried away by the current into the roiling river. The tube sliding out from beneath him. Sam smashing against a boulder as his inert body hurtled downstream.

Trembling, she shook her head to clear it and checked where a natural barrier of rocks and boulders narrowed the stream, leaving only a small opening. One that his tube would not fit through.

But his tubeless body would.

Stop! she chided herself.

"The other kids are allowed to play "Tube-On-A-Rope," he always nagged when she lectured him on stream safety.

She, in turn, always cautioned, "Don't pull on the rope, Sam."

He always insisted, "You know it can't break, Mom. It's too strong. 'Sides, why do I have to get all tied up? When can I tube down the river like Scott and Anthony?"

"When you're *their* age." *Maybe.*

"It's the pits," he always complained, but usually resigned himself to the confines of the little pool.

Now he was examining another school of rainbow trout drifting in the underwater shadow of his tube. "How come the fish swim in schools?" he asked her, his smile curving into mischief.

"Nature made it that way?"

"Uh uh. They want to get smart." He laughed. "Got ya!"

A pair of gulls, emigres from the Hudson River, arced over the water, shrieking. Sam's head shot up, and, in seconds, one of the birds held a writhing trout in its beak. Katya had been surprised to see gulls foraging for food scraps in the parking lot of the supermarket outside of Deer Falls; stranded, homeless creatures spilled into the flotsam and jetsam of Mother Nature turned upside down.

Sam's cry of "Awesome!" followed the gulls' dizzying dance. He picked up a river rock resting on a high bed of gravel and studied two brown nymphs, natural residents of the stream, and questioned her with wide eyes.

"They'll be hatching into mayflies soon," she explained, again drawn back into the bittersweet memories of her childhood when her father had explained the life-cycles of nature to her, the balance of stream life; how nymphs were transformed into mayflies, some to fall prey to the voracious appetites of fish and birds.

Whipping her flyrod back and forth, she sailed the line out, depositing her fake fly on the opposite side of the stream. Earlier, she had witnessed a feeding frenzy in that very spot. On her next cast, a trout bit, leaping out of the water in protest. The late afternoon sun illuminated its rainbow hues.

Sam became a rapt audience, sitting perfectly still on his tube, absently playing with the straps on his neon orange life jacket as she played the trout, her mouth dry with excitement; and gave it slack. The next move was the trout's and it shot upstream. Kneeling at the edge of the water, she fed it more line, toyed with it, until they both grew weary. Finally, with her net, she captured its flailing body. Grasping it gently by the mouth, she crimped back the barb of the hook with a needle-nosed pliers. The hook slid out with minimal damage. Cradling the fish beneath the surface of the water with gentle hands, she faced it upstream.

"We going to eat this one, Mom?"

"Don't think so. This one's got a lot of growing up to do, like you." She loosened her grip on it, watched it hesitate for a second, twist and shoot upstream, a bright dart of silver. After it disappeared, Katya turned to her son. "The current's getting stronger and your lips are blue. I think it's time." She motioned to the stream's bank.

He started to protest, when his eyes widened with excitement.

Katya instinctively looked to her left, where the stream curved around a bend. Shielding her eyes with one hand, she studied a figure wading around the curve, casting with a flyrod. Something about the tilt of the head, the cap, the long legs under white shorts was familiar.

It couldn't be. Katya had seen to that when she had so callously rejected Chris that fateful evening when she phoned. She busied herself with her flyrod, but it only made her think of the reason she had been so cold. Loren. The wound still festering inside her. Guilt.

It struck Katya that maybe she didn't want it healed, wanted, instead to have the past restored. Wanted Loren to be there for her. Before Chris's phone call she had been crying, the aftermath of an anguished week set off by their kiss in the kitchen. Her recent erotic dreams had been replaced by nightmares in which she lost control of herself and was falling through space. It seemed as if she was passing through a new, and hopefully, final stage of mourning. But she needed time. She had tried to convey this to Chris, but Chris had cut her off. And in spite of herself, when she closed her eyes at night, Chris' face filled her thoughts.

All week she had talked to herself: *A relationship with her can only lead to heartbreak.* Over and over, she lectured herself, as her lips still tingled from the memory of that electrifying kiss, from the frightening chemistry that had exploded in the kitchen.

Coward, she said silently as the figure waded closer, playing havoc with her heart. Maybe it was a mirage—someone else. But just as the figure stepped into a shaft of sunlight, Katya saw the dark cap she wore turn purple.

"It's Chris, Mom!" Sam splashed water as he bobbed up and down.

Her pulse raced. She tried to quiet it by busying herself with another dry fly, but the knot failed her fumbling fingers, and to her dismay, the fly dropped into the speeding downstream current and disappeared.

Chris was only a few feet away; Katya's ears roared, above the rush of the stream.

"Funny running into you like this...," was all Katya could think of to say when she found her tongue.

Chris shrugged, rubbed the cleft in her chin and couldn't meet Katya's eyes, instead gazed fixedly at some boulders jagging out of the water. "Maman sent me out for some fresh trout. For the dinner menu." With a sigh, she patted the wicker creel attached to the belt of her white denim shorts. When she finally looked up, her eyes reflected, not only the green T-shirt she wore, short sleeves rolled up over well-defined biceps, but the surrounding spring foliage. And vulnerability.

Breathless, Katya admired those eyes. They were so deep she could drown in them. And then they looked away. Chris seemed so hesitant, so unsure, that Katya's heart melted. Chris reminded her of a child fascinated with something she could not touch. Like a flame.

Katya's body sprang to life. Chris could have gone fishing in the stream closer to *Le Provençal*. She pondered teasing her about it, but was afraid she'd drive her away. If only she could get a grin out of that face then everything would fall into place. Could they start over as friends?

Chris leaned her flyrod against a flat boulder, reached into the back pocket of her shorts and drew out a box of licorice candy. She popped one in her mouth without offering any to Sam or Katya, which she would have done before.

Katya could almost feel the retaining wall the younger woman had built around herself.

"I should move on," Chris spoke softly, with a weak smile at Sam. "The current is getting unmanageable."

"And sneakers aren't the best defense against slippery rocks," Katya observed with concern.

"The traction's enough," Chris countered and gave another shrug. She paused, as if she didn't know what to do next, bent down and submerged her hand in the stream. Searching along the gravel bottom, she grabbed some rocks and straightened up. Swiveling her head, she studied the woods across the way, paused and hurled one with precise and amazing speed. It grazed off the center of a knot in the trunk of a maple tree.

"Neat!" Sam exclaimed. "Wish I could pitch like that."

Chris's face brightened. "When I was a little girl on my grandpère's vineyard in Vieux Ville...my brother and I went target-shooting with rocks." She fingered the remaining rocks in her hand. "We used grandpère's old grape trellises for targets. And we would get a point every time the rock went through an empty space. We practiced every day. We became such good shots we dreamed about moving to America to join a baseball team."

"Didn't your grand, uh, pear, get mad? Mommy gets mad when I throw rocks in the stream. Says it scares the trout."

Chris chuckled. "Grandpère angry? He taught us how to throw! But your mother is right, Sam. You do not want to scare the fish."

"Hit that," Sam demanded, pointing to a hornet's nest dangling from a branch in a sweet birch tree.

Chris squinted, and shrugged. "It is very far away." Pausing just for a beat, she fired another rock, and with uncanny precision, it hit the target. A hazy, yellow cloud of hornets rose up, then shot into the air as the nest shattered against a boulder underneath.

"Awesome," Sam complimented, and looked at his mother to second it.

Katya was feeling mixed emotions: admiration and annoyance. "I'd rather you didn't throw rocks. Some nature lover could be on the other end." She wanted to be angry with Chris. It would make things simpler.

"Sorry," Chris looked down at the water, opened her hand, and the remaining smooth stones she had held disappeared below the surface.

But she couldn't contain the small smile she shared with Sam, and looked approvingly at the way his tube was fastened to the swamp maple behind Katya. "It is a fine day to go tubing down the river."

Katya could have strangled her. Sam opened his mouth to reply, when to her horror, she saw his rope snap off.

The current caught the tube and spun it in crazy circles. What was left of the rope whipped the water like an enraged snake.

Shrieking, he was knocked backwards. His tube careened against a cluster of rocks that threw him clear. Skidding into the dangerous current, the tube whirled around in circles.

Frozen in place, Katya stared with disbelief and horror as Sam got swept downstream, heading toward the barrier of rocks that dammed the entrance to swifter waters.

The river lay just beyond.

Sam panicked and flailed his arms frantically as the swirling current claimed his little body. He was like a flimsy toy sailboat in a stormy sea, his orange life jacket doing little to sustain him.

Just as Katya snapped out of her shock, Chris was already free of creel and sneakers, her baseball cap arcing into the air. She dove into the center of the stream and surfaced a few feet from the granite outcropping where Sam's life jacket had snagged. Reaching out, she desperately tried to grab him, but the current knocked him loose again.

Katya raced down the shoreline, heading for the rocks, crying, "Sam!" all the way. She scrambled up on the barricade and lost her footing on the slippery surfaces. Then Chris's head popped out of the surging current, a handful of Sam's life jacket in her grasp. She quickly flipped him over on his back, for he had been floating face down.

Endless seconds later, crouching on the barrier, Katya reached out a trembling hand.

Chris had Sam in a cross-chest hold and struggled against the current to bridge the small distance between the thunderous channel of water and Katya's outstretched hand. She gasped, swallowed water, but managed to grasp the edge of the boulder.

Clinging to it, she lifted Sam and pushed his inert form up to Katya.

Katya dragged him up on the ledge to safety, ran back and extended her hand to Chris, who was clinging precariously to a partly-submerged tree trunk now. "Hang on!" she ordered, adrenaline surging through her body, flooding it with strength. "Okay. Got you."

Chris wormed her body halfway up on the ledge and lifted her head. A stream of blood ran down her face from a gash on her cheekbone. She struggled to her feet, drenched and trembling, but quickly recovered.

Now she was crouched at Sam's side. She gathered him in her arms and dashed for a level strip of land, ripped open his life jacket, and pressed her ear against his chest.

Anxiously, Katya hovered over them, torn between calling the paramedics and anticipating Sam's first breath. His lips, fingernails, were frighteningly blue.

"His heart is beating," Chris assured her. "And he did not swallow much water."

"Why isn't he breathing?" Katya wailed.

"Shock." All the while, Chris prepared Sam, clearing his airway with one finger, tilting his head back, parting his darkened lips. Pinching his nose, she blew air into his lungs.

"Please, Sam. Please breathe," Katya murmured. She needed just one sign. Nothing could unglue her from the spot. Gathering solace from Chris's confidence, she waited. If she withdrew her vigil over his still form, he might not be alive when she returned to the stream.

Chris continued the rhythmic mouth-to-mouth breathing. It was only seconds, but seemed hours.

Katya watched Sam's narrow chest rise slightly with each forced breath from Chris; swallowed the panic in her throat. Then, miraculously, he coughed. A small trickle of water squirted out of his mouth. His eyelids fluttered open and he shivered violently, coughed again and began to retch.

Katya couldn't believe she was happy to see Sam vomit.

She ran to the spot where she'd been fishing, grabbed the blanket they had used for a picnic lunch and hurried back.

Dry-heaving now, Sam finished and lay spent as she tucked the blanket around him.

"Mom? What?" He shuddered and sat up with her help. "Don't feel so good."

"Oh, baby. Baby." She rubbed warmth into the shriveled flesh of his hands, watched with relief as color returned to his face. His blue lips gradually turned back to their natural color.

"He will be just fine now," Chris promised. Her own lips began to chatter, more from shock than chill, Katya gathered. Something shifted inside her. Staring into Chris's black-fringed green eyes, she felt her universe come together. "Thank you," she whispered. "You saved Sam's life."

She thought, how appropriate it was that it was Chris who had saved his life. Loren had given her the gift of life one memorable afternoon in a restaurant. Now things had come full circle and Chris had done the same for their child. Gazing up at white clouds scudding across the sky, she wondered what shapes Loren would pick out. A swan?

Would Chris, with her artistic eye see the same thing or her own fresh vision?

Goosebumps popped out on Katya's exposed flesh. A few of the clouds broke up into fragile wisps as if Loren were answering her, giving her a blessing. Then Loren faded from her mind.

"I should drive you both to the emergency room," Katya said in a voice husky with feeling. "I won't rest easy unless I do."

Sam winced at the words "emergency room" and shook his head vehemently.

Katya knew why. The last ambulance he'd seen had carried Loren to the hospital on a stretcher. It was also the last time he'd seen her alive.

A distracted look clouded Chris's face. "Take Sam. I am all right." Her breathing was still ragged; her soaked green T-shirt clung invitingly to the tight curves of her slender, strong body.

Katya stood beside her, scooped up a few drops of blood with her thumb. "You're going to have a scar." Her heart wrenched at the thought.

"A reminder of today, no?" Chris's eyes searched Katya's and she gasped when Katya leaned toward her and kissed her quickly on the mouth.

"Gross, Mom. Don't get icky," Sam scoffed, but he was smiling.

Katya touched her lips where she still felt the voltage of that brief kiss. "I'm sorry I hurt you," Katya explained. "But I was very confused the night you called. Forgive me?"

Chris's nod eased into a slow grin and Katya's heart settled in place. "What *am* I going to do about you?" Filled with relief, she felt as if she could light up a city, and glanced briefly at Sam. There was no sign of anything out of place in his demeanor. He had been accustomed to her quick embraces with Loren when the mood struck them.

"No hospital." He made a face. "They stick you."

"Come, little man." Chris swept him up in her arms, blanket and all, and followed Katya back to where they had been standing before.

"How do you say?" He flicked a quick glance at his mother, then whispered in Chris's ear: "Shit, in French?"

Chris laughed, holding him tighter.

"Mom won't let me say it in English."

Katya chuckled to herself as Chris whispered back, "Merde."

"Merde," he repeated softly, savoring the word like a precious tool that would come in handy. "Merde. I hate hospitals."

"Me too, but they help people get well."

"I don't want to be responsible for a scar on that beautiful face," Katya objected, gathering up her things, hearing in the background how Chris was going to paint a special mural with chocolate trees and vanilla mountains—a gingerbread house with lollipop trees for Sam. She heard his huge sigh of happiness and Katya wondered when the shock of his ordeal would register. He had an uncomfortably familiar way of burying things. She'd have to make sure he talked about his near-drowning, that it didn't result in a permanent fear of water.

"I love you Chris," Sam said. "You saved me."

About to start up the incline leading into the woods behind her house, Katya turned, expecting to see the two of them behind her. But Chris was circling the swamp maple tree with Sam. Her face pinched with worry as she parted the overgrowth of brambles, weeded vines with one hand and studied the remaining coils and knot.

For some reason, a thread of alarm pinched Katya's gut. Searching Chris's face for a clue provided nothing. If something was bothering her, she wouldn't say it in front of Sam.

What she did say was: "Katya," and the word went through Katya like warm honey. It was the first time she had heard her name on Chris's lips.

Katya stood poised at the edge of the woods and waited expectantly.

"Oh it's nothing.... Let me help you dress Sam and get him in the car. Then I will go to my cottage and change. Maman can patch up my cut."

Katya felt suddenly jealous of Chris' mother. As they started after her, she led the way home. She intended to give Chris the key if she couldn't talk her into seeing a doctor at the hospital. She didn't think she'd have to work too hard to talk Chris into starting the mural as a surprise for Sam, after what she knew would be a wrenching hospital ordeal.

Would Chris have the patience to wait for her? Perhaps an intimate candlelight dinner by the fire? Her body shivered pleasurably at the thought.

But why had Chris been staring at the knot? Had Katya done something wrong? Caused Sam's accident?

When Katya heard Chris's belated response to Sam's declaration of love she melted.

"Je t'aime, Sam. I love you, too."

Just now, love had allowed him to acknowledge his rescue from a near-drowning. Perhaps it was love for her and his doting grandparents and the legacy of love that Loren had left him, that had sustained him this past year.

And now there was love for Chris.

Ɋɘ   Ɋɘ   Ɋɘ

❦ 13 ❧

*K*atya studied her son's vulnerable face as he slipped into deep sleep beneath his Ninja Turtle comforter. On the way to the hospital, a flood of repressed tears started pouring out of him, rapidly escalating to panic. The nurses could barely contain him—pry him loose from Katya's arms.

She hated to consider how he might have carried on if he had been forced into an ambulance. He still jumped when he heard sirens. It was only recently that those nightmares with sirens and ambulances rooted in the last, grave stages of Loren's illness, had dissipated.

Between waiting for his pediatrician, blood tests, chest x-rays and a neurological workup, hours had passed. Dr. Mescalaris had finally prescribed a sedative and an antibiotic to counter any respiratory complications before releasing him.

As the hours slipped by, all Katya could think about was getting Sam back to the sanctuary of their log cabin. She didn't dare hope that Chris would still be waiting.

But she was...and in her familiar pale blue workshirt and jeans, the aroma of wood burning in the fireplace, the crackle of sparks in the background. Smiling broadly at Chris, Katya promised to come right down.

Despite Sam's protests, Katya had urged him upstairs. After planting a kiss on his forehead, Katya turned to the one sheet-rocked wall opposite his bed. A charcoal sketch of Chris's vision of Candyland jumped out at her, framed by the adjacent log walls. On a dropcloth sat stacks of unopened paint cans, two empty tins, one filled with brushes. Katya pored over the mural, fastening her eyes on the little boy with Sam's face standing on a candy wafer path in front of a gingerbread house. Ice cream mountains were topped with cherries and whipped cream slowly melted into an ice cream stream; all surrounded by spearmint leaf bushes bearing lollipops. The lack of color didn't detract from Chris's intent. What most took Katya's breath away, what most delighted Sam before he succumbed to his bed and pillows, was how the fantasy scene in front of them was so much like the layout of their own log cabin and property—the trees, bushes, stream.... It was just like Chris to soften reality and provide Sam with an inviting dreamscape to distract him from his close brush with death.

Katya wondered what other demons, besides her brother's horrible death, plagued Chris. She flicked off Sam's bedside lamp and began to tremble with anticipation.

Almost by rote, she wandered into her bathroom and showered. She toweled off, standing mutely by the full-length mirror in her cedar closet. Running her hands over her nude body, she imagined them as Chris's hands.

With a sigh she slipped on a long, pink nightshirt, and another quiver of desire snaked through her. Her weakened legs carried her down the spiral staircase. A gust of wind rattled the windows. Tree branches scraped against panes of glass. Her heart pounded.

In the great room, Chris was thoughtfully shifting some logs in the hearth with a poker. Katya's mouth dried up. She watched the curling tongues of flame until Chris turned. Their eyes touched.

Drawn closer, circling the couch facing the fire, Katya saw a pulse beating in Chris's throat; naked desire in her light green eyes as they quickly flicked over Katya's aroused body under the revealing pink nightshirt.

"Please forgive me for not going to the hospital with you." Chris looked down at the poker in her hand, sat down and replaced it in the wrought iron stand on the hearth.

"You don't have to explain," Katya assured her, absorbing the beautiful, troubled face before her, its fresh wound now patched with tiny butterfly strips of adhesive tape.

"I must explain," Chris disagreed as Katya lowered herself to the couch, "why I could not go with you." Sparks popped and crackled in the fireplace behind her. She began to knead her hands. "I told you about my brother, Simon. How he was a casualty of New York City violence. What I did not tell you was what really took place the night he was murdered. How it affected my life in so many ways afterward." Her eyes wandered up to the cathedral ceiling and lingered, as if she could draw strength from it.

"Nothing you tell me will matter, Chris. You saved Sam's life. I owe you."

Chris shook her head. "You do not owe me anything, but I owe you an explanation at least. It could not have been easy for you in the emergency room with Sam. He was so frightened." She drew in a breath and continued in a monotone: "The police phoned me at the women's bar where I had my first commission to paint a mural. I was filled with myself—that is, until the call. I cannot even remember how I arrived at the emergency room." She tapped her forehead. "A blank. What I do remember is the white glare, the blood...cries of pain. Curtains separating patients, victims of one kind of violence or another...."

"Go on," Katya urged, nerves still jangled from her own wait just hours before.

"The charge nurse had me sitting in that waiting room for hours. Promised to get word to me as soon as there was news.... I did not mind the waiting...it meant that Simon was still alive." Her voice caught.

"Finally, a doctor came out. Looked upset, explained about an error.

"An error," Chris repeated, running a hand over her face. "He asked me to go down to the morgue to identify Simon's body." She shuddered. "You see, my brother had died in the ambulance hours earlier."

Katya half-rose from the couch, but Chris's hand went out to stay her.

"I shall never forget how pale his skin looked when they pulled the sheet back. And the tag on his toe like a brand on cattle. I forced myself to stare at the terrible wounds on his body." She pounded her chest with a fist then shook her head as if to erase the image. "They gave me a small plastic bag with my brother's belongings." Touching her earlobe, she forced herself to go on: "I wear his gold earring here. My mother, his high school graduation ring, around her neck. On a long chain. So the ring is deep down where no one can see it. But where she can *feel* it. A...terrible secret."

She looked up through tear-filled eyes that pleaded for understanding.

Katya felt tears sting her own eyes. She rose from the couch, skirted the glass coffee table, and knelt in front of Chris. "Hush," she soothed. "Hush now." The cut on her cheekbone was deep and would leave a V-shaped scar like a dimple. Somehow, Chris's face was made more endearing by the wound, as a crack might make a fine piece of porcelain.

Clasping the cold hands resting on Chris's knees despite the fire, Katya ran her lips below the fringe of dark lashes shadowing the younger woman's cheekbones. The breath was sweet; the shudder bittersweet.

How exhausted she must be, Katya thought. This amazing creature who had risked her life for Sam; who had walked past the "No Trespassing" sign on her property as if it were fate. Their fate. She cringed at the thought that she had almost allowed Chris to walk out of her life with the same swiftness that she had entered it.

The grandfather clock chimed in the vestibule. A sudden flash of lightning illuminated the room. One roll of thunder preceded drops of rain that splattered the roof; tinkled down gutters; marked time. But time had stopped for Katya. Only a heartbeat divided them.

Katya would never be sure who bridged the gap first, whose moan broke the stillness. Their lips met tentatively, then with hunger. First hesitant, Chris's tongue explored Katya's mouth, probed deeper, demanding a response. Her hands captured Katya's head.

But now it was Katya's turn to stay Chris's hands. She pressed them close. Above her breasts. She kissed every lovely feature on Chris's face; gently followed those kisses with the fingertips of one hand.

Eyes glazed, stunned with passion, Chris trembled. She tried to free her hands, but Katya held them fast and continued her loving exploration. Now her ears; the lobe with Simon's earring, the graceful neck, the pulsating throat.

"Katya...."

They kissed again. Katya didn't even realize she had let Chris's hands go until they were on her, hot and urgent. Katya felt her body grow as taut as an arrow on a drawn bowstring.

Under Chris's lips and tongue, her own mouth answered. A rush, fiery and wet, exploded from Katya's core. She trembled with desire. Managing to cup Chris's head, absorbing heat from the fire, from Chris's lips, she devoured that mouth, eliciting a string of guttural cries. Katya was a woman consumed, desperate to consume in return.

Chris gasped. With abandon, they tumbled on the Navajo rug. Katya pulled off Chris's T-shirt. She kissed and tasted the strong, hot body she had captured under her own. She was delirious with pleasure and urgency. Even more brazen now, her hands moved down, unzipped

Chris's jeans before she could object, for Katya sensed along with the younger woman's wild response, some hesitation.

"Wait...please," Chris murmured against her mouth.

Katya didn't listen. Couldn't. Chris's jeans, her panties came off. The only sounds Katya heard—their shared moans. A sense of feverish need seized her body—consumed her as another flash of lightning lit the room.

Bracing herself on her hands, Katya lifted her body up and looked down at Chris's face. She saw conflict. She was not sure that it was the same hesitation she had sensed earlier. And why was Chris trembling so violently? Eyes half-closed; thrashing her head back and forth on the rug; animal cries. That was not conflict. A rush of tenderness eclipsed Katya's urgency. She murmured soft, endearing words to Chris, kissed her face, enveloped her in a cocoon of warmth.

Chris gasped. "I...cannot."

So deep and powerful were her feelings, that Katya could only explain them with her body. She lowered herself again to Chris, slowly moved against her, pulled away teasingly, came back, circling her hips rhythmically now, touching and not touching.

Chris's eyes shut tight.

"Look at me," Katya demanded in a thick voice.

Dazed eyes opened to her.

Rising again, Katya unbuttoned her nightshirt, slipped it from her shoulders.

"Goddess." Chris's eyes fastened on Katya's full, upturned, hard-nippled breasts; her own smaller ones darkly-puckered, tips erect.

Smiling tenderly into Chris's wondrous eyes, Katya resumed her slow, horizontal dance. Then there was no hesitation at all, just bliss.

Katya dipped her head and bit the slender neck beneath her mouth. "Make love to me in French."

"You are scaring me," Chris gasped, her hips moving involuntarily under Katya's.

"I don't want to scare you. I want to love you. Let me love you." With a gently-prying knee, she parted Chris's reluctant thighs and pressed the cleft of her passion against Chris's. Chris moaned.

Chris grabbed hold of Katya's buttocks and arched up.

Under the urgent rhythm of their hips, the floor seemed to shoot up from beneath Katya. She was flying. Oh, God was she flying.

Barely, she heard low ragged cries from Chris's throat. Taking the lead, she undulated, climbed higher, certain that the next peak would be the last, that she would hurtle up to orgasm. But the peaks were endless.

Chris's hands seemed to be everywhere.

Even higher, Katya rose; a thousand shooting stars. From somewhere deep and primal inside her, a scream gathered momentum, reached her vocal chords, shattering the silence.

They kissed as their orgasms finally blended into one glorious explosion.

℘ ℘ ℘

❦ **14** ❦

*C*hris woke up to an overwhelming sense of well-being. Shaking off her confusion at opening her eyes in a strange bed, she gazed around the room. She liked the log walls, the complementary colors of mauve, burgundy, lavender and white in the cushions, rugs and comforter. Turning her head, she saw Katya's blonde hair partly buried under a pink satin pillow, and her heart opened with such love and passion that she could not swallow.

It was far from the reaction she had experienced in Molly's embrace five years earlier, she mused. She had come for physical release, but had been frightened by Molly's aggressiveness. Gazing at the large picture window, she admired the laughing Goddess surrounded by adoring nymphs, and realized she was not afraid of Katya.

Her breath caught. She remembered the abandon that had overtaken her by the fireplace last night, her body responding, despite itself, like a wanton woman. A *woman* crying out for more. Fingering the cut on her cheekbone, she winced, then gradually moved her hand down over her satiated body as if to assure herself that it was still intact.

Feeling somewhat disloyal to Simon, she realized that her vows of celibacy were a thing of the past. But had she lost anything in surrendering to Katya as she could not to Molly? Had she shown weakness in loving Katya? In being loved? If anything, she felt stronger, her senses vibrating like finely-tuned antennae.

What to do now? Leave? Outside the window, a shaft of post-dawn sunlight filtered in, accompanied by a symphony of bird trills. Shards of light from the stained glass window glowed in pastel patterns on the oatmeal rug.

A pair of Katya's sneakers on the polished hardwood floor, bordering the rug, caught her eye and triggered a stab of alarm. She pictured her jogging alone on the road. At some point today, she had to talk to Katya about the recent attacks on Deer Falls women. When Sam was out of earshot. There was something else she had to tell Katya, too. What she had seen after Sam's near drowning. The remaining piece of rope on the tree that had been used to anchor his lifeline looked like it had been tampered with. She was not certain of this, but nevertheless it gnawed at her. There might be a connection with the Deer Falls Attacker.

Katya stirred and Chris smiled, careful not to wake her—for selfish reasons. She wanted to study and savor the relaxed form next to her. Propping herself up on one elbow, she admired Katya's smooth, firm back and realized that today she did not have the urge to flee that had been her pattern in the past. She dipped her head down and sniffed her pillow, caught the aroma of Katya's herbal shampoo and another, more heady feminine scent. Never, in her wildest imagination, would she have pictured herself waking up like this, a contented woman. Rising again to her consciousness was the image of the two of them downstairs, bodies pressed together; the texture of the Navajo rug under her naked back; Katya's damp, hot body undulating above her. The memory turned her on again. Katya stirred and shifted, as if Chris's thoughts had aroused her, too.

Still smiling, Chris lightly caressed the blonde silky hair near her hand and felt a rush of tenderness; the slow burn of need. *This woman will turn me into a sex-crazed maniac.* Her hand strayed to the comforter, turned it back. Swallowing hard, she studied the length of Katya's lush, smooth body, down to the soft blonde tuft of hair where she was now half-turned toward Chris. It was just waiting to be kissed. Had her lips touched there last night?

Mon dieu. I would remember that. Her hungry gaze swept over the gentle slope of hip curving into flat belly; long legs...her desire fanning into a flaming bonfire.

One of Katya's hands lay stretched out in Chris's direction, the other curled over her pillow, her long, elegant fingers tapering into coral oval nails. Chris groaned inwardly, rested her own hand beside the outstretched one. How different their coloring—Katya's soft pink; her own, tawny.

But how did I end up in this bed? She tried to force her memory when Katya shifted again. *Mon dieu, I would love to paint her like this. Make love again and again, then memorize with a brush, where my fingers have stroked.* The need was so intense her body ached.

Beyond the closed bedroom door, she heard padded feet, the flush of plumbing, footsteps retreating, a door closing. Vaguely then, she recalled Katya leading her upstairs after the fire had died down; the deliciousness of sinking into this bed; then oblivion.

Sometime during the night Chris had felt a disconcerting blast of cold air when Katya left her side and crawled out of bed to check on Sam, but afterwards...the incredible warmth and security as they rejoined, cradling each other, content to sleep. It was a sensation she would long for again and again—the cradling of her once bereft heart as well. Settling in, belonging, opening up as if the world in its rightful place was theirs to explore.

She wondered where Katya had learned to make love with such abandon, such passion. This Loren must have been someone special. Too many questions, not enough answers. It did not occur to Chris that perhaps *she* had unleashed the flood of passion inside Katya.

She eyed her clothes neatly hung on an oak rocker. Again, she allowed her gaze to sweep over the log walls, anticipating a wave of claustrophobia that did not come.

As her eyes searched for signs of Katya's former life, a warm, insistent hand touched her back, releasing the blood in her veins with a violent surge. Chris's body arched beneath the touch. She faced Katya.

The sleepy face was at first shy, then smiling, the blue eyes clear of pain or remorse. So relieved was Chris that she wanted to bury her face in that graceful neck and hide from the world. Instead, she returned Katya's smile.

Lazily, a hand went up and caressed Chris's cheekbone. "Hurt?"

The lump in Chris's throat blocked any response.

"Hmmm." Katya shifted her naked body to get a better look at Chris's nakedness. "Perfect."

Still speechless, Chris sighed. "You ambushed me last night."

"You sound surprised," Katya murmured huskily. "As if you hadn't been ambushed in years."

Chris's laugh had an edge to it. "You do not realize how close you are to the truth.... I have been celibate for five years."

Katya's jaw dropped. "You're putting me on."

"No, cherie. After my brother died, I...."

Katya silenced Chris's mouth with a gentle finger. "It's all right, I'm flattered that you chose to break that celibacy with me."

"Oh, Katya." Chris buried her face in Katya's breasts and felt close to tears. Hungrily, she engulfed Katya's nipple in her eager mouth. Katya's gasp thrilled her. Playful now, Chris pulled back and teased the now erect nipple with a fingertip. "One good turn deserves another, no?"

Closing her eyes, Katya breathed, "Don't tease me!"

Five years of abstinence seemed to melt away. Chris's hands tingled as they brushed Katya's skin. Soft, but so hot. "Now, where did I leave off last night before you attacked me?" Chris pretended to think. "Ah, yes...I remember you saying, 'Make love to me in French.' "

"I said that?"

"Oh, yes." Chris smiled wickedly. "Is this French enough?" She captured Katya's face in her hands and lightly tongued her mouth, feeling beneath her now, Katya's body quivering.

"Let us start here." Chris kissed the smooth strip of skin separating Katya's upper lip from her nose. "Le bacchante," she instructed, nibbling the contour of Katya's lip. "Say it."

"You're embarrassing me."

"Le bacchante," Chris demanded.

"Don't. You're driving me crazy," Katya said. "What does bacchante mean?"

"It means," Chris laughed. "Your mustache."

"My what?" Katya's eyes widened. Grabbing a pillow, she pummeled Chris. "I don't have a moustache!"

"Cradle robber," Chris accused playfully, tickling Katya's ribs until tears rose to her blue eyes. Lowering her mouth again so that Katya's waiting mouth was just a breath away, Chris teased the outline again with her tongue-tip and was rewarded with shivers. "Very well, no more jokes. Just serious business. Very serious." She nibbled Katya's eyelids shut. "Les yeux," she breathed. "Beautiful blue eyes," and "Nez," against Katya's nose. "Les babines," and she trailed her tongue over Katya's lips.

Reaching up with a groan, Katya encircled Chris with her arms, pulled her down into a deep kiss, her body wracked with tremors. She bit Chris's underlip, pulled at it with her lips.

Chris moaned. "So delicious." As she returned the exquisite kiss, she felt the body under hers move in an ever-increasing tempo, taking her with it, sweeping her up.

Chris drew back again. "Not so quickly. Our lesson has only just begun." She lifted Katya's hand and pressed it to her lips, noting how the blue eyes had glazed over with passion. "Le main. I love the way your hands touch me. I must return the favor, cherie."

"I'm burning, Chris. Make love to me now. I'll scream if you tease me any more."

"Then Sam will hear us and come storming in, no?"

"Shut up and come here," Katya demanded.

Suddenly, the urgent rhythm of Katya's body consumed Chris. She blew into the soft pink ear below her mouth, intoxicated by Katya's shivers.

"Les esgordes," Chris continued in a caressing voice. "Your ears...are like exquisite seashells." Her tongue explored the delicate grooves and swirls, probed deeper until Katya cried out.

"Aha, I have discovered your weak spot."

Katya trembled as Chris kissed her way down her body, pausing at her belly, licking around her navel; then lower, lower, until Chris herself turned molten. Her throat tightened. She grasped Katya's hips with desperate hands, her face hovering over the golden triangle, worshipping it with her eyes.

Katya purred as Chris's tongue parted the delicate inner lips, coaxing the tiny pink fruit until it swelled, ripe for her mouth.

"Don't stop," Katya implored. "I'm so damn hot."

"Then I will cool you off, cherie." Chris blew on the expectant, throbbing flesh that was begging for release.

"Oh, God. Please." Katya's hands grasped at Chris's hair.

Unable to contain her own passion, Chris drew Katya's pearl into her mouth and entered the pulsating opening below it with one finger, searching, finding, pressing upward against Katya's hungry center.

"Ahhhh!" Katya cried out, arching her spine to give Chris deeper access. "What are you doing? I'm going to explode!" Her body thrashed on the bed.

Chris felt her own climax build as the impatient body beneath hers undulated in ever-widening circles. "L'extase!" she cried, her tongue stroking Katya's pearl, keeping a constant rhythm while the finger enclosed by Katya's tightening flesh pressed harder. "La praline. Little piece of candy," Chris murmured around the hard, smooth knot of flesh in her mouth.

"Oh my God!" Katya exclaimed. "This can't be happening...no, stop! I can't stand any more," as she held Chris's head tightly.

"I want to paint you with my tongue, cherie," Chris mumbled.

"I...oh, I'm coming. I'm coming.... Please don't stop," she cried raggedly, bucking under Chris. Her body tensed, quivered, as Chris brought her over the edge—stayed there until the last passionate explosion dissolved into throbbing pulsations, the final long sigh of release. Breathing heavily, Katya's languid hand stroked Chris's cheek. "That was beautiful."

"I hope that Sam does not think so, too," Chris answered.

"With last night's medication, he's probably unconscious. But next time I'll put a pillow over my head. You're dangerous."

Chris murmured, "You can always say that you were practicing aerobics." She smiled with innocent mischief.

Her remark had Katya in hysterics, pressing her hand against her chest as if her heart hurt. Then she grabbed Chris and drew her down beside her. Chris lay her head on Katya's thrumming chest and felt again, the delicious descent into shared sleep. She experienced, not the thrill of conquest, but a tenderness that almost made her weep.

ஐ ஐ ஐ

🦎 15 🦎

*U*sing a stick and one careful hand, Chris parted the thorny vines hiding the knot where Sam's rope had broken loose. She had not imagined it. An inch below the most vital knot, a piece of rope had been cleanly cut. With a knife. Halfway through and sufficiently to start the treacherous unraveling that the pressure of Sam's weight, on the tube in the swift current, would finish in tragedy.

"Merde!" How was she going to break the news to Katya, already burdened with the weight of yesterday's near-drowning? With a last glance at the frayed portion of the rope, she threw the stick away and headed back to the log cabin, her feet first crunching gravel, then giving way to softer loam as she threaded her way through the small patch of woods.

On her way back to the kitchen, Chris patted Sam's head as he played with some fire trucks outside . She took the same seat that she had swiftly vacated earlier, to "digest her breakfast," as she had put it to Katya.

Katya had been pouring two cups of camomile tea on her butcher block and smiled questioningly at Chris. "You didn't have enough exercise this morning?"

Chris blushed. She began to peel dry paint off her nails, from the preliminary work she had managed on Sam's mural while waiting for breakfast. Before her little walk to the stream, she had basked in the afterglow of their lovemaking, watching Katya's every move at the cast-iron stove. *If only every Sunday could be like this.*

"Please sit down, cherie," she requested, still working on her nails.

Katya nodded, pushed aside the sheer white curtains above the sink to check on Sam. Joining Chris at the kitchen table, she asked, "Sugar or honey?" and slid a cup of tea in front of Chris.

"Honey, honey."

Katya smiled and this time it was all there. "I love *your* honey." Her clear blue eyes now danced with light, like the golden highlights in the amber jar of honey. She looked radiant in her oversized yellow shirt, tied at the waistband of her tan chinos. Despite her sense of foreboding, Chris felt the heat rise inside her again.

Idly, Katya plucked a yellow thread from the sleeve of her shirt, glancing up when Chris spoke.

"About last night...you did not make love like an innocent." Embarrassed, wishing she could have just gotten to the point, Chris stared into a wisp of steam curling from her teacup.

After a thoughtful pause, Katya offered. "I've only known one other woman, Chris. If that's what you're asking. You turn me on so...I just did what I think comes naturally for me." For one moment, Katya's eyes sparked with mischief before they turned inward.

"Watching Loren's painful struggle with ovarian cancer affected me, I guess, the same way your brother's death affected you. I lost all my sexual energy. I'm making up for lost time now. So what'll become of us? Think we'll turn into sex maniacs?"

"I want more than that," Chris responded, overriding Katya's attempt at humor with sobriety. "I want you safe."

"What is that supposed to mean?"

Chris paused, unsettled by the defensiveness in Katya's voice. Reaching over, she took her hand. "Katya...Sam's rope was intentionally cut. I am very concerned for you both."

Katya opened her mouth to respond, but Chris stopped her. "Partially cut on the underside—the rest just gave way. There was no way for you to see it because it was hidden under all those vines. Somebody knew what they were doing."

"And you're saying that someone did it *deliberately*?" Katya retorted. "That's crazy. Who'd want to hurt Sam?"

"I thought that you could tell me that. Perhaps someone from your past."

"There's no string of jilted lovers," Katya declared, with a hint of anger.

"I did not mean to worry you, Katya." Chris was equally annoyed.

Chewing the inside of her lip, Katya shook her head. "It could have been beavers. They like to gnaw on things...or bears," she added with confusion. "Bears rub their backs up and down trees—marking the trail to their dens. The rope could have gotten in the way. Damn, I don't need this now. Sam certainly doesn't need it."

"But you cannot ignore it. Check the rope yourself. Pretending that it did not happen will not make it go away," Chris argued, sensing that Katya's automatic response to danger was rationalization. "Have you noticed any strangers on your property recently?"

"No."

"I may be wrong, mon amie, but humor me. Call the sheriff. Report it."

"If what you say is true, of course I will, but the last time I called, the deputy was ready to lock me in a padded cell. You know, just another neurotic woman complaining about crank phone calls."

Chris' eyes widened. "You have received threatening calls?"

"Please, don't look at me like that. You're frightening me."

"What else have you neglected to tell me?" Chris retorted, and just then the phone rang.

Katya jumped, startling Chris. "Calm down, cherie," she offered, feeling guilty. "It may all add up to nothing...."

But Katya was already at the phone, snatching up the receiver. As she listened to the voice on the other end, she slowly, unconsciously, started to wrap the white telephone wire around her index finger. Chris saw her fingertip turn red and stiffened, on the alert, poised, as if her worst nightmare had been realized.

"Who is this?" Katya asked in a panic-laced voice, frantically motioning Chris over. "What did you say? I didn't hear you." She thrust the receiver at Chris.

Listening intently, Chris made out a whispery, indistinct voice with a menacing rasp that sent chills through her:

"That bulldyke's there, right? You were with her all night, right? You don't look queer, Katie. Did the bitch seduce you? I'll take care of her. You, too. Make you a liberated woman. A queer's life is misery, Katie. I'll take care of you.... Make you fly...."

The phone clicked off in Chris's ear. Outraged, she stared at the receiver, then at Katya. "The bastard seems to know you."

"Could be pretense," Katya suggested. "To throw me off."

The first person that rose to Chris's mind was Vera Hudson's lover, Bobbi Jean. "This is the same caller you have heard before?"

Nodding, Katya went to the window. "Maybe I should get Sam in here."

"I will have a look outside, Katya."

A puzzled look crossed Katya's face. "Was it a man or woman? I couldn't tell. But why...?"

Would a woman want to harm me? Chris finished silently for her, recalling what Toni had said at the meeting in Molly's store, counting the possibilities off on her fingers: *Someone gay with internalized homophobia; externalized homophobia—a straight woman; a closet case with psychotic tendencies.*

The last thing Toni said rang in her ear. "If she's a lesbian, then we have to face the fact that the hets don't have a franchise on mental illness."

A sicko who likes to peek up the skirts of female profs at Bear State? Chris thought. Who resented the female staff because she felt they looked down on her? Frowning, she tried to remember what else Toni had related. Then it came to her. "What made Margo think her attacker was female? It was dark out."

A man in drag? Toni had hinted.

Setting Bobbi Jean aside for a moment, Chris' mind went into high gear. There were other possibilities. It could be a very sick, straight male with a twisted view of gays. No, not gays. This was definitely a vendetta against lesbians. All right then, a man with a warped history who had an agenda he was exacting on the women of Deer Falls. It struck her, when she had been staring at Katya's sneakers in the bedroom, that the stalker and Katya's nemesis could be one and the same. But what was the tie-in? Katya certainly did not even remotely resemble a bigot's image of a dyke.

Passing through the laundry room, she opened the door to the yard, stood at the corner of the house facing the woods and studied Sam, who was still playing with his toy trucks. He saw her and grinned, pretending to squirt her with the miniature hose on one of his fire engines.

"Ooo la la. A fireman has come to rescue me," she teased.

His red-cheeked, freckled face beamed up at her. "I can get the *real* hose," he warned, pointing to a roll of green lawn hose wrapped around a circular rack near the deck. "It's real hot out," he added hopefully.

"Maybe later, little squirt." She studied him fondly. Who would want to hurt him? The thought triggered a surge of outrage. Crossing the side yard, she followed the edge of a dense patch of woods that separated Katya's property from the closest neighboring parcel of land. She passed the garage with Katya's Toyota, and took the gravel driveway leading to the road on the opposite side of the house rather than the wood chip path.

She didn't realize her fists were tightly-clenched until she stood on the road scanning both ways. Nothing. The crank call put a whole new light on things. For one, she had no more time to waste. Love had made her head soft, distracting her from the job she had set out to do when she placed the personal ad. It was time to start trusting her friends more.

Her next thoughts were of the sheriff. He was a man she did not trust in the least. For all she knew, he or one of his deputies could be the psycho, using their twisted minds to rid the town of Chris's friends. She trudged back to the house thinking that Katya could be torn from her as easily as Simon had been.

"Sam is fine," she assured Katya, patting the chair next to her at the kitchen table. "And I saw no one out there." Anxiously, she popped a licorice candy into her mouth. When Katya sat down, Chris asked some questions, careful to keep her voice calm. She learned, to her horror, that there had been a total of four calls like the one just before, and a white station wagon sometimes followed when she went out to jog.

Chris groaned.

"But the calls stopped...until today. And I haven't seen the station wagon in a few days."

Chris had no patience with her rationalizations. "Stop it, Katya. You are behaving like an ostrich."

Katya tapped a coral fingernail on the white marble tabletop. She swallowed with difficulty. "Okay, what do I do now? I don't want to scare Sam."

"First you must call the sheriff and report the incident with the rope, the phone calls, the white station wagon. Get it on record. And I think you should phone that prison in California and make sure that Sam's father is still there. If you cannot bring yourself to make the call, I will do it, or one of my friends." Chris watched Katya's face pale. "Forget it. I will take care of the last part. Sara, with her whiz computer, can get all kinds of information. Even registrations on white station wagons." She smiled encouragingly. "I am with you. We are in this together. And I will not tolerate the sheriff or his deputies patronizing you."

"Oh, Chris...."

Chris took Katya's hand in hers and kissed it.

"Help." Katya covered her forehead with her other hand. "Maybe I should move back to the city."

"At least you have not lost your sense of humor, cherie."

Katya grew thoughtful. "You mentioned calling the prison. The last thing that Marty DeLeon would do is come back here and face us. I told you, although he's in prison, he's getting a tidy sum of money every month. My in-laws mail it to his wife. His jailhouse bride. Blackmail money. To keep him away from Sam. He'd never jeopardize that."

"But he could get more if he took Sam," Chris pointed out softly.

Katya bolted out of her chair. "He may be crazy, but he isn't stupid. Besides, why would he hurt his own son? *If* the rope was cut."

Chris shrugged, chewing her candy pensively. "You implied that he was a bigot *and* homophobic that Friday I stayed for lunch."

"Just like a good portion of the population. Besides, I think he only felt threatened because it was so *close* to him. His sister-in-law, Loren, actually flaunted her love of women, *and* her contempt for him. Damn. I wish it would all disappear."

"It will, cherie. But someone has to make it go away. And our community of women is willing to do just that."

Katya blew out a breath. "Break out the lavender berets." Nervously, she began to polish off the bowl of sunflower seeds and raisins she had put out for Chris during breakfast.

"Lavender berets?" Chris's eyebrows shot up. "Where did you hear that?"

"From a woman after my own heart—your friend Sara."

Chris grinned and just then the side door flew open and Sam rushed in, his face pale. "Mom, Chris, you gotta come out."

When she recovered from her surprise at seeing him so perturbed, Chris noted how alarmed Katya looked before she ran out after him. She shot to her feet, all her reflexes alert. If there was trouble, she was ready.

ða ða ða

❦ 16 ❧

*K*atya watched Chris vault the wooden railing and land on the deck where Sam had seen what scared him, her heart pounding with impending disaster.

Minutes later she uttered a small cry of relief as Chris cupped, in her palm, a tiny, inert ball of feathers.

"Ooo la la—a hummingbird," Chris exclaimed excitedly. As it stirred, its feathers caught the sunlight and glowed like ruby, emerald and amethyst gems.

Exchanging relieved glances, Katya and Chris smiled at each other.

"A good omen," Chris pronounced, whispering French endearments to the tiny bird. As if in response, it smoothed its feathers and wrapped its long, black spindly feet around her forefinger. "Goddess, I have made a friend."

Katya's breathing had returned to normal and she smiled at Chris with affection. "Do you blame it? *Your hand* is the *bird's* good luck." From where she stood on the lawn below the deck, she stared up into Chris's eyes until the familiar blush arose, rekindling the low simmer inside her. *Yes*, Katya thought. *This is what it's all about*, envying the little bird its perch on the gifted finger which, just hours earlier, had circled her nipple.

"Is it hurt, Chris?" Sam asked, closer to the deck now that he was assured he had not uncovered some humongous flying insect, but a beautiful hummingbird.

With the lightest of touches, Chris probed the bird's fragile green breast, her eyes widening in awe when it allowed her to spread its violet-gray wings. "I see no blood. What happened to it, Sam?"

He showed her the narrow space between the deck and a border of wildflowers. "That's where my fire engine got stuck. I went to get it and heard a scary buzz and this thing flew out. I thought it was a giant bumblebee!"

Katya touched his sunburned cheek where freckles dotted the surface like so many tiny brown rafts in a pink sea.

Lifting one hand, he exclaimed, "It went up, up, just like a helicopter and flew around the deck real fast. Then it went crazy, Mom. Just smacked right into the glass door. I guess I scared it. Is it crushed bad? Is it going to die?" His bottom lip quivered.

"It was not your fault, Sam," Chris assured him. "I think the bird is just frightened." Again, she stroked its breast, sending an electrical charge through Katya. Her throat tightened, and when Chris gazed into her eyes, her mouth parting, her eyes answering with shared passion, Katya blew Chris a silent kiss and received a small, teasing flick of a tongue-tip in return, turning her knees to jelly.

"I want to see," Sam said, unaware that he was disturbing their quiet erotic exchange. A lock of blonde hair tumbled onto his forehead as he went over to take a closer look. "Wow, cool! Look how long his beak is." Moving still closer, he placed his face against the deck railing when Chris bent down to show him the bird. He laughed with delight when it spread its feathers. "He likes me, too!"

The tiny creature stood contentedly on Chris's finger after Sam reluctantly retreated. She cooed to it in French, conjugating "love" in all its forms.

"I wouldn't mind getting a French lesson on Chris's finger," Katya confided impishly to Sam. "Now if we can just find a shrinking machine."

"You're silly, Mom." Sam giggled.

"Très bien. Then I would keep you both in my pocket...forever," Chris declared.

"Forever?" Katya demanded.

"Oui, cherie."

Smiling, Katya approached the deck and suggested in a low voice: "...Between now and forever we could enjoy a little bit of French conjugation...upstairs...later?"

Chris's blush traveled up to her ears, thrilling Katya, who realized with a pang that their time together was running out, that this afternoon they would be going their separate ways.

Katya sighed, saddened by the thought, "Lucky bird."

"It's a lucky duck, Mom."

"The way it just sits there trusting Chris."

"'Cause she's a real piece of work," Sam informed his mother.

Chris laughed, a lilting, melodic sound that thrilled Katya further, and made the pain of their impending separation even more poignant.

"Sam?" Chris asked. "Where did you learn to talk like that? From your friends in school?"

"Nope." Folding his arms across his chest, he stared at her as if she had just landed from outer space. "*I* taught *them* 'cause I'm the New York City dude." He swayed back and forth on the balls of his feet, hooked his thumbs in the pockets of his overalls, and looked very pleased with himself.

They both cracked up. "Blame it on T.V.," she declared. "And his Grandpa's collection of macho videos. Grandpa thinks it's his duty to make up for the lack of," and when Sam's attention was diverted by the bird, she mouthed: "a man in my life."

"A man, eh? Then the next time you see me...I shall be sporting le bacchante." And she twirled an imaginary moustache.

"Ah, zat eez just what I need in my life, cherie, a moustachioed womeen...," Katya responded, painfully aware of the growing need in her groin, the way Chris had so mercilessly teased her that morning. She had to close her eyes as a tremor of desire passed through her. This would never do. It was torture.

"Sam." She quickly shifted gears. "See if you can find a small carton in the basement. Some newspapers, too."

Pointing to the woods with her free hand, Chris added, "And a bundle of twigs and branches would make a fine nest for this lucky duck. So she can recover."

Jumping up and down, Sam was beside himself. "Then we're keeping it?" He made a dash for the house.

"*She?*" Katya questioned.

"This bird is too beautiful to be a male," Chris assured Katya.

"Well, I'm sorry to disillusion you, but the male of the species is usually more colorful than the female. She blends in so she can protect her young."

Chris feigned amazement. "You do not blend in at all, cherie, and *you* protect Sam."

It was a lovely compliment, a validation of her motherhood, and Katya tucked it into her heart.

"Found this one in the basement," Sam cried, panting, as he ran back with a carton. "Newspapers, too. Oh boy, we're keeping it. We're keeping it!"

"Chill out, dude," Katya warned. "Don't you want him to go free? Release him like we do the trout?" It had taken her weeks to ingrain the "Catch and Release" philosophy that her father had passed on to her when they went fishing.

Thinking this might be a good time to put in his bid for a pet, he bragged, "Bet nobody ever had a hummingbird for a pet. I'd take good care of him, Mom. Promise. I could bring him in for show and tell." He dropped the carton and tugged at Katya's yellow shirt, adding, "If we keep him in *my* room, he won't fly away and get hurt again."

Gently, Chris intervened. "In a cage, Sam? After being in the wild? Would it not be wonderful to watch him fly free? Wild birds belong in the wilderness, just like you belong with your mother."

Katya was touched deeply by Chris's sensitive interception, and suddenly believed the promise the younger woman had made at the kitchen table: "We are in this together."

Sam shifted on his feet and seemed to come to a decision. "Can I get him some water before we let him go? I get thirsty when *I'm* scared."

His remark brought a smile to both Katya and Chris.

"Its beak is so long," Sam said. "How does it drink?"

Resting her elbows on the deck railing, glancing at the bird on her finger, Chris explained, "Their beaks are long so they can drink the nectar deep inside flowers. It is why," and she looked meaningfully at Katya, "hummingbirds are called *Flower Kissers.*"

Katya melted at the erotic picture Chris's words painted in her mind. "Flower kissers." She smiled at Chris.

"So I'll get some nectar," Sam suggested, ready to run off again. "How do I squeeze it out of the flower?"

"Honey and water might be a nice idea," Chris put forth, laughing.

"I'll make it," Sam offered. "Please, Mom, let me mix it."

"Just be careful. The water in the teapot should still be warm. Don't turn on the burners, hear me? There's a jar of honey on the table."

"Okay, Mom," and he disappeared.

In seconds, carefully balancing the bird on one finger, Chris was standing behind Katya on the back lawn, her other arm encircling her waist. "Do not move," Chris warned gently in her ear. "Or he will fly away." Extending the hand with the hummingbird, she rested that arm lightly on Katya's shoulder and began nuzzling her neck, exploring the inner recesses of Katya's ear with the tip of her tongue. "Mmmmm. I am a flower kisser, too, cherie. I love your flower bud."

Katya was paralyzed, her bud swelling.

Lifting the thick hair at Katya's neck, Chris swirled her tongue around, moved up, bit her on the earlobe, forcing Katya's breath out in short gasps, sending rushes of syrupy heat through her center.

Aching, barely able to stand, Katya swiveled her head hungrily and grabbed Chris around the neck. Their teeth gnashed together in the intensity of the kiss. Katya opened her mouth, could have swallowed Chris whole. She was that sweet. An orgasmic wave shot up from her groin, hovering there. She tore her mouth away. "This is impossible. I don't believe it," she breathed, leaning back against Chris, Chris's free hand now circling her stomach. "But, I'm coming." She gasped.

Holding her tight, Chris murmured in her ear as she approached the top. "Oh, God!" Katya uttered between clenched teeth, suddenly aware of Sam in the house.

"Let it go. He is still inside. Come, Katya. Come for both of us."

Katya's body tightened into one convulsive knot before a shudder ripped through her, releasing waves of throbbing pleasure. She quivered in the last throes of ecstasy before collapsing totally against Chris, stunned and spent.

A deep laugh of pleasure escaped Chris's throat as she released Katya. "Imagine what a two-armed lover could have accomplished."

Katya began to laugh just as Sam turned the corner balancing a shallow aluminum tin of honeyed water. Too distracted to notice her flushed face, he placed the tin in the carton and took off for the trees.

"Stay where I can see you." Katya shouted after him. Dipping her finger in the sweetened solution, she tasted it and shuddered. "Too sweet."

"Not as sweet as you and Sam," Chris responded, chuckling, it seemed, at his efforts to make the hummingbird comfortable. Katya watched her bend down and transfer the bird from her finger to a tree branch, then rubbed her wrist as if it ached before casting a protective eye at Sam in the woods. "It is a good thing he does not run on gasoline. You would be broke. He is such a sweet child, Katya. I never thought I would feel such fondness for a boy child knowing that some day he will turn out to be a man," she said, seemingly amazed. "But you have given him something special and I believe he will grow up to be special, too.

Unfortunately, that is rarely the case, in my opinion with males." She looked down at the bird in the carton.

"Now you have two males whose lives you've touched," Katya said, warmed by Chris's compliment to her son. "That one," she pointed to the hummingbird, "is already missing your finger."

"And I thought he did not approve of my seducing you just now," Chris joked.

"Well, that just proves he's gay," Katya quipped with a chuckle. "I don't think I could deal with a lesbophobic hummingbird, too."

Chris laughed and then grew serious. "We must talk some more about the white station wagon. About jogging when it is not safe. Early morning may not be a good idea."

"Chris, I can't turn my life around." She was unwilling to deal with that subject right now, and wondered when Chris was going to mention the rope again. She didn't want to look at it while Sam was around. She didn't want to look at it period, but knew that she must.

"Change your schedule a bit, cherie. Just for now. Please...."

Katya sighed, reached out and touched her cheek. "Okay, I wouldn't want to turn you into a professional worrier like me."

When Sam came back with an armful of leaves they both smiled, but for Katya the smile had an edge of panic as she studied her son.

"Très bien. Now we must take care of the bird. I think the best thing would be to call my friend Bev Dillon. She is a veterinarian and would know what to do."

"Chris...we hardly have any time left. I promised Sam we'd go to the college flea market...and you said you had some errands to run."

"Then you can meet me at the sheriff's office afterward," Chris reminded Katya, her thoughts back on a more ominous note. "Let me call Bev. She usually goes to the hospital to visit Randi and Margo on Sunday."

"I can drive the bird to the animal sanctuary on my way to the flea market," Katya suggested, in a last attempt to restore some magic to their day.

But Chris was stubborn. "If you liked Molly and Sara, you will like Bev, too. And I know Sam will love Bev's animal stories. I promise."

((((((((((

And to Katya's surprise, she did like Bev. Very much. Bev was a woman who seemed as natural around children as she probably was around animals. Sam took to her right away.

Katya felt a genuine tug of warmth when Sara appeared too.

After a quick tour of the house, they sat on chaise lounges on the back lawn between the woods and deck. Sipping iced tea, they chatted about Randi's slow but positive recovery, Margo's last attempt to check herself out of the hospital without her doctor's okay, and Katya's winsome little boy who stood by the deck guarding the hummingbird.

Chris wasn't prepared for the abrupt turn in conversation.

"What happened to your cheek?" Sara asked sharply.

"A stream hit me in the face."

Sara's eyebrows shot up. "Damn, girl. You find danger in the most unlikely places."

Running a restless hand through her short, unkempt brown hair, Bev Dillon leaned forward in her chair and added: "The Deer Falls Attacker struck again. Last night." Her voice was a whisper.

"The fucking psycho pushed a woman off the cliff at Eagle Point," Sara added tersely.

Katya's mind flew to the recent newspaper headlines about the Deer Falls Attacker—the frightening conversation she had overheard in *Le Provençal* at the table of women.

Eagle Point. A wave of paralyzing terror gripped her. It was an incredible vista, she had been told by the former owners of her cabin. The highest point in Deer Falls. All you had to do was turn right out of the driveway and follow the road as it curved slowly up the mountain.

Katya barely heard the rest of the conversation. Although tempted by the talk about the view, she had postponed going up there and having to deal with her fear of heights.

Chris's voice melted through the chunk of ice she'd turned into. "Tell them about the crank calls."

"No, you tell them," Katya objected. *What did it have to do with the conversation?*

"Are you all right, cherie?"

Katya nodded. But she was not all right. Her mind was racing.

"The pervert on the telephone called her Katie," Chris shared with Sara and Bev, directing a concerned look at Katya.

"Then he knows you," Sara surmised, her chocolate brown eyes flashing.

"Only my father...and a...close friend ever called me Katie." Katya didn't believe in resurrecting the dead. "Chris...," she began, feeling exposed. "Enough."

Bev's soft voice intervened. "We don't want to pry, Katya. I get the feeling you're a very private person, but the women in our community are getting beaten or killed, and we're scared. Scared and ticked off. If there's anything you can share with us that might help stop this psycho, please...the incidents could be linked."

With a reluctant nod, Katya agreed. "The station wagon Chris mentioned was white and had a tinted windshield. There was a woman behind the wheel. At least I think it was a woman."

"Just like Randi and Margo said," Sara offered thoughtfully.

"She had dark hair pulled back in a ponytail.... No, maybe it was a braid. It was hard to tell behind the tinted glass. But I did make out a light colored shirt, brass, maybe gold buttons. Like someone in the military might wear," Katya added as an afterthought.

"Or someone who likes to dress in military surplus," Sara said. "This is a college town, so it computes." A flicker of realization lit Sara's eyes. "That guy that followed you into Molly's store two weeks ago. Does he dress like that? There was something suspicious about him that threw me off. Maybe the way he was looking at you."

Suddenly weary, Katya murmured, "Geoff Holden. But I don't know. I think he's harmless. He just has a crush on me."

They all sat forward, regarding her with interest.

"There is no more," Katya said helplessly. "Oh, wait. She had...a substantial chest."

"Merde." Chris rose from her chair, accidentally knocking over the tall glass of iced tea she had placed on the grass. She seemed to study it without really seeing it. "I was also given this description."

"By whom?" Sara asked.

"It was a real estate agent in Deer Falls. Her name is Vera Hudson. Someone I met through the..." She glanced uncomfortably at Katya before falling silent. A few moments passed. "Katya? Did you ever notice a female maintenance worker up at Bear State? A gardener who fits the description? She...well...seems to have a love/hate relationship with the female professors."

Thinking about it brought a flicker of recognition. The day she had walked from the Creative Arts building and Geoff Holden had carried some of her manuscripts; his remark as they passed the statue of

Icarus and the woman kneeling in the dirt planting annuals: "That woman gives me the creeps."

Katya admitted, "I think I've seen her. But you can't go around accusing people."

There was a long pause before they rose from their lawn chairs and ambled over to the deck to join Sam, willing, for the present, to shift the conversation to lighter things.

"Bev's really an animal doctor," Sam confided to his mother. He had been impressed when she examined the bird before.

Bev grinned. "Sam, an animal doctor is a doctor that has a tail."

Sam giggled. "You know what I mean."

"Okay, kid, you've got me pegged. An animal doctor." Bev slipped a pair of granny glasses from the chest pocket of her wrinkled safari shirt. "I think he's ready to be transported. Can you deal with that, Sam?"

"I guess. But I want to keep him. He likes me." To show Bev, he reached into the carton and tentatively stroked the bird's breast with one finger, just as he had seen Chris do. "See? He's not scared of me."

"That's because he's still in shock. A hummingbird usually wouldn't be tolerating our company, and I don't think it's wise to get him used to people. The animal sanctuary will do what's best for him. Sam? Just one more thing. If you ever capture a hummingbird again, put sugar, not honey in his water. If he fell into that, his feathers would stick together." She glanced at Katya and blushed. "Hope you don't mind my interference. I know you wanted to do what was best for the bird."

"Can I change the water, Mom? And see how he drinks with his long beak?"

Katya questioned Bev with her eyes and got a nod. Sam was determined to provide his little captive with the best care before giving him up. Was he hoping that it might fly back to him one day? Katya wondered, feeling somewhat guilty about depriving him. Nonetheless, she preferred this feeling to the panic she had felt just moments earlier sitting with Chris's friends.

It didn't take him long to replace the solution in the tin with sugar and water.

Bev placed the bird on his finger, poured a small amount of sweetened water into his cupped palm and said, "Watch."

Greedily, the bird accepted the offer, its long, thin tongue darting in and out, sucking up nourishment from Sam's willing hand.

"Way to go," he cried, sparking a chuckle from Sara and Katya who considered changing his initials to T.L.C.

"Hummingbirds can fly backwards, Sam," Bev told him. "And their wings beat seventy-eight times a second." Her eyes scanned the deck, alighting on the sliding glass door that led into the dining room. "I'll bet he was headed for the plants behind the door. Never knew what hit him when he collided with the glass. We lose a lot of birds like that." She gingerly took the bird from Sam and placed it back in its carton. Holding the carton she said, "Making friends with a hummingbird is special." She paused and studied Katya. "Can Sam come to the animal sanctuary? Sort of end the story on a positive note? Before I bring him back, I can show him the pony I've been treating for colic."

"Mom? You've gotta say yes."

As if sensing Katya's anxiety, Sara chimed in, "We'll take very good care of Sam."

Katya studied her son's expectant face. "Just don't come back with a mountain lion."

Katya felt Chris's hand slip into her own.

"We shouldn't be more than an hour," Bev promised.

The hand holding hers moved to her waist as they walked out to Bev's van. Katya covered Chris's hand with her own and gazed into loving light green eyes. Eyes that said, thank you for accepting and trusting my friends.

She whispered in Chris's ear as Sara fastened a seat belt around her son: "What I'd like right now is to sit by the stream with you, close my eyes and dream about a candle-lit dinner for two."

And she got that promise in the eyes she so loved.

🐾   🐾   🐾

❦ 17 ❧

*A*s she waited for Sam to be returned to her, Katya tied her hair back in a ponytail, cuffed up her chinos and slipped on a pair of comfortable sandals. After a little nap on a sun-warmed boulder near the stream, she felt revived. She had been wonderfully content to simply sit with Chris, until they had parted. Meeting with the sheriff later didn't seem so fearful any longer.

Her heart leaped with relief when a horn honked outside. Katya bounded down the steps buckling a denim fanny pouch above her hips.

Bev, standing near the brown van that Katya noted was shinier than her boots, smiled shyly.

Sam was in a pitcher's stance, to Katya's consternation, throwing rocks into the woods dividing theirs from the next property. "Watch me hit that sucker, Bev," he boasted, pointing to a wide oak. "Chris taught me how. She throws awesome!"

Biting back her disapproval, hoping that no unsuspecting nature lover was roaming the woods, Katya wondered if a little boy existed that didn't like to throw rocks. A quick appraisal of Sam showed him to be surprisingly clean. "Who combed your hair?" she asked.

Bev shifted on her feet, seemingly at a loss for words without Sara and Chris, but with a twinkle in her hazel eyes. "There was a nice clean rest room at the ranch...I didn't think you'd appreciate getting him back up to his ears with hay and manure."

"That was thoughtful. Thanks, Bev. I hope we can get together soon. Sam would love that. Oh, by the way," and she moved closer to the shorter woman. "I'm thinking of a pet for Sam, but I don't know what dogs are good around children."

Bev rubbed her chin with strong, squarish fingers. "Beagles make great pets. If you decide on a puppy let me know. I'll check it out for you. My practice puts me in touch with dog owners looking for good homes for their litters. And I can give your puppy all its shots." She glanced at her watch and frowned. "Speaking of litters, I've got an appointment with an expectant mother—an Irish Setter hussy who keeps getting herself in the family way." Extending a hand, still shy, she shook Katya's, then dropped it as if it were hot, and blushed. "It was real good meeting you. And a real treat having Sam today."

Her eyes shone, but Katya could see the same loneliness she had noticed before when they first met.

"Where's Chris?" Bev asked.

Katya threw up her hands. "Beats me. She's a woman of mystery."

"Oh, yeah." Bev's words were accompanied by a sheepish look. "That's Chris. She's probably out on some mission."

Suddenly alarmed, Katya asked, "Do you think she'd do anything dangerous? About this attacker business?"

"Chris can take care of herself. Now don't you worry, hear?"

"Thanks, Bev. And I wish you the best with Randi. Maybe I'll get to meet her, too. If there's anything I can do, please let me know. I mean it. You must be very worried."

Another smile appeared on Bev's face. "Oh, well." And she glanced at Sam. "See you, kid...." He ran over, unexpectedly flinging his arms around her, which made Bev jump like a startled deer, then break out into a huge grin.

Katya and Sam watched the van disappear before Katya pulled the car out of the garage.

Sam's blonde hair was slicked back with water, but the part was uneven. And the new green neon laces on his scruffy white sneakers were coming loose. She watched him tie them. As soon as they climbed into the Toyota, he couldn't stop chattering, tripping over words in his excitement to tell her about the wild animals he'd glimpsed at the animal sanctuary. Winding down as she made a left into town, he noted, "We're both wearing yellow."

She smiled. "Maybe it means that sunshine's coming back into our lives," she offered, but found herself checking the rear-view mirror for a white station wagon. It brought Eagle Point to mind. Her stomach turned over. She had finally checked the rope with Chris at her side and she couldn't deny that it looked suspicious. She tried to block it out in order to get through the rest of the day with Sam. He was so looking forward to the flea market. To wipe the frown off Chris's face, she had called the sheriff's office. The same deputy she had spoken to before,

Fisk, had been on duty. This time he had sounded overtly nasty, whereas the first time she had telephoned he had been just patronizing. With Chris pressing her, she extracted his reluctant promise to stop by and check the rope.

Why can't it all go away?

Afterwards, she had doubts. Maybe she and Chris were overreacting. The teeth of beavers and bears could be as sharp as knives, she had rationalized.

Pushing aside these thoughts, she cast a quick glance at Sam. This was his day and she didn't want to spoil it. "Want to go swimming at the reservoir after school tomorrow?" she asked cautiously. He didn't respond. Though she wanted him to talk about it, she bit her tongue. "You can learn to dive this summer. You know, your Grandpa Michaels was a diving champ in college."

Finally, he said: "I almost drowned yesterday, right, Mom? Chris saved me."

When her heartbeat returned to normal, she agreed, "We're lucky she was around."

"Know what, Mom? She breathed into me just like Loren breathed into you."

An unexpected stab of loss pierced Katya's heart. "You're right, honey." Glancing at her son again, she marveled at the depth of his perceptions. "I love you, Sam."

"Love you too, Mom."

"I guess you have a little bit of Chris inside you now, huh?" she asked.

"And you have Loren inside you."

Her throat constricted.

"Is Chris going to live with us like Loren did?"

Slowing the car down, she faced him for a moment. "Would you like that?"

"Yeah. It'd be real cool. She could paint a mural on your wall, too."

Katya didn't know if she could take any more of this conversation. Hooking a right onto Main Street, she followed it to the Bear State campus where the parking lot was filled with cars. Sunshields, bear ornaments, student stickers dotted the metal and glass landscape. A cluster of motorcycles claimed six parking spaces. Katya pictured the bearded, tattooed bikers and their rough looking women taking over Deer Falls, and flinched.

They could be responsible for the recent attacks on Deer Falls women. She found a shady parking lot, courtesy of the descending afternoon sun, and grabbed Sam's hand as they strode up the manicured lawn.

"Ouch!"

"Sorry," she replied nervously, not realizing how tightly she had been holding it. "Guess I'm a little wired."

Sam smiled up at her. "You're talking like me now."

Feigning horror, Katya pressed a hand to her mouth. "Oh my God! What a terrible fate. Tell me it's not true!"

Sam giggled. "You're weird."

"Just your average modern mother."

He gingerly touched his blonde pompadour, making sure it was in place. "Okay, so you why are you wired?"

Katya turned serious. "Remember that time at the Jersey shore when we couldn't find you?"

He cocked his head at her. "And all the lifeguards came looking for me?" Despite the gravity of his tone, a mischievous smile played around his lips.

"Please don't wander off today. You were only five then. Now you know better."

"And I don't have any money in my pocket."

She didn't laugh at the remark which he probably didn't even realize was funny. It had been a heartwrenching experience. Loren had given him his two dollar allowance on the beach because he was excited about the pocket zipper on his new bathing trunks. Then, one moment he was beside them, the next vanished. The lifeguards had combed the surf, but then Loren, who had been cooler than she, found him happily standing on a milk crate completely absorbed in video games. Frightened out of her mind, Katya had spanked him, the first and last time. His stunned expression, giving way to tears which quickly dissolved, had left more of an impression on her than it had on Sam.

But now his mind was on other things. "You should'a seen the animals where Bev took me," he bubbled. "There was a raccoon with babies in a cage. It had a broken leg. And in the lab I saw an owl who almost poked the eye out of one of the rangers."

"Wow!" As they headed toward the athletic field in the rear of the college, Katya cut a glance to her left. The statue of Icarus seemed to dominate the other bronze sculptures in front of her building. It led her thoughts to Geoff Holden and then to Icarus himself. The idea of his joy in flight; his wings melting; the horrible plunge down to earth. Why was she thinking these terribly morbid thoughts?

An icy sliver of recall from that morning's phone call pierced her: "A queer's life is miserable. I can make you fly," the caller had suggested.

Grab hold of yourself.

"Mom? They had this humongous pond with swans and ducks, and Bev took me to the ranch where the sheriff keeps his horse. He let me sit on it and it ate salt out of my hand." He smiled dreamily as if he could still feel the animal's hot breath on his palm.

"You met the sheriff?" she asked.

"Yeah. He was real nice. He looks like a cowboy."

Well, she'd be meeting him too, make him work for his money.... That decided, she gave Sam her attention. "I'm glad you had a good time. How's the hummingbird?"

"Okay. Can I go back when Bev lets it fly away?"

She nodded absently, impressed with the flea market. It was decked out with brightly-striped umbrellas and lean-tos, tables covered with colorful wares for the crowd of eager buyers. Their purchases would help support the college's new handicapped facilities as well as the Deer Falls Women's Center, where Women's Studies majors interned.

The aroma of hot dogs and french fries filled the air, and off to one side, in a bright kaleidoscope of motion, a mobile amusement park was attracting children like magnets, Sam no exception.

"Check it out, Mom, it's neat!" In his excitement, he tripped over one of the green neon laces unfurling again from his sneaker.

"We'll get to everything," Katya promised, and asked him to tie it. Strolling down the jewelry aisle, she spotted, to her delight, a tiny gold artist's palette with miniature multi-colored gems. She pointed to the pin and the vendor, a woman with long gray hair framing a weathered face, unhooked it from its black velvet bed.

"Fifty-two dollars," she pronounced.

Katya contemplated bargaining for price, but felt uncomfortable because it was for Chris, and the vendor's hands were workworn and trembling. The woman reacted to the indecision on Katya's face by hedging. "Take it now and I'll only charge you forty-two. Cash. It's fourteen karat."

Eager to have it, Katya felt jubilant when it rested in a plastic bag in the zippered pocket of her fanny pouch. Sam fidgeted and started to nag her about the amusement park.

"Have I ever broken a promise?" she asked him, and after he thought about it and shook his head reluctantly, she assured him that he'd be on the rides in no time. "Just don't nag me, Sam."

He muttered something under his breath. She could have sworn it was, "merde."

Halfway down another aisle, she recognized a familiar voice and turned to the Women's Center booth. There was Toni Cabrera presiding, a few devoted female interns at her side, handing out leaflets.

A tall, striking woman, athletic in build, with a shock of short auburn hair, paused at the booth, chatted with Toni a bit, then vanished into the crowd. Crossing the aisle with Sam, Katya said hello.

Toni's face brightened. And after Katya introduced her to Sam, she leaned over the table and pinched his cheek. "Heard a lot about *you*."

She seemed much friendlier than she had been in Molly's store when they first met. Katya thought that maybe it was because she was in her element. Then again, she might have warmed up as a result of Katya's involvement with the frightened teen-ager that day she bought the painting.

"Toni?" she asked. "The woman who just stopped by your booth—tall, very attractive, auburn hair. She looks familiar."

Pressing the eraser of her pencil against her bottom lip, Toni's face squinted up. "Oh yeah, you must mean Nicki Random."

"Nicki Random the writer? The famous hermit of Deer Falls? I've only seen her picture on the back of her books. But I've been trying to get her to lecture in some of my classes."

Toni raised an eye brow and smiled doubtfully. "Keep trying. It might be enough motivation to get you past ninety."

"That bad, huh?"

"I can't even believe she stopped to talk. Must be my charm. Here, take these." She handed Katya several pamphlets listing the services of the center. A trio of women parked themselves to chat about a recent pro-choice lecture she had given. Before Toni gave them her full attention, she winked at Sam and told Katya she'd see her soon, and not to forget her promise to visit the Women's Center. Katya moved on.

She and Sam stood by a refreshment stand drinking iced tea when Katya felt her eyes drawn in the direction of the amusement park. She almost dropped her plastic cup. A tall, hefty woman with frizzy brown hair, wearing a navy flight-suit, stood next to a makeshift fence. Her nervous dark eyes alighted on Katya and locked.

Shaken, Katya noticed how her fingers gleamed with heavy silver rings. This was the woman she had seen gardening on campus the last week in April. The woman Chris seemed so concerned about. Could she also be the driver of the spooky white station wagon?

Wondering what to do, she just stood there. She had scolded Chris about accusing people, but before another thought could take root in her reeling brain, Bobbi Jean disappeared.

Shakily, Katya said: "I'll take you on a few rides, Sam, but I don't feel so good. We might have to go home right after..." The hairs prickled on the back of her neck. Was the woman now standing by the exit, staring at her?

Sam's face fell. "You promised. I want to go on all the rides."

He looked so disappointed that she immediately felt guilty. Then she spotted a familiar form, someone she would never have dreamed of turning to for a reality check, and maybe comfort. But she knew him, and he liked her, and that was all she cared about right now. He was conversing with a vendor hawking military souvenirs and uniforms. Drawing a few breaths, Katya took in Geoff's olive drab T-shirt and tan cargo pants. A camouflage suit was draped over one arm.

She had never seen Geoff Holden so animated. She realized with a shock that he had shaved off his sandy blonde, wavy hair. He looked the same as he had the first day of class. *Who cares?* she thought. *The man is a war hero.*

"Planning a reconnaissance, Geoff?" she asked jokingly as she tapped his shoulder lightly.

He spun around and grinned.

Katya's stomach dropped. His usually alert and intelligent dark eyes were glazed and overly-bright, the pupils dilated. With a sigh of disappointment, she listened to him carefully enunciate the simplest words. It became clear from his nonsensical conversation and giddiness that he was on some kind of high. Whether it was drugs or alcohol, Katya could not tell. She didn't smell any liquor on his breath.

When Geoff noticed Sam he seemed startled.

She thought his reaction strange. "I mentioned my son...."

"Uh, sure.... Hey, man, what's up?" Geoff extended the palm of his hand for a slap of high fives, but Sam, to Katya's surprise, backed away.

Puzzled by Sam's behavior, at a loss for words, Katya shifted her attention to the chain Geoff wore around his neck. It bore dog-tags, but also a large silver cross, and his right eyelid did its familiar slow dance as the tic displayed his discomfort. She sensed it had something to do with Sam.

She tried to allay Sam's fears, though nervous herself now. "Sam, this is Geoff Holden, one of my most promising students. He was in the Gulf War."

Slightly mollified, Sam edged forward. They shook hands.

"Hey, man, you can do better than that. Only girls shake hands like cooked spaghetti."

Irritated by Geoff's remark, Katya observed her son take a firmer grip of Geoff's hand. *She* could have taken a firm grip of his neck.

Grinning again at Katya, Geoff bared small white teeth, one of which was discolored. He faced Sam. "Your Mom's always talking about you." His quick eyes darted around the flea market. "How about some ice cream? One of my buddies owns the food concession."

Sam shook his head. Another surprise. *Sam reject ice cream?* "I want to go on the rides now," he tugged at her hand impatiently.

Katya sensed that it might be unwise to turn Geoff down again, especially since she had approached him. She stood there indecisively while Geoff took out a roll of bills, turned to the vendor and pointed out a medal. Kneeling in front of Sam, he pinned it on before she could object.

Sam opened his mouth with delight. "Neat."

"It's yours, little soldier. I got a few myself. No, don't give me that look again, prof. It's not like he's taking a gift from a stranger. Now how about that ice cream?"

"After the merry-go-round," Sam decided.

"You've got it," was Geoff's satisfied response. "Meet you back here?"

Her heart wasn't in it, but Katya said yes.

Unwilling to see her go, Geoff confided, "Just finished another story, but I'm not sure about the ending. I wish I could call you." He shifted on his feet.

As kindly as she could, Katya reminded him of the administration's policy. *Don't give out your home phone number.* And hers was unlisted, which made her wonder how the crank caller had gotten it. "Stop by my office after class on Monday, and I'll look at the story," she suggested

"That's tomorrow. Can we do it over coffee? Maybe in the cafeteria?"

Deflecting his question, she looked at Sam. "You didn't thank Geoff for the medal." Sam murmured his thanks and Katya gestured at the camouflage suit Geoff was holding. "Are you re-enlisting?" she teased.

"I wish. I'm starting a little business. Selling military gear. There's a big market up here."

Sam pulled her arm. For once she was grateful. "Well...I really must be going, Geoff."

Out of nowhere it seemed, he leaned over and shocked Katya by planting a swift kiss on her cheek.

"Don't." She stepped back, annoyed, and briefly touched her cheek. It felt coldly damp.

A shadow darkened his face momentarily, but he quickly recovered. "Don't get mad. I couldn't help it. You knock me out."

"I *will* knock you out if you ever do that again," she warned, trying to keep her tone light.

He stared at her intently. "Does anyone ever call you Katie?" he asked suddenly, "You look like a Katie."

Katya's stomach twisted into a knot of panic. The person on the other end of the chilling phone call had called her just that. Searching for hidden meaning, maybe even a warning in Geoff's eyes, she found them inscrutable. "Come on, Sam." She grabbed his hand.

"See you later?" Geoff slurred. "Ice cream? Okay, Sam?"

But Sam was focused on the amusement park.

Once he was strapped on a carousel horse by a bored ticket taker, Katya idly gazed at a bunch of kids clamoring for the horses of their choice, preferably ones that moved up and down to the honky-tonk music.

The merry-go-round eased into a lazy spin and gathered momentum. After three rounds, Katya felt dizzy keeping track of Sam. Then, for the second time that day, the hairs on the back of her neck stood up. She raised a hand to wave at him with the next rotation, but stopped in mid-air. The pink and white horse that had been his was undulating vertically to the rising wail of organ music. But it was empty.

Oh, God. She had to be imagining this. Frantically, she searched the whirling ride with desperate eyes, but her son was gone.

❧ **18** ❧

Squeezing into a parking space across the street from Molly's, Chris was curious as to why the sheriff's car was parked out front. She checked her watch. Strange. All the lights glowing in the store when it was Molly's habit to close early on Sundays. It was three o'clock. Curbing a rush of alarm, she hopped out of her Jeep and entered the store. Molly was thankfully in one piece, in her usual place behind the cash register. Relieved that her friend was safe, Chris was nevertheless worried about why Sheriff Wendell was questioning her and busily taking notes. Accustomed to seeing him dressed in stream gear or riding chaps on Sunday, Chris studied his neatly-pressed brown and beige uniform. One shirt button strained against his pot belly. He did not look happy.

A deputy entered the store from the back room and began dusting for fingerprints. Chris frowned, observing longish, coarse brown hair that could easily be pulled back into a short ponytail. The brass buttons on his uniform reminded her of the gold metallic buttons Katya thought she had seen glinting out from the tinted windshield of the white station wagon. His name tag read: "Deputy Fisk."

Suddenly, it occurred to her that she was examining everyone with suspicious eyes since Katya had become a target.

Wendell smoothed the waxed ends of his brown handle-bar moustache. It was peppered with gray as was his thick shock of brown hair. An admirer of the Old West, Wendell was addicted to John Wayne flicks and horses, even went by the nickname, "Duke," in honor of the movie hero.

"*Allo*," she greeted, cocking an eyebrow, laying on the French accent.

His gray-tinted eyeglasses barely masked a lazy right eye which often drifted into a disconcerting orbit. When this occurred in the middle of an interrogation, she had heard it could spook the most stubborn perpetrator into confessing.

"What happened to your cheek?" Molly demanded sharply, pushing up the sleeves of her white peasant blouse, setting off a tinkle of silver bracelets on one wide wrist. "Can't let you out of my sight, Chris."

"Really Molly, it is nothing. A slight cut. But you! Mon dieu, I half expected to find you in a pool of blood." Chris kneaded damp hands in a worried gesture. "What is going on?"

"You two can gossip later," Wendell barked, facing Molly. "Let's go over this again." One of his beefy, freckled hands curled around a pencil as he scribbled something on his pad on the glass counter between him and Molly. It was then that Chris noticed the glass top was cracked. She also noted how the floor behind his shiny brown western boots was littered with glass.

"You want an investigation? Then give Deputy Fisk an inventory of your stock—what's missing, what's damaged. Otherwise, forget it. There wasn't much damage, far as I can tell." With the tip of his boot, he kicked aside some shards of glass. "Probably just some local kids into mischief."

"Forget what, Molly?" Chris asked testily. Her hackles shooting up like the feathers on one of Molly's dry flies.

Pointedly ignoring Chris's militant attitude, Molly addressed the sheriff. "I want an investigation, Ollie. Period. The door was locked when I went out to lunch. We've got breaking and entering, vandalism...and robbery. No way am I going to forget it. You wouldn't tell any of the men who own stores in Deer Falls to forget it."

"Bull," Wendell muttered, but looked ill at ease. "Still, this wasn't much of a robbery, now was it?"

Deputy Fisk dusted his way to the door and exited, setting off the bells hanging from the archway. Chris heard him mutter: "You bitches are nothing but trouble."

Picking up on Fisk's thoughts as if he had invisible "Good Ole Boy" antennae, Oliver Wendell grumbled, "Before you people bought businesses here, Deer Falls was a quiet town." He half-turned and glared pointedly at Chris, who lost whatever cool she had left.

"It was *quiet* in Deer Falls? *Quiet* like Southern California before the earthquake? Or like after you allowed the motorcycle gangs to take over Main Street? *Merde*," she spat, as blood rose to her face. "There is a maniac running loose out there. Women are terrified to go out at night...and now this?" Her arm swept Molly's store.

Molly cut her a look that said, *enough already, shut up before you make it worse.*

Wendell fixed his lazy eye on Chris. "Put a lid on it, Benet, or you'll get her more worked up than she already is, and then I gotta calm *her* down again. I don't need no *amazons* running around outside breaking anymore noses. What went down here is just a prank, plain and simple, and like I said before, nothing really valuable was taken."

"Exactly what was stolen?" Chris asked Molly, dismissing the sheriff. But Molly would not look at her. She fumed as she thought about Sam's near drowning, Katya's ominous phone calls, the break-in. And the day was not even over yet.

She glowered at Wendell. "I am getting pretty sick and tired of watching you ignore the danger Deer Falls women are in. You can't blame everything on teen-agers." Still consumed by outrage, it was now her turn to ignore Molly, who rolled her eyes with exasperation. "A few weeks ago, someone poured lavender paint all over my red Jeep, and when I reported it, you said there was nothing you could do—call the insurance company.... The Women's Center has been trashed and vandalized, and a friend of mine, Katya Michaels was threatened on the phone this morning. Not to mention harassed on the road when she went jogging." Raking a frustrated hand through her short dark hair, Chris added, "And, when *she* reports her first crank phone call, your deputy twists her words to make *her* feel crazy.

"Margo Silver and Randi Ortiz went jogging too, and they wound up in intensive care... Alors! What will it take to make you take us seriously?"

Wendell shook his head, slipped a cigar out of his shirt pocket, carefully unwrapped it, and stuck the cigar into his thin-lipped gash of a mouth. He did not light it, instead regarded Chris with suspicious eyes. Then he rolled up the cellophane, leaned over the counter and tossed it into Molly's wastebasket. "This Michaels woman. She live up on Route 204?"

"With her seven-year-old son, Sam," Chris said, waiting.

"Met the kid. Real live wire. Bright as a new copper penny."

Chris shoved her hands in the pockets of her jeans, and nodded, already missing Katya, sorry she had left so abruptly to run errands and drop in on Sara, who insisted on driving Margo to her mother's to recuperate. She had thought that perhaps Sara could help her get a make on the white station wagon with her whiz computer.

Wendell stared at the wet end of his cigar. "Yep. She's the one who called Deputy Fisk a couple of weeks back, reported an obscene phone call. Never mentioned any trouble on the road, though. Fisk said she sounded hysterical."

"How would *you* sound if someone threatened one of your grandchildren?" Chris shot back.

Defying optical gravity, Wendell's right iris wandered away from the center of his eye like a planet drifting away from the sun.

In spite of herself, Chris shivered.

"The Michaels woman called this afternoon. Something about a rope being deliberately cut...seems it was attached to the little boy's tube." He tugged at a hairy earlobe.

"I was with her. Did you go up there and check?"

"Fisk drove over about an hour ago. She wasn't home. And he didn't find no rope. Woman ought to have her head examined."

Chris's fingers curled into fists. "It was there. It certainly was there, zut! Dammit, I saw it myself." Inching toward Wendell she pointed to her cheek. "See this cut? I had to jump in the stream to save that little boy because that rope was cut."

"Chris, please," Molly implored, coming around the counter. Chris held a hand up to stop her. "Do you believe me, Molly?"

"Of course I do."

"And you met Katya. Did she seem unstable to you?"

"Just the opposite. Very level-headed the way she calmed that teen-ager down. Ollie, you're really off base here. I think it's something you ought to investigate further. Obviously, whoever cut the rope in the first place returned and took it to make Katya look crazy. *I* wasn't there and *I* can figure *that* out."

Cornered, Wendell reverted to form. He took the offensive. "Fisk suggested the little boy's mother change her telephone number. Did she?" he challenged Chris.

"You can ask her yourself. She...rather, *we*...will be paying you a little visit later. So do not put your fishing tackle in the pick-up yet. We will be at your office, Sunday or not."

Oliver Wendell shoved the cigar back in his shirt pocket. "Hold that nasty tongue of yours, or you'll find yourself staring at steel bars."

"Mon cul." Chris threw her hands up in a gesture of helplessness. She was getting nowhere. Perhaps she should try a different tack. One that went against her grain. Like it or not, she needed Wendell. Calming herself, she conjured up a fake smile. "Sheriff, you are the expert. Perhaps you have a suggestion? The car tailing Katya Michaels on Route 204 is a white station wagon. And the driver could be the Deer Falls Attacker. Can you send out an A.P.B. or something? Also how about a phone tap on her telephone?"

Wendell hoisted his gun belt up over wide hips, seemingly relieved that her tirade had passed; that his bluff would not be called and he wouldn't have to put her behind bars. "I'll lay you odds the Michaels woman don't even show up at my office. You women are a bunch of alarmists."

"Hah!" Chris scoffed.

"Cool it, Chris," Molly warned under her breath and returned to the cash register.

"Been hearing lots of rumors that you women intend to take matters into your own hands in this attacker business. Not very smart. Vigilantes don't sit well with me." He directed a stubby finger at Chris. "A deputy witnessed you asking questions and stirring up trouble at *Ruby's*. We have a stake-out there. You want to blow the case, be my guest. I'll just stick all of you in jail for hampering an investigation. Then there won't be anyone left to attack.

"So smarten up, Benet. Your mother know you're involved? If there's one slip-up in the investigation, one false arrest—one broken link in the chain of evidence—the perp walks. No court could hold him. And you'll be to blame for setting him free."

"Not a him, Ollie. A *her*." Molly corrected. "Check the statements."

"Oh great, now *you're* a detective?" He tapped the glass counter. "You want an All Points Bulletin on that station wagon? Get me some corroborating evidence. I doubt the Michaels' complaint is tied in with the attacks."

Chris glanced at her watch. Sara would surely be gone by now. She did not flinch under Wendell's glare. Venting anger always relieved her. But it was serving no purpose here.

Turning to Molly, he suggested, "Explain this to your hot-headed French pal over there: Justice spins on its own wheels; in its own sweet time."

Chris couldn't stop. She felt like a teething puppy gnawing on a leather slipper. "It would not surprise me that you enjoyed watching us getting picked off one by one. Fisk would declare a holiday, and that woman deputy supposedly staking out *Ruby's*...well, perhaps *she* is the killer."

Molly's mouth opened. "Chris!"

"Okay, okay." Chris held up a conciliatory hand. "I am just frustrated." She saw that Wendell was ready to explode and apologized, again, hating herself for it. "What happened with that white male biker you arrested last week?"

The sheriff suddenly looked his age. In answering Chris's question he actually sagged and directed his response to Molly. "We showed his photo to the two women in the hospital. They couldn't give a positive I.D..., so I had to let him go. Shit, I'm getting too old for this. I'm supposed to retire next year."

Pressing him while he seemed vulnerable, Chris continued probing. "I do not understand. His description fit the attacker's. It would not take much to add a bit of padding and impersonate a woman. What did Randi and Margo actually say when they saw his photo?"

"Whatsa difference? They're a couple of basket cases. The Silver woman swore her attacker had a brown ponytail; the ditsy librarian was sure the hair was black. They also couldn't agree on height and weight; eye color...."

"But it was dark out!"

"The biker had alibis for every night there was an attack."

"They stick together," Molly argued.

Chris still believed that Bobbi Jean was the most likely suspect, but she had to consider every possibility. The official indifference was wearing her down. It would be so much easier just to go after Bobbi Jean herself.

"Well, ladies, I've had my fill of this pleasant little conversation." Wendell donned his sheriff's hat. "Waste of taxpayers money," he mumbled under his breath.

Before he could escape through the door, Chris stopped him. "If I can get the license plate number on the white station wagon, would you check out the registration?" She waited, holding her breath.

"Jesus, You know how many people in the county own white station wagons?"

"No, but I am sure you will tell me."

"Sarcastic little bitch, aren't you?"

"You cannot jail me for that."

"Enough!" Molly cried out. She looked ready to pull her hair out.

Chris was deriving an almost perverse pleasure in upsetting him.

"I reckon there's close to thirty of those suckers," he snorted. "Recall that plastics company that went belly up? They sold off all their company cars—white station wagons. Good deal, too. Sorry I didn't buy one myself."

"This one had a tinted windshield," Chris informed him.

"So what? Lots of people have them.... Well, good day, ladies." He nodded in Molly's direction. "I'd think twice about stirring up the town over this break-in. Why get worked up about some broken glass and three stolen paintings?"

"Two," Molly corrected him. "Nicki Random, the writer, bought the summer seascape; and a couple of days ago a tourist, the Autumn scene. There were originally four of Chris's work. Spring and winter were the ones stolen. I want them back."

The air went out of Chris, her gaze immediately shifted to the wall. A blank space glared where the canvasses had hung. Her favorite one was the scene of the blonde woman and child bathed in the golden glow of spring. She broke out in a sweat. It was personal now.

"I'm sorry, Chris," Molly said softly and there were tears in her eyes.

"Oh, Molly...I know you loved them so."

Wendell cleared his throat. "Think about that offer," he advised Molly as he opened the door. "Maybe this store's too much for a woman to handle. That businessman I mentioned would give you a good price for it...and he knows how to turn a profit."

And turn a profit for you, too, Chris thought, looking again, with a sharp pang of loss at what was left of her work: nail holes and scuff marks on a wall.

When the door shut behind him, she bridged the gap between her and Molly. Her friend looked so crestfallen about the paintings that Chris could not bear to make an issue out of them. "Were you thinking of selling the store, Molly?" she asked, aware of glass crunching under her sneakers. "Would that not allow the sheriff and all the other lesbophobes, perhaps even the killer, to win? We settled here with a dream. To make a home in Deer Falls. To have a sanctuary."

"Of course I'm not thinking of selling it," Molly said with a hint of surprise in her voice. "Wendell always tosses one or two offers out a week. A ritual. Ask Sara—the two women who just bought the health food store in town. He bugs them, too."

"I hate him, Molly. I would not be surprised if that deputy of his removed the rope on purpose."

"Then *humor* him. He's got clones in every small town." Reaching across the counter, she touched Chris's injured cheek. "One day he just *might* throw you in jail. You're walking a tightrope."

"Perhaps I enjoy tightropes," Chris chuckled. "As long as he has the hots for my mother, I am safe."

"You're impossible!"

"Fou. He makes me so mad I could spit."

Molly laughed. "Well, I have something to tell you that might make you spit too." She paused and watched Chris's face. "Katya Michaels put a deposit on your spring canvas. She was going to pick it up today."

Chris' jaw dropped. "Mon dieu. She did? I mean she was?" The revelation stunned her. "This is terrible. Who could have stolen it?" Her mind worked, bringing her back to her conversation with Vera Hudson at *Ruby's*. Somehow, all the clues seemed to bring her back to that. Was the motive behind the theft revenge because Chris had not invited Vera up to "see her etchings?" Was it rejection? She could see the hungry blonde turning mean, putting her lover Bobbi Jean up to stealing the paintings. She could not picture Vera taking them herself.

"How involved are you with Katya?" Molly asked suddenly. "You know where a relationship with a straight woman can lead."

Chris did not answer. She felt it was up to Katya to tell Molly or anyone else what her sexual preferences were. "Not now, Molly, please. I thought you liked her."

"That has nothing to do with it. I don't want to see you hurt."

But Chris had other things to think about. Tonight she had plans to meet another "Mystery Woman," the last of her post office box respondents; the woman cloaked in anonymity. Suspicious. *Damn!* A twisted, self-loathing psycho was answering the personal ads of innocent women and making them history. Someone cunning and slippery was leaving notes tucked into the rocky barrier that separated the edge of Eagle Point cliff and the treacherous drop below:

Another Dyke Down, had been the latest horrifying message. Edgy with rage, she jumped when the telephone rang.

Molly's face brightened at the caller's voice. "You must be psychic, love, I was just thinking about you."

A brief tug of jealousy surprised Chris, swiftly dissolving to alarm when Molly's face paled. "When? No! What happened?" She avoided Chris's eyes. "No...stay there with her. We'll be right over." A few seconds later she hung up, visibly shaken.

"What is it, Molly?" Icy fingers crawled up Chris's spine.

"That was Toni up at Bear State...."

Chris nearly choked. "Something terrible has happened to Katya."

"Her little boy is missing."

"Oh, no...Goddess no. Not Sam!" Chris's hand flew to her mouth.

"I don't know the details," Molly explained, "But the sheriff's department is closing down the flea market and cordoning it off. It seems that Sam was on the merry-go-round one minute, the next gone. That's all Toni told me. Katya is hysterical and Toni is trying to calm her down. I'll bet those thick-headed, insensitive dicks are giving her a hard time. Wait till the FBI gets involved. Oh, shit."

"I cannot...will not assume the worst, Molly" Chris forced through clenched teeth.

"That asshole Fisk who was dusting for fingerprints is grilling her like she planned it herself," Molly said with disgust. "He must have had a nasty divorce."

"It would not surprise me," Chris muttered, already at the door. "He wants to believe Katya is unbalanced. And as far as her planning it? That woman loves her child more than life itself. Let's go, Molly, please."

After Molly found her purse and locked up, they raced for the Jeep and screeched out of the parking spot.

"Goddess, this is really turning into a nightmare," Molly said.

❦ ❦ ❦

❦ **19** ❧

*R*eflected in the glow of the lamp beside the couch, Katya's face showed horror and disbelief. It pained Chris to look at her so she kept a steadying hand on her quaking shoulder and stood beside her, speaking softly, reassuringly, promising Sam's return. The voices of Molly and Toni in the kitchen were somehow reassuring, too; the thought of Bev driving the Deer Falls streets, patrolling with her C.B. And as soon as Sara returned from driving Margo to her mother's, she would join the search.

Chris felt her friends as a powerful, loving force, neutralizing the harsh reality of the kidnapping, as two deputies installed a direct tap into Katya's phone line. It would be linked to a surveillance van concealed outside the property. They explained that it was the kind of device that could monitor incoming calls, as well as trace the caller's location.

Just let the bastard call.

Again, Chris thought. *It is the waiting.* So much of her life spent waiting.

Molly and Toni entered the livingroom just as the deputies finished. "There's a plate of sandwiches and some coffee in the kitchen," Toni told them abruptly as if their presence was an affront to her. Molly placed a cup of hot coffee on the end-table closest to Katya. "You should try and eat something."

Katya shook her head.

"It could be a long night," Toni seconded, but Katya just sat there like a zombie.

Chris picked up the cup and held it close to Katya's lips. "Drink, cherie."

With a resigned nod, Katya took the cup from her and sipped. Her hands trembled.

Chris's mind wandered to her own plans. *I should leave and head for Ruby's.* Afraid that the sheriff's investigation would proceed at a snail's pace, she wondered when the FBI would intervene. She knew Wendell would hate that—the bastard was not the kind of man who liked taking orders from anyone.

Chris was impatient. She was eager to meet with the "Mystery Woman," and if that did not pan out, then she would try to dig up some background information that might point the finger at Bobbi Jean.

"Chris?" Katya whispered after the deputies left the room. "They think I'm an unfit mother. How could I have allowed Sam to play that foolishly dangerous game on the stream? Why didn't I watch him more closely on the merry-go-round?"

Kneeling in front of her, taking her hand, Chris soothed: "Knowing you, Katya, not even a seeing eye dog is more watchful. And almost every child in the county has played the tube game at one time or another. The sheriff's grandchildren included."

Katya drew a sigh.

Chris wanted to kiss the glistening blue eyes near her lips and drink the tears gathered there. "Yes, cherie. There has never been a near-drowning because we have never had a psycho in our midst before."

"That deputy...Fisk? He asked if Sam was happy at home, if he might have run away...as if I abused my own son."

"Katya, I think their questions were just routine." But Chris was boiling inside, ready to tear Fisk apart. What were they thinking? That Katya was automatically guilty, in their eyes, because of her association with them, the most militant of the women's community?

"Routine my ass," Molly interrupted as she collapsed into an armchair near the cold fireplace. "They're using her as a scapegoat...a smokescreen...to get at us."

Chris could have killed her. She was trying to *calm* Katya, not agitate her.

When Molly was on a roll, on a soapbox, she tended to be oblivious to Chris's murderous looks. Whether that trait had been fueled by Toni, or the other way around, Chris now had the two of them to contend with. For it was obvious to her that they had bridged the gap from being friends to lovers.

About to protest verbally, she noticed that Molly's remark had drawn Katya out of her semi-catatonic state and sparked her eyes with outrage. Better to be furious with the sheriff's department than wallowing as a victim.

Suddenly, Chris was proud of Katya. It would do more harm than good, she realized, to continue what she was inclined to do: protect Katya. The realization rocked her. Protecting maman had gotten her nowhere.

Toni lowered herself to the Navajo rug in front of Molly's chair and leaned against her leg. "As usual, the media gives us bad press. Statistics show that women rarely kidnap their own children, even if they face a losing custody battle. The new underground groups that help mothers and their kids find safe places, even if it is through illegal channels, are one of the only options a frantic mother has. Look at the woman doctor who was recently imprisoned for refusing to reveal her child's whereabouts to a judge. It didn't matter to His Honor that her ex-husband had raped and molested the child. The law, in its black and white rigidity, decided that he had the right to see her. The *boys* win again."

"I dread the thought of the sheriff's department botching the investigation, spooking whoever kidnapped Sam. Putting him in further jeopardy," Katya stated, punctuating her concern with an audible sigh. "I have more faith in *you*," and her eyes swept from Toni and Molly to Chris. "In *me*, damn it, than the officials."

"Then we will have to get to Sam first," Chris responded with finality. "Because Wendell would hate our interference worse than he probably hates the FBI. I would not put it past him to throw us off with false clues." Considering this possibility for the first time hardened Chris's voice. "The one thing most kidnappers threaten is to harm their victim if the police are called in."

Katya visibly flinched. Chris squeezed her shoulder forcefully, so that she would feel that discomfort rather than her inner pain. A reality check. Chris was determined, as difficult as it was, to stop herself from overprotecting this woman she was coming to love.

"I must go," she said, prepared for the panicked look in Katya's eyes. As if in response, a crack of thunder shattered the cabin, and lightning illuminated the dark sky outside. Chris stood up.

Glancing at her watch, she was astonished to note that it was already ten o'clock. The longest Sunday in her life.

"Please, wait..." Katya pleaded, the hand holding her coffee cup trembling again, as her eyes pulled Chris in.

A rush of love flooded Chris. "I am going to find Sam and bring him back to you," she said with conviction. "Toni and Molly will stay and keep you company. They can answer the phone so you can sleep.

I am not sure how reliable the two deputies in the kitchen are, but at least they are not Fisk. What I *am* sure of is the worth of my friends." She smiled at Toni and Molly to show them how much she meant it.

Another burst of thunder followed in the lightning's wake. It seemed to shake the very foundation of Katya's log home. Its boom rolled into the distance, like the a receding sound of a kettledrum. As the sky erupted with a deluge of rain, Chris reflected on how appropriate a night it was to solve a crime. She hoped that Sara had arrived back in Deer Falls, for she needed her help. Kissing Katya gently on lips bruised from biting, she started for the vestibule.

"Maybe there'll be a ransom note. *Something*. Waiting is the worst part," Katya expressed, her voice trailing off.

Chris motioned for Toni and Molly to join her at the door while the rain gained momentum, as if it, too, was racing against time.

Glancing back, Chris fixed her eyes on the oak mantle above the fireplace. It would have been the perfect place to hang her painting, she thought sadly. Magnifying her empty feeling was the constant tick of the grandfather clock.

"You'll get soaked," Molly said when she and Toni stood beside Chris.

"I have my rain slicker in the car. Besides, I intend to go home and change first."

Molly touched Chris's arm. "Don't do anything stupid. Simon's murder happened a long time ago. Maybe one of us, or Bev should go with you to *Ruby's*."

Chris shook her head vehemently. "I must do this part alone. Not arouse suspicions. If I need you I will call. But for now, I am asking you to trust me." She paused, considering them. "You remember what we discussed?"

Toni glanced at the grandfather clock. "If it's after ten here, then it's after seven o'clock in California. I'll make the call to the prison and hope I get through. It's Sunday, and there was a minor earthquake in Southern California this afternoon, which could affect the phone lines." She played with the rings on her fingers. "I wonder if Wendell called the prison to check out what Katya told him at the flea market. I'm not sure he believed that Sam's father actually sold his son...that he gave up custody to pay for his trial costs."

"Wendell will keep us in the dark, and on the defensive as much as he can. The last thing he wants is for us to be involved in the search. Goddess forbid, anyone should steal *his* thunder," Molly offered, as Chris opened the door to another burst of lightning.

A rush of emotion overcame Chris. Turning slightly, she said, "I love you guys. Do not worry. I will be very careful." She noticed Toni slip her arm through Molly's, and for the first time since she had known Toni, an irksome woman to be sure, but intelligent and perceptive, the other woman gazed directly into Chris's eyes. In those hazel depths, Chris saw an apology for all past misunderstandings. She hugged them both. This was not the way she would have wanted Katya to come to know her friends better, but somehow, it seemed right. She slipped out the front door into an onslaught of rain.

A blinding fork of lightning split the dark sky. Skirting the log cabin, she reached her Jeep, shivering as a gust of wind whipped her wet body. Once settled in the driver's seat, she started the engine and wiped her wet face with a rag she kept handy. Outside, raindrops danced in the headlights, slanting toward Katya's home.

She hoped it would let up before she reached *Ruby's* to keep her eleven-thirty rendezvous, dressed all in black, like the night. Playing amateur detective was difficult enough when it was dry out.

Shutting her eyes briefly to ward off anxiety, she saw a little boy's face, but it was Sam's, not Simon's, and she suddenly realized that getting him back safely was the only thing she cared about now.

Finally, the living were taking precedence over the dead.

ℑ℘   ℑ℘   ℑ℘

❦ 20 ❧

*C*hris studied the thin Sunday night crowd at *Ruby's* rest-lessly. More and more, she felt removed from their loud reveling and flirting as her feelings graduated from a state of desperation and fear to cold calm. She almost resented their light-heartedness. Especially the jubilant team of softball players who were making up in noise what the room lacked in patrons. Her rage, buried silently like a time bomb all these years, ticked darkly now; as black as the T-shirt and cargo pants she wore.

It was hard to believe that just hours earlier, in the promising rays of daybreak, she and Katya had made such exquisite love; hard to believe that her vows of celibacy were irrevocably broken. Had Sam really come close to drowning? That, too, seemed like a dream.

What seemed less a dream was the realization that within a few dizzying weeks she had fallen in love with Katya. She could picture herself living with Katya for the rest of her life.

At the same table where she had sat just a little over a week ago, awaiting Vera Hudson's arrival, she now awaited another stranger who might turn out to be the woman stalking Deer Falls. She was determined to rid the town of the maniac who was hell bent on destroying her community.

Nervously, she checked her watch. Twelve-twenty-four. Tensely, she watched the door for a woman she knew nothing about, but who would know her by her black outfit and short hair. After meeting her first "date" in the wheelchair; and Vera Hudson, her gut assured her that tonight she would come face to face with the Deer Falls Attacker. She pondered the possibility of Bobbi Jean and the "Mystery Woman" being one and the same. Was it also possible that she was the deadly psycho?

Her eyes scanned the candlelit room again. A few couples danced to Heather Bishop's music. Her "date" was an hour late, and she was growing impatient. Starting to doubt that her post office box respondent would show up at all, she ordered a glass of the insipid house wine, just to look like a normal patron. Having that in front of her might keep her from glancing at the bottles of hard liquor lined up behind the bar with longing. A few more stragglers entered *Ruby's*. They would not stay late, Chris knew. Tomorrow was a work day.

As the softball team broke up and began to drift onto the dance floor, Chris's mind raced: *Was* she *among the drifters right now? Was she measuring Chris, planning to attack at a later date?*

But Chris was not Randi or Margo. If the killer messed with her, she would get much more than she bargained for.

Come and find me, tu salope...you bitch. Show yourself.

Then, just as she took out her pen to sketch away her impatience, her foot began to itch. An old sign of perceived danger. A shadowy figure passed in front of the bar, partially blocked by the dancers. The woman moved quickly, her gaze scanning the room as if she were looking for someone. She showed her back to Chris as she went past the kitchen door. Chris pinned that broad back with a piercing gaze and the figure turned; caught and held her gaze. An icy hand squeezed Chris's heart.

Through the gyrating dancers, Chris made out kinky brown hair, frizzy strands escaping a short ponytail fastened at the nape of her neck. She was dressed in a navy blue flightsuit that gleamed with military epaulets and shiny metal buttons. Instantly, Chris recognized the face.

A brazen young bleached blonde, who had been flirting with a member of the softball team suddenly headed in Chris's direction, totally blocking her view of Bobbi Jean. "Like to dance?" she asked Chris with a postured, cocky stance.

Frantic, Chris waved her away. "Some other time." And when she looked up again, past the miffed blonde, Bobbi Jean was gone as mysteriously as she had appeared.

She bolted out of her chair and headed for the bathroom, checked it, doubled back and swung open the kitchen door. Empty, except for a harried short-order cook—a calico cat glancing up at her from a bowl of milk.

Merde. Chris checked out the bar, glanced at the dance floor, before she desperately headed for the exit.

Opening the heavy wooden door brought a whiff of warm May, rain-washed air; the thick moist blanket of humidity that promised a night filled with soft drizzles. But the thunderstorm had passed and the outside lights in the parking lot cast shimmering reflections on the wet asphalt. It was not the kind of night to induce chills, but Chris shivered. The itch in her foot intensified.

As she stood gazing out over the dark parking lot, she wondered if her assumptions about Bobbi Jean had been correct. Could she be the "Mystery Woman," pinning Chris with her glance, or just a frustrated woman searching for her restless lover?

Then she saw, in deep shadow, a white station wagon parked three cars up from her Jeep. Licking dry lips, Chris cautiously crossed over to it. Fishing her key ring from the lower pocket of her pants leg, she directed the beam of her pocket flashlight into the wagon. Her pounding heart was deafening.

Through the wagon's rear window, she made out a jumbled array of shapes. The back seat was turned back to make room for an assortment of clay flowerpots, bags of manure; a tool belt.

Not much to suggest a kidnapper or killer, Chris mused, relentlessly circling the beam of light, wishing she'd had time to retrieve her heavy-duty flashlight from the Jeep. And now she could not chance going back for it. All she could discern were the tools and supplies any maintenance worker or gardener might use in her job.

"Zut!" If only this was the station wagon that had frightened Katya. Sheriff Wendell's words echoed inside her head: "There's close to thirty of those suckers."

The flashlight beam swept the messy interior once more, paused, circled, when something caught her eye. A small jeweler's saw. And on its steel-toothed edge, unprotected by a plastic sheath, and fastened to the tool belt by a small strap, was a narrow strip of some kind of green, glowing material. Like a shoelace? A ball of fury again fisted inside Chris's stomach. She had almost missed that strip of fabric. Hand shaking as she steadied the narrow light beam, she recalled how incongruous Sam's fluorescent shoelaces had appeared against his worn white high-tops.

Do not get too excited, she warned herself. *It might not be Bobbi Jean's car. It might not be a shoelace.*

Pausing for a moment, Chris pondered what circumstances would have motivated Bobbi Jean to do this? Jealousy over Vera's obvious sexual restlessness? Bobbi Jean's fear of being cast off into a social world in which she was out of place? But why kidnap Sam?

It made sense and yet did not. There were many successful and happy butch women Chris knew. Betrayal was the only motive she could comprehend. And perhaps revenge. An unstable and self-loathing psyche which lashed out at the world.

She recalled Vera's eagerness to have a child. Could Sam's kidnapping have been Bobbi Jean's warped way of fulfilling her lover's fantasy? Insurance that Vera would never desert her?

She had to stop analyzing and *do* something. Time was running out. Cutting a look at the bar's entrance, she searched the station wagon, not sure of what she was looking for. Reason prompted her to call the sheriff, then she remembered Katya's concerns. No, she would not risk spooking Sam's kidnapper by adding an incompetent, bull-headed law enforcement officer to the explosive mix.

The door of *Ruby's* pushed open. Bobbi Jean emerged with a scowl on her face. Crouched down behind the front fender, Chris's pulse raced. She carefully backed up and inched her way toward her Jeep.

Bobbi Jean headed in her direction just as Chris reached her car. Looking up as the other woman passed through a shaft of light cast by the parking lot floods, she noticed Bobbi Jean's eyes dart to the left and right, before she froze.

With a screech, a patrol car entered the parking lot.

Chris watched helplessly as it slowed down and made a loop. Her nerve ends tingled. The blue and white completed its quick surveillance and braked at the exit before speeding away.

During this time, Bobbi Jean had made a production out of tying the laces of her boots, straightening up only when the patrol car was out of sight.

Holding her breath, Chris waited to see if the large woman would claim the station wagon.

This she did. Chris's heart flew into her throat. Sacre bleu! She had been right all along.

All she had to do now was follow her and get Sam back. She was prepared. In barely a moment, the station wagon's engine hummed. When it paused at the exit, Chris slipped quickly into her Jeep, and watched it hook a right. She started her own engine and followed, nervously maintaining a two-car distance with first a black Corvair, then a red Honda between them. As the car wound through a maze of dark side streets, Chris's adrenaline surged. Sam was the only thing she could keep her thoughts on. Near a small, all-night shopping area with a gas station, pharmacy and convenience store, the station wagon abruptly stopped, sending the Honda's driver behind it into a spasm of honks. Chris slammed on her brakes to avoid hitting it. The Honda stalled, restarted, then swung around Bobbi Jean's vehicle and sped away. Cursing in French, Chris imagined the driver of the small red car cursing in English. The humor of the situation did not make her smile.

She soon saw that Bobbi Jean planned to stay where she had parked in the middle of the street opposite the drug store. Careful not to be seen in the wagon's rear-view mirror, Chris pulled over to her right and waited. A moment later, a petite woman emerged from the pharmacy. Bobbi Jean stuck her head out of the driver's side window and yelled: "Where the helluv you been?"

The figure looked startled, but continued holding the door open for someone behind her. The startled woman was Vera Hudson.

Another figure exited. Small. A child, head lowered as if counting change in the palm of one hand.

Chris was so shaken she forgot to breathe. Clutching the steering wheel, she tried to make out the child's face, but the street lamp did not fully illuminate the recesses of the store's outer alcove. She could barely discern that the child was wearing a baseball cap pulled down low. A child as tall as Sam. _Please, goddess, let it be him._

Poised to spring, she watched, with astonishment, as a man exited the drug store and grabbed the child's hand, nodding his thanks to Vera, who finally released the door. She seemed reluctant to acknowledge Bobbi Jean's shouting presence.

Moments later, the man and child stepped into the light and proceeded to walk to the convenience store. Affectionately, he pulled the baseball cap off the child's head and a cascade of long brown hair spilled out. The air hissed out of Chris like a punctured inner tube. Cursing, she slammed her hand against the steering wheel.

Vera crossed the street, edged around the station wagon and eased into the passenger side.

It began to drizzle. Chris turned on her windshield wipers. She had to steady herself before following them, her thoughts fixed on Sam's shoelace. The wagon seemed to be heading in the direction of Bear State College, and now a tan Chevy squeezed between them, reminding Chris to keep her distance. Bobbi Jean obviously did not know she was being followed.

In an impulsive spurt, the station wagon sped up and took a quick right. "Damn!" Chris cursed aloud, almost slamming into the car in front of her again. She had no patience for the startled driver in front of her and swerved around him. But when she turned down the same street the wagon had taken, it was empty, the station wagon out of sight.

A quick search along a series of side streets, with her headlights cautiously turned off, left Chris frustrated. Doubling back to the shopping center, she switched the Jeep's lights on again and pulled into the gas station adjacent to the pharmacy...her mind racing. Sprinting toward the pay phones while fishing for a quarter in the pocket of her pants, she dropped it on the ground, where it rolled into a puddle. She was ready to tear her hair out, grabbed the key ring flashlight and found it. Once inside the booth, she dropped it in the coin slot.

She said a silent prayer. *Sara, please be there.* The press's number rang and rang. Chris pounded the steel wall of the phone booth with the side of her fist. It rang nine times before she hung up; her face, her clothes, damp with sweat and drizzle. Collapsing on the metal stool, staring at, but not really seeing the graffiti on the wall, she tried to calm herself. When her breathing was under control she tried Sara's number again. "Come on Sara, answer." Just as the sixth ring buzzed in her ear, a breathless voice answered.

"Merci, Goddess." Chris wiped her soaked forehead with the back of her hand.

"Chris? Hey, baby, what's wrong?"

What is right? Chris wondered. Her mouth wouldn't work. Finally, she managed: "Sara, can you do me a favor, no questions?"

She heard k.d. lang's plaintive wail drifting through the receiver of the radio on Sara's desk. It was the first time, Chris realized, that their connection was not filled with the sound of presses. "Shoot," Sara said.

"I need a name and address on your mailing list."

After a pause, Sara explained. "Honey, you know I can't give those addresses out."

"Please, Sara. Trust me." Hastily, Chris filled her in, and once Sara heard about Sam she went right to her computer.

"Hope there aren't too many Bobbi Jeans subscribing to *Women's Network.* And that's the first time I've wished that, from a business point of view."

For the first time since Chris had raced after the station wagon, Sara's quip made her smile.

"Okay. I've got two Bobbi Jeans."

Chris's knees went weak. "Do either of the listings match an address for a Vera Hudson? It might be a business address. She is a realtor in town."

The tap of computer keys sounded like miniature earthquakes to Chris. She was so edgy and energized she could have lifted the phone booth off the ground just as easily as she had picked the receiver off the hook.

"Nope. Just those two home addresses."

"Quick then, mon amie." Chris's ballpoint was poised over a mangled phone directory. She scribbled the addresses down before tearing off the corner. "Merci, Sara. I hope I'm not too late."

"Hey, girl. Hold on a sec. Don't tell me you're going out there alone at two-thirty in the morning. Call the sheriff."

"Sara, if this maniac sees a patrol car...."

"How about old Sara? I can be there in..."

"Oh, no. This is something I must do myself. Look, if it is something I cannot handle I promise to call you."

"Just bought a car phone. It's the same number as the press. Keep in touch with me, *okay?*"

"Okay. Somehow I will find a telephone."

Sara tried to object again, but gave up. "Just have to keep reminding myself that you're as smart as you are gorgeous." But her voice was tense.

"Again, mon amie, merci. You are a good friend," and Chris hung up, a ball of nausea rising to her to her throat. Pulling open the phone booth door, she sprinted back into the rain, heading for her Jeep.

ʃɔ ʃɔ ʃɔ

❦ **21** ❧

Chris picked up the trail and finally found Greene Street, the address she had chosen first because of its proximity to the college. It ran parallel to the river. She could hear it rushing along in the darkness.

With her headlights off again, she craned her neck to see numbers on a few houses illuminated by outside lights on the old residential block, and saw she was headed in the right direction. Her windshield wipers arced a clear crescent across the wet windshield.

Number one-twenty-one was a sprawling old white clapboard structure with a wrap-around porch and ornate facade. It was like something out of a turn-of-the-century Gothic tale and her body responded with a shiver.

Surrounded by dense, untended shrubbery, it was not an ideal advertisement for a gardener, and sat far back and apart from the other homes tucked into the dead-end street.

A detached garage had windows above that hinted at a second story, perhaps a separate apartment. It piqued Chris's curiosity.

She decided to back up and park further down the street, then climbed out of her Jeep. Armed with a Kiyoga stick, a steel weapon that was legal in New York State, she tested it with one flick of the wrist. Its flexible, but deadly steel rod whipped out. Telescoped this way, it gave her more leverage when she was at some distance from her adversary. Closed, it was a lethal black club easily tucked into a back pocket where she could feel its reassuring weight. She also took her heavy-duty flashlight, and the short, lightweight black slicker she kept in the Jeep.

Pulse racing, she crept back to the house and peered over a row of hedges. She paused, her blood suddenly surging with fresh adrenaline. The white station wagon was parked in the driveway.

Bobbi Jean Overton: Get ready to taste steel.

All systems in her body sprang to life. But she would not make her move until she spent time observing, planning, thinking. In the light rain, she staked out a surveillance position behind a stand of evergreens that sheltered the ranch house opposite, and was relieved to find all its windows dark and no cars in the driveway.

The minutes ticked away, broken only by a passing train in the distance and her own heartbeat. To the far left, a few curtained windows flickered with the blue-white lights of after-midnight televisions. Would these insomniacs ever dream that something more terrible, more gripping than the movies they were perhaps watching, might be happening on their quiet street?

She glanced at her watch. 2:50. Had Katya been able to get any sleep, she wondered, and drew in a breath. Would she find Sam? Quickly, she turned on her flashlight to test it, when a clatter of metal spun her around.

"Merde," she muttered under her breath as a pair of masked faces froze in the beam of her flashlight. Two raccoons, as startled as Chris, scurried away, leaving her alone again in the dark. The inky sky was hazy, the moon veiled with clouds. The ball of her foot started to itch again. Her hands were cold.

The rain had turned into a steady down pour. Momentarily placing the Kiyoga stick and flashlight on the grass, she slipped into her slicker. She had not worn it since the rainy Tuesday night her Jeep had been splattered with lavender paint.

Something prodded her to pat one pocket. Chris smiled. She pulled at the snap and fished out the two smooth, hefty, white rocks she had picked up from the edge of Katya's wood chip path. She had saved them like a lovesick puppy buries a choice bone. Pressing them briefly to her wet cheek, she dropped them back in her pocket. Re-discovered good luck charms.

And then she heard the scream. A bone-chilling, keening wail that shattered the silence with heartbreaking intensity.

Grabbing her weapon and flashlight, she raced toward the house. She moved swiftly and erratically across the expanse of ragged lawn. The last thing she wanted was to be an easy target.

A dim light seeped through a downstairs window; impossible to determine its origin. Her body tensed up. She quietly crept up the porch steps, and hesitated, so keyed up that she felt confined by the slicker.

Frantically, she placed the flashlight and weapon on the wooden floor, shucked the slicker and tied its sleeves around her waist. Prepared now, the weapon tucked into her belt, grasping the flashlight with her left hand, she reached for the cut-glass doorknob and her right hand froze. All her training told her that she should be circling around back, peering through a window. But time was precious. It might have been Sam's scream. He might be seconds away from death.

To her surprise, when she turned the doorknob, the door easily opened. A dark, stuffy interior enveloped her, tinged with an acrid, bittersweet odor that reminded her of the cap guns she and Simon had played with as children.

When she cautiously entered the eerie, dark vestibule, she saw that the source of the dim light was coming from two places. One a lamp in a small living room packed with old, overstuffed furniture to the left of the corridor, the other facing her. It seemed like just seconds since she had heard the scream, but the house was ominously quiet. Not even a clock ticked.

Gripping the Kiyoga stick now in her sweaty right hand, she ventured one step, then another down the hallway. Trying not to step on a squeaky floor board, quickly glancing left and right where darkened rooms branched off like the tentacles of a hydra, she approached the second source of light. It shone through a slightly-cracked door at the end of the hallway and cast eerie shadows on the wall. Prickles of fear raced from the back of her neck down her spine.

Where had the scream come from?

Shadows on the wall undulated in the sheen of sweat that had dripped into her eyes. They burned. She blinked, swallowed hard. Afraid to call out Sam's name, she advanced slowly on leaden legs.

The hand tightening on her weapon did not shake. The shadows were only shadows, she told herself. Gritting her teeth, she paused near the door. A faucet dripped inside. She heard the hum of an oil burner, the click of the thermostat before the pilot light roared up.

Extending one foot, she slowly nudged the door open. A light above the sink barely illuminated the kitchen, but it was enough for her to see a sight that paralyzed her.

Vera Hudson lay on a blood-splattered floor, and to Chris's right, slumped against a refrigerator, lay another figure. Terror stabbed at her. Now the hand holding her weapon trembled as she readied it, desperately searching the kitchen with her eyes.

She moved closer. A tiny hole pierced Vera's neck, still pumping blood from the carotid. It matted her ginger-blonde curls. Chris gagged. The startled blue eyes staring blankly up at her were devoid of the energy she had seen at *Ruby's.*

Choking back a rush of vomit, Chris allowed a flood of rage to consume and enervate her. It would have been directed at Bobbi Jean for killing her own lover if Bobbi Jean was not the other body on the floor.

She wore a dark blue flightsuit wetly stained just below the left shoulder. There was a pool of blood around her, too, broken china, spilled coffee on the cracked linoleum.

A hand with heavy silver rings moved, brown eyes glazed open. She moaned. Confused and wary, Chris tightened her grip on the Kiyoga stick. Bobbi Jean tried to sit up. Her eyes went from Vera's inert form, to Chris. Her face betrayed not only her own pain, but the pain of what she had seen in that kitchen.

It was *her* scream, Chris suddenly realized, rushing over, kneeling in front of the wounded woman.

"Son of a bitch killed her," Bobbi Jean breathed incredulously. "He killed her when we went into the kitchen...he was waiting." Tears ran down her cheeks.

"Who?" Chris asked and quickly zipped down Bobbie Jean's flightsuit, revealing a bullet wound, not fatal, but still bleeding heavily.

Is he still here? she wondered. *Did I scare him off?* she hoped fervently.

Disturbed by the amount of blood, Chris set her flashlight down with a sigh, transferring the weapon to her left hand. With her right, she reached up to the kitchen table and grabbed a handful of napkins, anxiously pressing them against the wounded shoulder. "Why did he do it?"

"Because...." Bobbi Jean winced with pain, her breath coming in short gasps. "Vera had left a note on his door...said if he took the station wagon again without asking first, she'd report him to the sheriff...and.... Son of a bitch. Never would have rented this house if I knew *he* had rented here first."

Frantic, Chris asked, "Was that your scream a few minutes ago? Chris stopped breathing, waiting for Bobbi Jean's reply. She leaned in closer to the face twisted in agony and grief. "Did you hear a child scream?"

Slowly, Bobbi Jean lifted an arm, gasped, and pointed to the window. "Check...the garage." Then she beseeched Chris with pleading eyes. "Why did he have to kill her? She was the only woman I..." Another moan escaped her lips. "We had a fight in the car. Just got back...didn't even have a chance to say...I was sorry." The tortured body convulsed in heartrending sobs.

"Where is he? The man who shot you?" Chris demanded, supporting the other woman's face with one hand, willing the bereaved unfocused eyes to look at her.

"He's..." And then Bobbi Jean looked up, her eyes wide with terror. Wildly, she tried to push Chris out of the way.

Swinging around with the Kiyoga stick, Chris blocked the descending arm that grasped the butt of a gun in its hand. She quickly switched the Kiyoga stick to her right hand and clubbed his forearm.

He howled, caught the gun before it flew out of his grasp and managed to trap her right wrist in a viselike grip, twisting it, cursing, trying to force her to drop the weapon. Eyes tearing with pain, Chris swiveled on the floor and delivered a ferocious kick with the heel of her boot.

It connected with his knee. Releasing her wrist, he fell backwards against the kitchen table, screaming. Her wrist burned, but she managed to slash at his forearm again with the telescoped end of the stick. The gun spun out of his hand and clattered to the floor. She leapt for it, but he tackled her, slipping in a pool of Vera's blood; clawing at her; spinning her around.

He was on top of her. She looked up into fanatical dark eyes, laughing at her; triumphant. Realizing she still had the Kiyoga stick in her hand, she raised it. He grabbed her wrist again and smashed it against the linoleum until she dropped it.

"Cul!" She went for his eyes with her other hand, but he twisted his head away. Laughing out loud now, he punched her hard in the face. She felt her freshly-healed cut tear open, warm blood seep out, the room spin.

Then, thankfully, the abominable weight was off her. Slowly, painfully, Chris rose to her feet and her loosened slicker fell to the floor. Watching him warily, she stepped out of it. The gun was back in his grip.

His cruel eyes tracked her hopeless gaze to the Kiyoga stick which had rolled away and was coated with Vera Hudson's blood. As if he was toying with a bug, he nudged the weapon with his army boot, daring her to make a move.

His eyes hardened. "Get over there, bitch!"

She obliged him and stood in front of the sink. Bobbi Jean whimpered.

And while she studied him, the rage simmering inside her reached a boil.

"Knew you'd show up sooner or later, dyke bitch. Got special plans for you."

"Where is Sam? What have you done with him? Who the hell are you?" she raged.

He laughed again, a chilling sound. A man of medium height and build, with close-cropped dirty blonde hair, he, too wore a navy flightsuit. The pistol he gripped had an etched black butt; a four inch silver barrel that ended in a silencer. She had seen its like in a gun catalog at *Grassroots Press* when Sara had contemplated buying a weapon after Randi and Margo were attacked; after the Women's Center was trashed; after threatening phone calls to her office.

The pistol was aimed at Chris's face.

She swallowed a cold lump of fear. Defiantly, she asked about Sam again. He ordered her to shut her mouth. Though he was average-looking, there was nothing average about his dark, hate-filled eyes, glaring like the heavy silver rings on his fingers. She wondered how he had managed the frizzy brown hair, the large chest of the woman he had clearly been impersonating.

Chris was furious with herself for getting caught, for getting so involved with Bobbi Jean that she did not hear him enter the kitchen. If she had, it might be him standing by the sink instead of her, defenseless. Her hands curled into fists.

"Bobbi Jean?" he said softly to the prone form on the floor, shaking his head as if she were a naughty child. "You and your dead dyke bitch over there almost spoiled my plans." And with that, he raised the gun, smiled, and shot her in the head.

"Batard! Salaud!" Chris cried, as the last breath left the mortally wounded woman's body; her beringed fingers slowly unfolding, going slack.

Hot tears filled Chris's eyes. She blinked them back. No way was this monster going to see her cry. Still stunned, she turned again to glance at Bobbi Jean.

"I never got to say I was sorry, either," she told the dead woman silently, before her head exploded in a hundred bursts of light.

❧ **22** ❧

*F*rantic with worry, Katya paced her bedroom floor. *Don't stop. Don't think*, she repeated to herself over and over. The mantra did little to calm her thoughts. *If I stop moving something unthinkable will happen to Sam.*

A flash of rage shook her body. She threw a slipper at the silent phone on her night table. *Ring, damn it!*

Out of habit, she perked up when the plumbing whined from somewhere inside the house. She found herself irrationally waiting for her son's customary knock on her door. If she wanted to sleep a bit longer, he kept himself busy in his room. It was their ritual, except for the one morning he did not knock. That was Sunday, just yesterday, she realized with a start. That sweet morning when Chris had awakened in her bed seemed like an eternity ago.

Surely it was all a bad dream. Something that happened to other people, not her. And it wasn't happening at all like it did in the movies—no ransom note; no phone call to end the interminable waiting.

Should she telephone her in-laws? Alarm them? They'd probably have a heart attack. And what could she say anyway? *I looked away for one unfortunate moment when he was on the merry-go-round?*

Jumpy, she sat on the edge of her fourposter bed as daybreak filtered in through the shutters, gathering dust motes. They danced like pin-sized snowflakes, in the diluted beam of light, and brought her back to Sam. His favorite movie, "Star Trek." What was it that one of the characters on the Enterprise always said that always delighted him? "Beam me up, Scotty?" Yes, that was it, she reflected with a heavy sigh.

Please God, beam Sam safely back to me.

Pulling a tissue out of a Kleenex box, Katya blew into it gingerly, her nostrils painfully raw and irritated. Gradually, she became aware of female voices, the smell of coffee wafting up from the kitchen, the sound of deputies changing shifts. She swallowed hard when she thought of the FBI man who was on his way to Deer Falls. More questioning. Maybe *he* could work miracles. Still, the idea of the FBI in her house filled her with dread.

Everyone was doing their part to get Sam safely back. Except *her*, his own mother. Had she allowed her own mother to make her so helpless? Wasn't it time to stop blaming her weaknesses on others?

She would always be grateful to Toni and Molly—literally dragging her drained, slack body upstairs to sleep—promising to keep an eye on the deputies monitoring the phones; promising to alert her if there was any news.

Try as she might, sleep had eluded her. She lay awake that long night with one ear cocked to the telephone, wondering why she had not received a ransom note—a message from Chris. Chris. Was she in danger this very minute?

Sam's well-being was her responsibility, not anyone else's. It wasn't fair to allow Chris to set herself up as a target. Why did she keep depending on other people to come to her rescue?

Because Loren always rescued me.

Standing up, she began to pace again, and that's when she saw the pile of mail she had forgotten to take out of the mailbox Saturday, remembering to do it only before they left for the flea market Sunday. Without thought, she had placed it on her desk, and in yesterday's confusion it had totally slipped her mind.

Frantically, she riffled through bills, catalogs, a note from her mother—noticed, with a jolt, a small, lavender envelope. Impatiently tossing the other mail back on the desk, she backed up to the bed, trembling as if her body knew something she didn't.

She tore it open. Her hands shook so badly she had to stop and count to ten before reading the typewritten message before her. It was the "Katie" that jump-started her heart. She read it, then went over it again with disbelief.

Katie:

> *It's time we got to know each other. You want to see Sam again? Then no police, no sheriff. None of your dyke bitches. Just you and me, Katie. You know where I'll be. All you have to do is go out jogging. I'm waiting for you. Don't keep me waiting long.*

It wasn't signed, but that didn't matter. Katya was already halfway into her grey jogging sweats, all the while thinking that the sly, confident bitch had been so sure of getting away with Sam's abduction, that she had placed the unstamped envelope in with Katya's mail. Probably before they arrived at the flea market yesterday. How did she know Katya's destination? Katya hadn't seen a white station wagon in her rear-view mirror. Obviously, she thought with distaste, this vicious stalker was very adept at keeping tabs on her.

A quick glance at the clock showed 6:30 a.m. Without realizing it, she had resumed her pacing. What to do? She had no plan. All she knew was that a psycho might have Sam in her car. She couldn't go out unprepared.

Her gaze fixed on the bottom drawer of the dresser. She yanked it open, hastily pushed aside some sweaters, and stared at Loren's gun. Vacillating between rage and reluctance, for she had never fired a gun, she carefully took it out and felt its weight. Removing it cautiously from the holster, she checked the cylinder. Though the safety was on, Loren had left its five chambers loaded.

Her mind reeled. She shut it down. It would have to stay in neutral in order for her to drive down such a drastic path. Katya found some adhesive tape, tore it in strips. As if by rote, she lifted the back of her sweatshirt and taped the gun to the small of her back.

Just you and me, Katie. No police, no sheriff. The words became her second mantra and propelled her in the direction of the bedroom door, when she realized that she had to slip out without anyone noticing. Scribbling a hasty note, leaving it on the bed with the kidnapper's letter, Katya locked her bedroom door and crossed the room.

"I'll be jogging south on Route 204. In the direction of town."

If enough time elapsed and Katya hadn't shown herself downstairs, or responded to either Toni or Molly's knock, then hopefully, the deputies would force an entry into her room. For now, she had to heed the kidnapper's warning. She was on her own. Though she couldn't confide in anyone, her gears had shifted from neutral to overdrive. *She* would not be stopped.

Unlatching the sliding glass door that led out to the upper level of her duplex deck, she silently thanked the contractor who had suggested it. Then she thought about the note again. It didn't have the sophisticated wording of one of her students, but that could be a tactic to confuse her. If it wasn't this Bobbi Jean; if it wasn't a jealous colleague on Bear State's staff, then it very well might boil down to a student trying to get her attention. She could only think of one person. *Don't start accusing people.*

Senses keen, she moved swiftly down the steps and out to the woods on the garage side of the house; paused to ponder where the surveillance van might be hidden, hoping that the deputies wouldn't see her.

When she reached the stream, she quickly walked to the next property and then to the road. She began to run. Gradually, her body adjusted itself to the weight of the gun, the pull of the adhesive tape. A another weight lifted from her burdened heart as she followed her usual route into town—the weight of helplessness. A breeze off the stream ruffled the hair she had neglected to tie in a ponytail.

Come and get me, bitch, she challenged, picking up speed. *Show yourself. Give me back my son.*

The small farmhouse loomed up ahead. Her leg muscles, her gut clenched, as she expected the German Shepherds to race out at her. But it was too early and quiet. Too quiet. Not even a car. And heartbreakingly lovely, too. If she could only appreciate the sun breaking through clouds scalloped with salmon hues like a benediction over her right shoulder. Above the farmhouse, a dark green canopy of trees was also illuminated with burnished highlights.

If she could only appreciate the sweet serenade of birds in their ritual good morning chorus. She had first heard their song at four a.m., trumpeting the new day. But she had been watching the goddamned clock. At least now she wasn't passively waiting.

Over her left shoulder, the stream thundered against rocks and boulders peppering the stream bed before snaking behind a crest of land where the houses began. Her eyes became vigilant, saw nothing unusual. Only cottages and the farmhouse just yards away. A quick tilt of her head toward the sun gathered some warmth, but only brought a sense of imminent danger, for she sensed where the kidnapper lay in wait for her. So she kept running, kept her thoughts, her fears at bay in order to keep her legs working; an unspoken contest of wills between her and her enemy.

An occasional puddle from last night's thunderstorm marked her journey. Her jogging shoes slapped against the asphalt relentlessly.

Don't think. Don't think! Blood rushed through her veins, forcing oxygen to her starved brain.

In the deserted field across from the farmhouse a glint of sunlight bounced off something metallic, and an icy knot of pure terror clutched her heart.

There it was, the front fender of a white station wagon. Slowly, the car pulled out, revealing its entire chilling shape. It idled at the edge of the field near the barbed wire fence it had crushed when it entered. Behind the tinted windshield, Katya could barely make out the dreaded silhouette of the driver. A white-toothed grin flashed spookily. Instinctively, she picked up speed.

Tentatively, she jogged a few more steps, daring the bitch. She seethed with fury.

Its engine racing, the wagon screeched out of the field. Katya glanced over her shoulder, expecting to find it right behind her and was astonished when it shot off in the opposite direction and kicked up a cloud of dirt. Smoky exhaust fumes spewed back into her confused face.

And then it reappeared in her lane, just inches behind her, slowing down. Whirling around, she faced it, her heart thudding.

The driver was taking all the time in the world, so confident that a car would not come along, so crazed as to ignore the possibility.

Katya's eyes frantically searched the tinted windshield for another small, familiar outline, a precious little head of blonde hair. But she only saw the driver. And with maddening deliberation, the car was nudging her gradually into the other lane—toward the field, its front fender a white, chrome-fanged monster like a creature in a grade B horror movie.

A maniacal laugh broke the early morning silence as the driver nosed her closer to the densely-weeded, unplowed field. She noticed longish brown hair carelessly pulled back and tied; brass epaulets on dark shoulders.

Her foot slipped in a puddle. Her ankle twisted, shooting up rays of pain. She half-turned, tried to brace her fall with her hands. They landed on barbed wire, forcing a yelp of pain from her throat. Then she hit the dirt with the wind knocked out of her.

Hands burning with cuts, irrationally wondering if the barbed wire was rusty; when she had received her last tetanus shot, she sprang to her feet and began to run faster than she ever had before.

She never saw what was in front of her, lost her footing again, screamed when her ankle hit the ground. Then she glanced up. What had tripped her made her stomach turn over. The two German Shepherds lay in the field covered with blood.

Again, she tried to get up. Terror-stricken, she reached behind her, clawed at the back of her sweatshirt, tugged wildly at the adhesive tape fastening the gun to her lower back, but a pair of arms encircled her.

"No!" she cried with outrage, twisting her body, kicking. A string of curses spilled out of her attacker's mouth.

There was no space to get at her revolver, but she fought with every natural weapon she had—her nails, her teeth.

One arm grabbed her neck in a choke-hold. One hand brushed against the small of her back.

"A gun, Katie? Dumb bitch...."

It was not a woman's voice. The revelation almost paralyzed her. He yanked the weapon off and the adhesive tape tore out body hair. The tender flesh of her lower back screamed in protest. Her arm automatically flew up. Her fist caught him by surprise. When he dropped the gun she kicked it as hard as she could and sent it flying into a patch of grass.

"You cunt. That was my back-up." He choked her so hard with his arm that she almost blacked out.

"Hell with the gun. Got no time for this."

She thought he meant to kill her, but he used both arms to lift her off the ground. Carrying her, he slammed her body, face down on his front fender.

"You like to fight, Katie? Good...shit, that's good. Cause you'll need it later." His familiar voice was deadly calm and chilling. While she was pinned to the white metal with one implacable arm, he used the other to wind coils of rope, with astonishing dexterity, around her own arms and wrists.

She struggled to twist around and see his face. He just laughed.

"What have you done with Sam?" she cried.

"If you behave I might just take you to him."

There was no other choice but to let her body go slack. He flung her onto the back seat of the station wagon, her face landed on sticky vinyl upholstery. A beat later, the car lurched forward. She just lay there, panting, for several moments, to ward off dizziness. Then she finally managed to sit up wedged into the right corner of the back seat. Gradually, her senses registered the back of his head and she blinked, perplexed.

His dirty-blonde hair was cropped close, military-style, his neck cleanly-shaven. And on the back seat beside her lay a brown wig with a short ponytail. It was thick and furry like the pelt of a skinned animal. And it immediately sent up a nauseating image of the two dead dogs. She gagged.

She noticed a pair of falsies, a torn bra.

When he spun around, her mouth opened with surprise, but nothing came out.

"Knew you'd show up, Katie. Knew you wouldn't disappoint me."

᠊ᢓ   ᠊ᢓ   ᠊ᢓ

❦ 23 ❧

*I*t was a slow drifting up toward consciousness and Chris's brain objected. Every movement sent tiny explosions through her skull. She tried to lift her sore right wrist, but her hands met resistance. They were firmly shackled behind her with heavy rope tied to a metal chair; both of her feet secured and anchored to the floor with two oversized eyescrews.

She struggled with her bonds, but they had as much give as iron. Directly in front of her was a table. Just trying to make sense of the photo album that was spread out, the shoebox—the assortment of papers, set up a wave of dizziness. Drawing a labored breath wreaked havoc on her bruised ribs. She tried to take stock of the situation, and found it easier to focus at a distance. A question kept nagging at her.

Why had the killer, who had so sadistically and coldly placed a bullet through Bobbi Jean's head, spared *her*?

"Got special plans for *you*, bitch," had been his greeting in the kitchen. It must have been hours. Dawn had just begun to chase the shadows in the room—a long, narrow rectangular room piled with cartons—some spilling out sleeves and other pieces of military clothes like so many dismembered boneless scarecrows. To the far right stood a bed hugging a pale green wall. Over it hung a large carving of Christ on a cross, which for some reason chilled her.

What chilled her even more was the pervasive smell of gasoline. In her befuddled state, she could not isolate the source of the vaporous fumes. Directly across from her, under a high row of dirty windows, a low bench was draped with a black cloth, and held one candle and a selection of framed photographs. She had the eerie feeling that it served as some kind of altar. And a note of dread sounded in her brain. It all spelled *disaster*.

There were so many images for her bruised brain to process that beads of sweat popped out on her forehead. She pictured the killer entering the gasoline-soaked room, striking a match to that candle, the resulting inferno. She wondered how long it took a cluttered room like this to ignite and become a funeral pyre. Did the candle represent a sacrificial lamb? Was she to be that lamb in the killer's plan to avenge something or someone from his tortured past? Even worse, was Sam the object of sacrifice? Katya? The altar, the cross, the gasoline. To dwell on the answer, the sum of those parts, set her teeth on edge.

Zut! If only she could get her hands around his neck and wring it, castrate him for what he had done to Bobbi Jean and those other unfortunate women; to her friends. But she had made a mess of her attempts to play lone hero. *Or shero*, she mused. Here she was more like a trussed goose, only fit for maman's pâté. *Une andouille.*

Her next move was to focus on the photos on the makeshift altar, searching for clues. The effort sent a spasm of pain through her skull. One photo showed a young blonde woman; a little blonde boy gazing at her with a trusting smile. Her focus sharpened. The mother and child bore an uncanny resemblance to Katya and Sam.

From the altar, her gaze climbed up. She made out treetops through grimy panes of glass. That, plus the shape of the room convinced her that she was trapped in the apartment above the garage that had first piqued her curiosity—the room where Bobbi Jean might have heard a child screaming. Had Sam screamed so loudly that his kidnapper took him elsewhere?

Leaning as far across the bridge table as the ropes allowed, she glanced to her left. There was no place to hide a child here. Only two half-opened doors she assumed were the bathroom and closet. If there was an occupant, she surely would have discovered that by now. With bone-chilling clarity she recalled the navy flightsuit the killer had worn in that kitchen. Identical to Bobbi Jean's. The Deer Falls Attacker and Sam's kidnapper had to be one and the same. She was dead certain of this. But what was the link?

As her mind cleared, she surveyed the room more carefully, starved for details that might help her neutralize her hopelessness. The peeling, pale green walls were dotted with Heavy Metal posters; a few shelves with books. A manual typewriter sat on a rusted television stand. Also to her left, a cheap clock hung over the stained sink, sharing space with a hotplate on top of a portable refrigerator. Trash littered the unfinished wood floor near a wastebasket with Snoopy's picture. The clock read 5:45 a.m.

It seemed to be a transient's room, perhaps one of the many students who settled for any affordable place near Bear State. Many of these old houses bordering the river rented rooms. Bobbi Jean, who had been employed by the college, had regretted renting the old house because of her unsavory neighbor. For some reason he had taken her station wagon without permission. The vehicle that had tailed Katya? The person behind the wheel not a woman, but a man posing as Bobbi Jean?

Who?

Slowly, she swiveled her head to the right. The neatly-made bed had surprised her. An army blanket was tucked in with precise hospital corners. A clean expanse of white sheet overlapped the blanket where a fluffy pillow rested. A soldier, or even a *convict* might have been trained to make such a bed. The realization brought her straight to Sam's father. But Katya had sworn he was still behind bars, and that even if he could get out would not jeopardize the "monthly allowance" Loren's parents doled out to keep him away.

But Katya tended to gloss over the grisly.

Toni would find out. She had promised to call the prison in California. Chris assumed that it would have been one of the first things a sheriff would investigate if he suspected a parent, such as he did Katya, of foul play. A normal sheriff. Oliver Wendell made his own rules.

Chris shut her eyes, fighting back a wave of dizziness. She knew that if she could touch the back of her skull, she would find a sizeable lump. Again, why had he spared her? She tried to picture him in that dimly-lit kitchen, could recall only hate-filled dark eyes, close-cropped sandy hair. A man who could have been anywhere from his late twenties to late thirties. Her mind refused to cooperate. It balked at that chilling image, the cruel voice preceding the even crueler shot to Bobbi Jean's head.

Stretching her head back, she tried to relax her stiff neck and resume her visual sweep of the room. A gallon can of paint sat in a cobwebbed corner near the door. It was the same color, lavender, that had been poured on her Jeep. Rage flooded her as she stared at the dried paint coating its sides. Each clue further confirmed her worst fears. He was a lesbophobic sadist, a lunatic who was affronted by the lesbians of Deer Falls. His solution—push the damn lot of them off the highest peak in the county.

"Make them fly. End their miserable existences," he had threatened on Katya's kitchen phone yesterday. This was truly a sick mind. Chris's eyes were drawn back to the bed, and as they journeyed to the paint can, and traveled up the wall adjacent to it, a slow burn of outrage consumed her.

She had to lean forward to see them clearly, but knew, with a sinking heart, what the frames held. One, a winter scene in white, with a joyful string of women skaters curving around an ice pond. It had been torn by a barrage of darts obviously thrown by someone with perfect aim, who had been reclining on the perfect pillow at the head of his perfect bed.

Un salaud. Bastard. The small feathered missiles pierced the heart of each skater. Chris felt their sting in her own heart.

Preparing herself, she checked the Spring canvas she had so lovingly rendered. Katya's painting. Expecting to find it destroyed, too, she was surprised to see it intact. Her mind wove a possible scenario. The bastard had stepped into Molly's store to purchase something. He noticed the painting. Something clicked in his twisted brain. He saw the blonde woman who resembled not only Katya, Chris realized, but the woman in the photo on the altar. His mother? Had he been driven to steal the painting? Destroy it? Erase the likeness, along with everything else in this room, including Chris?

Got special plans for you, bitch.

A sense of urgency overwhelmed her. She finally could focus on the objects placed in front of her, as if served up on a platter. Concentration did not set off the queasiness she had felt before. She found a pattern. He had arranged each clue carefully. Order in chaos. And she was his captive audience as she sat trussed up behind the bridge table. Clearly, he had wanted to ensure that she'd have something to pass the time, that she would sit gripped in the icy hand of terror.

And he made sure she would be "entertained." A large photo album revealed newspaper articles; some official-looking papers were scattered next to a shoebox filled with combat souvenirs. A folded sheet of lavender stationery was tucked under one corner of the album.

She rose to the bait, she was most intrigued by the stationery. But how to get to it with bound hands? It did not surprise her that he enjoyed games; wanted her to work for any small victory, for she found a pencil right under her very nose.

Leaning forward, she attempted to grasp the eraser end with her lips. After a few unsuccessful tries, she succeeded in gripping it between her teeth. A few downward sweeping motions dislodged what she was after. Flicking the note open, managing to keep it that way with the edge of the album as an anchor, she read the cryptic typewritten message:

Dyke Bitch:

> *Nothing I like better than a good fight. You haven't disappointed me yet, bitch. Not like B.J., the other dyke bitch. It'll be more fun watching you squirm. Seeing you fry. Kind of settle a score for me.*
>
> *Get this and get it good. While you're sitting there sweating your fucking, lezzie ass off, I'll be sending your bitch on the trip of her life, after I show her what a real man can do. Katya Michaels is gonna fly.... Too bad you can't watch bitch.*
>
> *If you think I'm joking just take a look at the album and think of the "hot" time we're gonna have together when I get back.*
>
> *The Avenging Angel*
>
> *P.S. I'll teach all of you a lesson.*

A string of French curses flew out of Chris's mouth. She strained so hard at her ropes that she felt as if the tendons in her neck would snap. The effort brought not only rope burns, but tears. The tears were for Katya. For Sam. She had failed both of them.

Scream, she ordered her vocal cords. But they would not obey. He *wanted* her to scream. Instead, animal sounds escaped her throat. She trembled with a fury born of helplessness. He was waiting to rush in and laugh mercilessly as he lit the match and tossed it.

You are bluffing, she thought, glancing again at the lavender stationery. There was no way he could have gotten to Katya. She would be surrounded by deputies, perhaps even the FBI by now, watching her closely. Protecting her.

Chris slumped in the chair, her mind drifting back to his words despite herself. *Katya Michaels is gonna fly.* Her stomach dropped as she pictured Katya tossed over the edge of the cliff.

The horror of that image was enough to re-awaken her determination. *This fucking psycho is not going to drive me crazy. He is not going to find a quivering mass of jelly. Des clous! No way!*

She would oblige him, though, by reading what he had spread out for her. She needed that edge. First the clipped headline pasted to the far left corner of the page:

Deer Falls Attacker Strikes Again! Carefully, as if not to stir up another emotional storm, she turned her attention to a large newspaper article that occupied one entire page. It was dated 1971 and clipped from the *Vermont Herald-Times*:

Local Arson Reads Like Dr. Jekyll and Mr. Hyde
Maple Gorge— *The charred body of a thrice-decorated Korean War veteran and private pilot was found early Tuesday morning. Authorities believe the decorated war hero may have driven his eleven-year old son to arson and murder.*

"He took that little boy up in a private plane and scared him half to death," stated county social worker Mary Nicolson. The boy (name withheld because of age) was placed in the care of juvenile authorities pending an investigation of the bizarre incident.

Shocked neighbors told a story worthy of a television drama. Dan Carpenter told this reporter that the father had custody of the son following a lengthy court battle and divorce two years ago.

Ruth Amiel, another neighbor, added: "He [the father] used to march around in his uniform and order the boy and his mother around. Beat up on both of them, too. Can you believe he even made the boy salute him, call him, 'Sir'? Always made fun of him in front of the other kids. When he drank, he was no hero. Just a bully with a foul mouth. I even heard him call his own boy a queer when he didn't fight back. And the boy was scared of planes. That's what did it, you know. That trip up in the plane...."

Chris's glance fell on the other papers. *"Irrefutable evidence shows the female plaintiff is engaged in an unnatural relationship with another female at The Sappho Commune in California...."* Another article caught her eye. *"Social worker reports that the boy allegedly set fire to another boy's bed when the latter fondled him...."* There was more, but Chris had read enough.

Badly shaken, she wondered what had taken place up in that private plane to turn an eleven-year-old victim into a merciless killer who threw innocent women off the most beautiful peak in the county.

She felt no sympathy for him. She felt violated by both the killer and his father. Violated by a society that spawned such beasts.

"Merde!" She wanted no part of that society.

"Je les emmerde! To hell with them! All of them!"

A moment after her outburst, and only after she had calmed herself, she heard, with disbelief, a scratching sound originating from the left side of the room.

Her first thought: *He is in here. Impossible!* The ball of her foot began to itch and when she heard the noise a second time, she listened closer. It was like a cat pawing at wood. Scratching.

The next sounds seemed fainter, followed by a thump, as if something solid had shifted its weight and met an immovable object. A wall, perhaps? Chris swallowed a white hot ball of fear. The newspaper article had done its job. She was petrified.

She began to sweat profusely. One ear was now cocked to the windows. Had she heard a car outside? She waited, but there was only silence.

Confused, her frantic eyes settled on a photograph of the same little blonde boy in the loving portrait with the blonde woman. Here, he saluted a stern looking man in full-dress air force uniform, his own little outfit identical. A little boy, possibly Sam's age, whose world was about to fall apart.

And then she heard an engine rumble in the driveway. It was worse than any nightmarish scenario her brain could create. A car door slammed. The sharp retort of leather soles on the driveway. Approaching.

Chris froze. He wasn't hiding nearby. That had been a cat. *He* had come back for her.

The footsteps paused, seemed to recede, grow fainter. Chris pictured him walking up the seedy lawn, into the house, to add one more body—hers—to the list of dead women.

Perspiration burned the freshly-opened cut on her cheekbone. She heard a door slam in the distance. Endless moments passed as she struggled with her ropes to no avail. How could she possibly hope to win in a no-win situation? Would her best weapon, words, have any effect on him? Did it matter anymore? He had probably gotten to Katya.

But you know his secrets, a voice whispered silently. *You cannot let him go free to kill again. Molly, Sara, Toni could be next.* At some point he would have to untie her. She would wait for her chance.

With a final glance at the boy saluting his hero in full-dress uniform, the man's mouth a thin gash in a harsh face, Chris could almost hear the boy uttering the required word "Sir," instead of "father." Even now, that boy was marching through Deer Falls following his father's murderous orders.

Footsteps approached. Her heart thundered. Just now someone was outside the door that led up to the garage apartment. Chris waited for the sound of a key in the downstairs door, but what she heard was the scratching, impatient sound over her left shoulder again. And, with a ray of hope, she thought: *Sam. Perhaps Sam is behind one of those slightly-cracked doors, after all....* If she did not win the war, she would settle for at least this battle. At least she could accomplish this for Katya...but she had to outwit him first.

What is he waiting for? The rope cut into her flesh as she twisted fruitlessly in the chair, not daring to cry out and respond to the intermittent scratching so close and yet so far away. A few seconds had passed since she heard the sound of footsteps again.

Finally, the click of a key in a lock. The first door between her and death opened. She dared not draw a breath. Footsteps ascended the stairs, outside the apartment door now. She had to squeeze her thighs shut to keep her full bladder from spilling over. She waited, dry-mouthed, for the last turn of a key.

The doorknob jiggled.

"Shit!" Sara Wenning's frustrated voice called out: "It's not the same damned key. Chris, you in there?"

"Merci, merci, merci...."

Chris had never heard a more welcome sound. "Sara! I am here!"

"Are you okay, Chris? Hang on. The key I found on the peg board doesn't fit this lock. Wait. I saw some split logs outside...hang in there, babe! The Lavender Berets are here!"

With exquisite relief, Chris laughed till tears came. She ordered her defiant bladder not to embarrass her, but was so grateful that she could have peed all over the floor. Grateful for her friend's impatience, heeding the call to arms even though Chris's phone call never came.

It did not take Sara long to break through the thin wooden door and cut the ropes binding her to the chair. "Honey-child, your face looks just how I feel after seeing those two poor women in the kitchen. Let's get the hell out of here."

Rubbing her wrists, barely aware of the throbbing in her ankles, Chris hugged Sara.

"Those women. I was about to call the police...."

Chris's head shot up. "No, no...."

Sara drew a long breath. "I didn't call because I wanted to check up here first."

"Smart move, mon amie. This monster will explode if he sees one badge....

"We'll talk in the car, Chris."

"Wait," Chris said.

They heard the scratching noise at the same time and while Sara checked the bathroom, Chris, hopefully, entered a small dirty closet. "Sam?" she said softly. "It's Chris." Hearing a muffled whimper, she tapped against the walls with the back of her hand.

Her heart leaped. The back panel was hollow. "Do not be afraid, Sam. There is no one out here who will hurt you," Chris promised, with a silent vow, her hands trembling with excitement. "You remembered our secret password, Merde? You scratched right after I said it. If you are in there now, knock on the wall."

At the same moment the knock resounded, she found the latch. Pressing it released the back panel, which popped into her startled hands. Sam sat bound and gagged, his brown eyes saucers of fear. She cursed the man who had done this to him, and gathered him up in her arms.

"Oh Sam, mon petit oiseau." Cradling his quaking body, she carried him into the room where she untied him and removed his gag. His eyes were still pools of horror. Tracks of dried tears stained his pale frightened face.

They tried to get him to speak, but he wouldn't say a word. Shaking her head with fury, Sara wandered back to the closet, found a light chain and pulled it. "Lord, will you look at this."

Chris had to calm Sam down and give him a glass of water before he would allow her to move even an inch away. She stood beside Sara and took stock of what else filled the crawl space: plastic bags of dried marijuana leaves; clear pouches of a white substance.

"Let's get out of here now," Sara said tersely, and then lowered her voice. "Before the motherfucker comes back for his goodies."

Chris's eyes were on Sam's feet, on the end of one green neon lace which had been torn off at his sneaker. Quickly, she retrieved the lavender note from the bridge table and handed it to Sara as they prepared to leave.

"Did you at least see the bastard's face?" Sara asked.

Chris nodded and described him. Sara drew in a breath. "Sounds like the creep who followed Katya into Molly's. Looked like he wanted her on his dinner plate...her own student," she said in a voice low enough to elude Sam. "This note could be another trap," she warned Chris. "And this time you're not walking into it alone. Lord, it stinks in here." They traced the gasoline fumes to a metal trash can near the sink.

"Don't you dare light a match," Sara ordered.

"How did you know I was up here?" Chris asked, taking Sam's hand.

Sara, who had reached the door, now held up Chris's black slicker. "Grabbed this from the kitchen floor and decided to have a look-see."

Managing a smile, Chris dug the two smooth white stones out of a pocket. "Good luck charms," she told a puzzled Sara as she pushed them into the lower pocket of her black cargo pants. She never wanted to see the slicker again and dropped it back on the floor. "We must call Katya's house. I pray that she is there."

"The phone in the main house is dead," Sara responded. "We can call while we're driving...by the way, if she isn't there, are we going where I think we are?"

Chris moved closer to Sara, out of Sam's earshot. "Eagle Point." She looked at Sam, lifting an eyebrow. "And there will be no time to drop him off if Katya is missing. Come on, Sam." She pulled his small, limp hand, then lifted him up and hugged him again.

In no time, they were down the steps and at the outside door, peering out cautiously. Moving fast. The minute Chris tucked Sam into the back seat of Sara's Datsun, he curled up and closed his eyes.

Chris checked her watch to gauge how much time had passed from when she was first knocked unconscious to when she had fastened her eyes on the clock above the sink. There was a possibility that the killer would have just gotten to Katya now.

Sara turned the key in the ignition, and seconds later her car phone rang. It was Bev. Sara listened intently before she hung up, turning to Chris in the passenger seat. "Bev's been up on all incoming police messages on her CB scanner. A mysterious caller got in touch with Wendell and reported a little boy with blonde hair walking along the interstate, dazed. The FBI's at Katya's house now. Wendell took his deputies to check it out."

"A smokescreen," Chris responded with chilling clarity. "The interstate is in the opposite direction from Eagle Point." She half-turned to make sure Sam was asleep and studied Sara's profile as they screeched out of the driveway. The jaw muscle was working under her unblemished skin. "Spit it out. What else did Bev say?"

"I was just trying to think of the best way to tell you....Toni finally got in touch with the warden in California. Sam's father was paroled six months ago. He violated his parole and disappeared. There's a warrant out for his arrest," Sara added glumly.

"Goddess." Chris rubbed a rope-burned wrist absently. "This throws another light on things. The psycho has a well-formed plan. Stop here."

Sara braked suddenly. "Why?"

"Back up. We must have a plan, too." When she had turned to check on Sam she had noticed two lavender baseball caps with the *Grassroots Press* logo on the shelf above Sara's back seat. "In case he's got Katya."

When they pulled up to her Jeep, Chris jumped out, fished the car keys out of her pocket and took her baseball cap, none the worse for wear after she had retrieved it from the stream on Saturday. "Okay, step on it," she told Sara as she got back in the car and fastened her seat belt.

Plunking the cap on her head, she said, almost to herself: "We must think up some diversionary tactics. I have an idea. It works in kids' games. It might just work for us. I will explain on the way. Drive faster, woman. I will pay for the speeding ticket."

Their lack of a weapon bothered her, for it would not be close combat. If she was not so petrified of losing Katya, she might even be enjoying this. A battle of the minds. Well, he had started it.

"Sara, the killer shot Bobbi Jean with the same weapon you showed me in your catalog. How many rounds did it have? I have to be sure."

"The .22 pistol? Six rounds. Semi-automatic."

"Then he does not have to cock it?"

"Right. Did it have a silencer? Being in such a quiet residential area and all...."

"Oui. He is not stupid. But he likes attention, and may not be using a silencer now. He might also desire to travel light." Her mind worked as Sara called for an ambulance to Bobbi Jean's address, then tried to get Bev back on the phone to alert the sheriff that he might have been sent on a wild goose chase by the Deer Falls Attacker.

"We must get him to empty that gun without hitting anyone. I know Eagle Point well. It is where I went whenever I was upset...after my brother was killed," Chris's voice trailed off. She was grateful to Sara for keeping her silence.

"The woods up there are filled with old trees. Nice and thick...and boulders. We can attempt to get from the park to the cliff without being seen." She checked her watch for the third time. The streets were empty. Too early for Monday commuters. The plan grew inside her head. Visualizing Eagle Point, she committed it to memory.

"I know this monster's mind," she assured Sara, reflecting on the newspaper articles, the crank phone call. "He believes that killing dykes is a mission of mercy,"

Sara tried Bev's number again and cursed.

"Call Toni," Chris suggested. They were now speeding up the road that ran parallel to the route in front of Katya's house. Chris mused that Katya could be the last link in a murderous chain to avenge his mother's abandonment of him for another woman, leaving him to fend for himself in the care of his abusive, tyrannical father, .

Chris had not realized that Sara had placed the call to Toni and was now holding up the phone, waiting, her face grim. "Katya's gone," she whispered. "They had to break her bedroom door down to find out. There was a note.... She went out to meet him."

"Merde." Chris clenched her fists. "Tell Toni and Molly to meet us at Eagle Point Park. Toni can stay in the park with Sam. She will know how to handle him."

Sara relayed the message. There was only Bev to contact to inform the sheriff, then rush up there herself and complete the circle of friends.

"Tell the sheriff no sirens," Chris instructed Sara as she punched in Bev's number. "Oh, Sara...I am going to wring that bastarde's neck when I get my hands on him."

"If I only had ordered the gun," Sara replied, regretfully, the phone to her ear.

"You know I hate guns, but I wish you had ordered it, too."
Chris touched Sara's arm. The stiffness of taut muscles beneath her light
blue workshirt was reassuring.

They were finally cresting the steep mountain road that would
lead them through the back entrance of Eagle Park. Her interpretation
of the Deer Falls Attacker's motive had only one loophole. Why had
Sam's father attacked the other women with such callousness and
cunning, if all he wanted was Katya?

And then she pictured the lone candle on the altar in his garage
apartment. One candle. One sacrificial lamb. She had been targeted for
that, just because she preferred women. That was even more personal
than her paintings.

❦ 24 ❧

A howling wind whipped through the canyon, eclipsing the sound of Katya's pounding heart.

"Beg for your life, bitch." Marty DeLeon dragged her petrified body further toward the two-foot high rock barricade that separated Eagle Point from a sheer, dizzying drop to oblivion.

Don't look down, Katya told her reeling brain. She shut her eyes tightly, afraid to look. At the edge, he yanked her head back by the hair and forced her to open her eyes.

His voice was menacingly calm: "Beg. Beg for me, Katie." His eyes cut through her like a knife.

"Marty, please.... Think of Sam, for God's sake."

"God? You filthy queer? You perverted my son!" He shoved his face so close to hers she could see the pores in his oily complexion, the dark sprinkling of stubble. His hooded, reptilian eyes, his sour morning breath made her stomach lurch. She almost welcomed the sharp pain in her scalp where he pulled at her hair. For if she concentrated on the pain she might not pass out from terror. Her next vision might be blinding light and cold air as she was flung into space.

Fascinated and repulsed, her gaze swept over the blue-glazed granite abutments on all sides; the skinny wisp of a stream so far below where foamy ribbons rippled through the churning blue-gray current. Her stream. Snaking along its rocky bed. She had gone fishing there Saturday, just two days ago.

"Ah, you're pathetic, bitch." With another sharp yank of hair, he shoved her back onto the rock-hard ground, sending up a sharp retort from the ankle she had twisted running away from him in the field.

Her left sneaker and sock were still damp from the puddle she had tripped in. The cuts on her hand stung and pulled as if a thousand tiny, sharp, metal barbs were embedded in her palms. But even this and the staggering height of Eagle Point took a back seat to thoughts of her son.

Warily watching his father, she inched away from the cliff's edge with imperceptible movements. Gradually, she sat up, wondering why he didn't just get it over with. Why he was toying with her.

Her attempts to distance herself from him didn't go unnoticed. Even though he wasn't looking at her, he laughed contemptuously at her feeble efforts.

Now, he stood near the edge, one army boot propped up on the rock barrier, as if defying space, while the wind screamed around him. An arc of screeching birds joined in the macabre chorus. It was odd to see birds dipping and swooping below, instead of above her. Graceful as they were, it made a chilling sight. And in just her light sweats, icy tongues of wind licked at her exposed flesh.

Katya felt as if she would never be warm again.

Deep in thought now, he stroked the barrel of his gun absently. She studied him against the granite backdrop and knew, as she had always sensed, but could never admit, that he hated what she represented. A dyke. Something sinister and threatening that uncoiled a serpent of fear deep inside him. Realizing this, even if it spelled death for her, Katya also knew that it somehow gave her an edge. In some strange way, Marty DeLeon was afraid of her.

He was only a few feet away. Why didn't she just bolt up and push him off? A bullet was better than that seemingly endless drop. A bullet was kinder. You didn't have to think, anticipate the rocks below as you sailed through space.

Do it! But her mind refused to relay the order. That shiny silver object in his hand, turned on her, kept her paralyzed.

Another gust of air lifted the collar of his navy blue flightsuit.

He stood as still as a statue, back turned to her, yet registered every movement she made. It was eerie. She might even believe him if he swore he could read her mind.

He was playing with her. This psychopath. She actually preferred his scalped blonde hair to the stringy hair that had been his style before prison. He'd had five years to build up his thirst for revenge. In his mind, Katya had been in on the heist; an accomplice in the theft of his son. Though in fact, he had forsaken the boy for money. Katya knew she was to blame in his twisted mind. After all, she had survived Meg and Loren. He had no one else to blame.

Whirling around, he faced her. Katya jumped like a startled doe. He raised the .22 caliber pistol as his shifty, dark eyes scanned the woods dividing Eagle Point from Eagle Park. He was in his own world, seemed to be listening to something in the distance.

Careful not to distract him, Katya half-turned and peered into the woods, a flare of hope sending blood coursing through her veins. Nothing.

He turned back to the cliff and resumed his meditation. Like a ticking time-bomb. She kept as still as she could, but her mind raced. Maybe, just maybe, Molly or Toni had knocked at her bedroom door one too many times. Surely one of the deputies had discovered that the sliding glass door leading from her bedroom to the deck was open.

She had ruined everything. Now she'd never see Sam again. He was going to kill her and take her son.

Let him be alive. Her eyes filmed over.

"You crying?" he asked, though his back was to her.

Dumbfounded, for she hadn't uttered a sound, Katya said: "Marty, please...just tell me Sam's alive."

Turning, he stuck a tonguetip in the hollow of his cheek, moved it around reflectively, then began to fidget.

His fidgeting scared Katya. He had gotten that way in the car when she mentioned Sam, then Chris. He hadn't said a word on the drive up the mountain. Then, without warning, he had stopped the station wagon, and with a small smile, crooked a finger at her. Too frightened to disobey, Katya had rejected the impulse to shrink further back into her seat, edged toward him instead. The slap had stunned her. Thinking about it now, she touched her cheek and shivered.

She turned her face away from the wind-swept cliff to the woods where rays of golden sunlight blinked through the trees. It was still low in the east, just beginning to lick the craggy, slate-gray wall of the opposite cliff, yet it seemed as if a whole morning had passed.

And then she saw a movement near a thick stand of evergreens. An animal? A crackling noise reached her ears. Her heart raced. Afraid he'd perceive what she just saw, Katya coughed, then took quiet stock of the woods, listening for a sound. Any sound.

She cast a guarded look in Marty's direction. He was walking down the length of the gray slate barrier, watchful, wary, the gun tight and ready in his right hand. He paused, ambled back, sat on the barrier opposite Katya and smiled.

"It's almost time, Katie." He cocked his head to the drop below. "Almost time to fly. Can't risk a tourist or some horny teen-agers come to see the sights."

Katya couldn't help looking at the gaping mouth of the canyon and starting to shake all over. *Don't show him you're afraid. He's waiting for that to finish the game.*

Use your wits. They're all you have. She forced a smile to her lips. Playing along. "There's nothing to worry about, Marty. It's not tourist season and most teen-agers are getting ready to go to school." Absently, she rotated her burning left wrist in the wind, tried another smile, but her face, from the bridge of her nose down, was frozen in a mask of ice.

"You got pretty hair." Marty grinned. He was just sitting there as though he had all the time in the world—as though they were friends.

Infuriated, Katya caught some strands of hair that the wind had blown away from her face. "Thank you," she forced herself to say. *And you have a great smile, you son-of-a-bitch.* It still unnerved her to see Sam's dimples on his father's evil face. His smile looked as if it didn't belong to him. She thought of his impersonating a woman when he tailed her in the station wagon—all those frightening, disrupted weeks. She wanted to ask why, but getting slapped again was something to avoid.

Now the pistol was pointed straight at her head. Playing with her mind. She pictured the two dead German Shepherds and shivered.

"You ever call Sam names?" he asked out of the blue. "My old man called me names all the time...before he died," he chuckled.

Katya was uncertain where he was headed and decided on honesty. Maybe it would spark some fatherly feelings in his hate-filled eyes. " 'Precious face' sometimes, and sometimes 'Dude.' He likes that...and at night? When I tuck him into bed I tease him with...." Her voice caught, " 'Honey Bunny.' " The tears were gliding down her cheeks now.

He stared hard at her. "Dyke bitch."

"Marty...Sam has your smile, your dimples...," she pleaded. "How can you hurt him? He's your son." Saying the word "son" choked her.

If she ever got out of this alive she'd make sure Sam's awful legacy ended with Marty DeLeon. She'd make sure of it by loving Sam with every fibre of her being.

"Go to hell," was his response, but it was said half-heartedly. His nervous eyes searched the woods—an excuse to look away from her. Then slowly, as if he couldn't help himself, he turned and really looked into her eyes.

Katya waited dry-mouthed. She sensed that he was seeing her for the first time. Really seeing *her*, and what he saw made him very uncomfortable and confused. It was information that his crazed, dangerous mind was not prepared to process. "Shit!" Bolting to his feet, he retreated back to where he had stood before, gazing trance-like over the canyon, then down below.

She thought she saw a momentary shudder, a mini-earthquake shake his body, and he tightened, as if to avoid any further thoughts that he might not be able to control.

Katya pondered the possibility that he might have written a script for all this, developing the plot, building his fury over the years he had spent in prison. The way he stood there with the expanse of sky surrounding him, brought to mind the statue of Icarus.

Allowing herself a script of her own, she pictured Marty DeLeon leaping off the cliff on wings of wax and alighting gracefully on the peak across the way. No danger because the sun was nestled low on the horizon. No melted wings this time. *His* father, unlike Daedalus, would have had a different tale to tell.

Like Daedalus, Marty's father had influenced his son, too—if he had been a name-calling tyrant. Just look at the trail of cold-blooded murders, Sam's abduction, the bigotry and hate he had created in his son. Her son's father. The Deer Falls Attacker. God. "The attacker takes victims up to Eagle Point and throws them off," the paper had said.

Marty's father, she realized with a start, had been Sam's grandfather.

"You knew Meg, didn't you? Sweet kid. Her car skidded off a cliff," he blurted, breaking into her thoughts.

Immediately, Katya wondered if he had played a part in that tragedy, too.

Involved in the past now, he muttered: "My old man was something. Gotta give him credit. Wasn't scared of anything. Know what made him like that? Flying. He promised it would make me brave, too," he said, then grew silent.

Katya couldn't understand how Meg had married this man. Maybe she took in stray animals. Maybe she felt sorry for him. Maybe he was good in bed, she thought with revulsion. *Or maybe he had gotten her pregnant with Sam.*

He began to talk again, and, hungry for information, she tried to enter his jumbled mind. As he poised on the rim of the cliff, he skipped from one topic to another, picking up loose threads after she could have sworn he had sewn the fabric. How could he scare her senseless one minute, then want to confide in her...want to *talk*, for God's sake? Had prison done that to him? For in his pre-prison days, she recalled him as quiet, abnormally so. When he wasn't hurling profanities in Loren's enraged face. At the trial, even at Meg's funeral, he had been first quiet, then abusive.

Marty droned on: "So I finally went up in his shitty old plane. Just to get him off my back. Just 'cause he dared me." Another tremor passed through him. Something in his tone told her to listen carefully.

A gust of wind stung her face. She knew she had to inquire again about Sam and Chris before she could concentrate on how to get past the gun and push him off first. Had Chris crossed his twisted path? Her stomach tightened at the thought.

What's he thinking now?, she wondered nervously, for he fell silent again.

If she broke that silence when he wasn't prepared, she might set him off again.

Casting a quick, concerned glance at the edge of the cliff, she pushed her dread aside. "Marty, is Sam okay?"

She jumped when he spun around. But all he said was: "You think I'd hurt my own kid?"

Katya wanted to believe him. If she knew that Sam was alive, was safe, she could survive anything.

"If you wouldn't hurt Sam, why did you cut the rope on his tube?" she asked cautiously. "You could have killed him. I don't think he's ever going to forget the incident."

"Shit, a little bit of fear's good for a kid. I used to be scared of things. But not anymore." To prove it he did a little skip dance along the rock barrier. "Heights scare lots of people, right Katie? *You're* real scared now."

"No," she lied. "I don't think you really plan to kill me."

"No. I don't think you really plan to kill me," he mimicked. *You are sick.*

She thought of Chris: "Your mind is your most powerful weapon, cherie...in love...in war," she had promised after Sam's abduction. "Together we will find him."

Just hearing that lilting voice in her head sent tingles through her. It was the first bit of warmth she'd had all day.

"I knew the kid wouldn't get hurt—watched him tubing a couple days before. Saw his life jacket. Smart move, Katie." But he smiled with malice. "Reason I cut the rope was to make *you* look bad. Bet that dumb-assed sheriff thought you were a nut case when he didn't find the rope." His crazed laughter bounced off the canyon walls.

It astonished Katya how invincible he thought he was. The way he had ignored the possibility of someone seeing them on the road that morning—all the other mornings. Dragging her up here with just an afterthought to tourists and horny teen-agers.

No sense of reality. No conscience, it seemed. A psychopath.

She paused. Her ears pricked up. Was that a crackling noise in the woods again? Footsteps on dried leaves?

Still seized by fits of demonic laughter, Marty didn't seem to hear anything.

Feigning a crick in her neck, Katya slowly rolled her head back, listened, her mouth dry with anticipation, hoping for a sign.

"Hey, bitch, aren't you curious about me?" His fanatical eyes bored holes into hers. "You know, I killed my old man and those other town dykes. Ya see, bitch, I'm on a mission—search and destroy." He was enjoying the terrified look on Katya's face. "And killing you is gonna be a real pleasure, Katie."

For some sick reason, Marty wanted to continue his confession, "And I'm gonna tell you why I offed him," he added. "Make your day. The secret dies with you— down there." He hooked a thumb in the direction of the canyon, his eyes stone cold.

"You were going to tell me about Sam's grandfather." *Keep him talking. Keep his mind off murder. Pray for a miracle.*

"Does Sam have a grandmother he doesn't know about?"

He started stroking his gun barrel again. "Maybe...you two have lots in common." His words were laced with bitterness.

Shifting her numb backside, she listened as a wail of wind tunneled through the woods, lifting swirls of burnished leaves.

Marty began to walk along the precipice. When he grew tired of that, he stared into the expanse below, seemed to be mesmerized. Accompanying his meditation was the muffled "tap, tap" of the gun against his leg before a torrent of words spilled out of his mouth.

"See, there was this kid whose old man liked flying better than anything. He took the kid up in his private plane one day. Wanted to make a man out of him. Called the kid a faggot 'cause he was scared.

"This kid was no faggot. Tossed cats off bridges. Liked to see cars squash them. Once he broke a bird's wing and tossed it over, too...just to watch it try and fly. Fly. That's all the kid ever heard: 'Flyin's gonna make you free. Brave like your old man,' his father said.

"But the old man was a liar and got punished. It *didn't* set the kid free. Somethin' else did that.

"When they got back from the airport that day, his old man hit the bourbon bottle, tied the kid up, beat him with a belt buckle for bein' scared of heights. It was an air force buckle—had an eagle. Real heavy...." Absently, Marty stroked a scar on the left side of his face.

" 'You're gonna go back up in that plane every Sunday, you little faggot, till you're shittin' engine fuel,' he told his son. But there was no way this kid would ever go up in his father's fuckin' plane again...

"Well, my old man got stinkin' drunk—sat at his fuckin' desk cleanin' his guns. Back and forth, back and forth, he rubbed those guns till I thought he was gonna rub all the silver off them." Marty stroked the barrel of his gun now.

"The old bastard lit a cigarette and left it burnin' in an ash tray...started swiggin' down that bourbon till he passed out." A malevolent smile curved Marty's lips. "That ash tray, well it was full of butts. Didn't take much for me to flick the lit cigarette on the desk where all his papers were...."

Katya listened with perverse fascination as the wind howled and whipped the hair back from her face.

Marty faced her slowly, propped one combat boot up on the barrier.

"There were no more planes, no more beatings. No way he'd ever call me a faggot again...

"Watchin' his papers catch fire was pretty. Fire's pure. Fire cleans. It was so easy. I just walked out the front door and hid while the house burned down." The face across from Katya was calm, the eyes burning with a vengeful light. He pressed the cool metal gun barrel against his cheek. "Died in the line of fire. A real war hero." He chuckled.

Aware that he had changed the noun in the middle of the story from "the kid" to "I," Katya saw her opening. "You're so clever," she told him. "You probably have Sam hidden where no one can find him." Holding her breath, she waited.

His eyes blazed. "Oh, you stupid, stupid bitch." He tucked the gun into the belt of his flightsuit. Shaking his head with disgust, he strode over, grabbed a handful of hair and shook her. Katya yelped with pain. Then he dragged her struggling body to the barrier again.

The awesome panorama in front of her loomed with finality. *This is the way it should happen. Fast. So I don't have time to think.*

"Maybe I don't talk as fancy as you, but I'm not stupid, so you listen, cunt, and listen good. *I'm not stupid!* You can't trick me and you can't butter me up. I can let you go over with your hands tied or you can go over free. Only reason I took that rope off before was 'cause I'm a nice guy and it's more fun that way."

A frenzied attempt to brace her feet against the barrier, just made him laugh scornfully. He kicked at her sneakers and pulled the gun out of his belt with his right hand, and with that arm, placed a choke-hold around her neck. His left hand clutched her hair as he shoved her up on the barricade.

"Look down!" he ordered, but she shut her eyes. A guttural cry of terror escaped her throat.

"Open your eyes!" She opened them to a bright blue sky, gray abutments softened by scattered clusters of pine trees and moss; the twisting stream below.

A wave of dizziness hit her so hard her knees buckled.

He shook her some more.

She started to cry, but the wind dried the tears as quickly as they left her eyes.

"Have a good flight. Happy landing," he whispered in her ear.

Katya smelled her own fear, tasted the canyon's chilling invitation.

"Dizzy..." she murmured. "Wait...."

He suddenly jerked her head back and forced her to look at him. His face was triumphant.

"Now you know how I felt when my old man did this to me up in that airplane. First showin' off to his flying buddy. Doin' stunts, sending the plane into spins. Makin' me read charts and study the control panel at the same time till I almost passed out. Vertigo. Comes when you're up so high, rockin' like crazy. When you think the fuckin' plane's gonna fall apart.

"Know what I said to him, Katie? 'Dizzy...gonna puke.' And the old man slapped my face. He gave his flyin' buddy the controls and shoved my head out the door so I wouldn't puke inside his precious Cessna.... Instead, I puked into the wind and it splashed back in my face. And that's why he beat me later. Cause I *embarrassed* him, the war hero's son got vomit on his plane; on his face; his friggin' flightsuit. So he beat the shit outta me. And then he got drunk...and then I killed him...and then I wasn't afraid anymore."

"And you killed those women. And now you want to kill me. You don't have to be afraid of me," Katya said softly.

He looked at her with surprise as if he had forgotten she was there. "Thought I'd never live to be twelve years old." His body sagged.

For a moment Katya expected him to release her, but in his mind he had gone back to where he was that day and was not on the ledge with her. He was up in that plane, God only knew how many feet in the air.

Sweat dripped down his flushed face. His tormented eyes found hers. He blinked away the image. "Afraid of you?" he spat. "I *hate* you, you queer."

"For Sam's sake, Marty, don't do this."

"Sam's sake? You pathetic cunt. Why should I care about a kid you poisoned? He's just gonna poison men with diseases someday. I'm doin' the world a favor."

"Let me go. Don't burden Sam with my death."

"But that's why I'm here, Katie. To make you and him pay. You, and as many dykes and faggots as I can get my hands on."

"I never did anything to you."

"Wrong, you helped Loren buy my kid and ruin him with those snotty parents of hers. Thought I wasn't good enough for them. You figured I'd just disappear? Huh? That you could buy me off? Well, you're wrong. I got Sam on *my* terms now. If they're rich enough to send me money every month, they've probably got plenty stashed away. And can buy Sam back with it."

His foul face moved in on her again—his hot, acrid breath—his spittle—while the cold breath of the canyon breathed another invitation. "Turnin' out better than I expected. Real simple how it went down." He yanked her closer to the edge. "Rented a room. Got the old man's military junk out of storage. Got your dyke lover tied up like a French roast in a fire trap...ah, justice..." He freed the hand with his gun from her neck and kissed his fingers. Only his left hand grasping her hair kept her from certain death.

"Too bad they're all dead and you're alive. Too bad for you."

"What do you mean, *all* dead?"

Cackling, he whispered in her ear: "Sam's really dead, Katie...those old farts are gonna buy dead meat."

Katya's heart broke. She grabbed hold of his wrist and dug her rubber soles into a crevice in the wide, flat rock that was inches between her and the edge. "Tell me you're joking."

"Relax, Katie. He didn't suffer. After all he's my kid. Only took one bullet." Marty chuckled. "He almost swallowed the barrel when I fed it to him."

"No!" Her anguish was mirrored in a chorus of echoes. "Oh, God, no! NO!"

He turned her around and shoved her to her knees. "I told you to beg."

Beyond caring what happened to her, she grasped his trouser leg. "He's not dead. He's not dead. Tell me he's not dead." Rocking back and forth on her knees, she sobbed.

"Time to die, Katie," he grinned sadistically.

"I don't care. If you killed Sam, you can kill me, too."

"But you gotta care or it's no fun," Marty cajoled. "And I've had a real party makin' you squirm. Was gonna kill you when I blew into town, then one morning I laid eyes on this lesbo bulldyke walkin' down the driveway to her white station wagon. Uniform freak like my old man. It was a sign..." he explained above Katya's tears. "And that afternoon I laid eyes on all those dykes walkin' around town like they owned it. Queertown. Went into a bar. Had me a nice talk with some 'Good ole boys.' They didn't much like the queers outside either, so I figured I'd do 'em a favor. Boy did I luck out. Had a much better idea. It'd make me a hero. Why just kill you when I could clean up the town? Just like in the movies." He laughed jubilantly describing in chilling detail, while Katya crumbled at his feet, the bloody rampage he had wrought on the Deer Falls community of women. And when he was done, he laughed. Was still laughing when he lifted her drained body and stood at the edge of the cliff.

Leslie Grey

Katya looked down with dead, empty eyes. Sam was gone and Chris, too, probably. Suddenly, so was her fear. She could never live with the fathomless sorrow she felt now.

"Say good-bye, Katie," Marty said with chilling finality. "Maybe you'll meet some other dykes where *you're* goin'."

"MARTY!" A voice barked from the edge of the woods.

Katya grasped a handful of his flightsuit. He froze, then stood there uncertainly, barely objecting when she slipped from his fatal hug.

He stared with disbelief at the slim young woman in a purple baseball cap, who had stepped out from behind a tree a few hundred feet away. She was holding up a sheet of lavender paper, waving it above her head.

"Was this an invitation?" Chris shouted over the wind. Moving cautiously away from the oak tree that had concealed her, she smiled reassuringly at a speechless Katya.

Marty blinked. His gun hand shook. As he raised it to shoot Chris, Sara appeared from behind a spruce tree.

"What the hell?" Marty snapped.

"I wouldn't do that, Marty. The party's over. Let Katya go. Now!" Sara warned.

"Oh yeah! Think you dykes scare me?" Infuriated, he tried to grab Katya again, but she twisted away and crouched on the ground watching him, watching the gun.

Then, he didn't know where to look first as two more lavender baseball caps shot up from a cluster of boulders. Spooked, he fired off two rounds. One off a boulder, the other sent a baseball cap flying.

"Shit!" He aimed the gun at Chris, but she moved swiftly to the safety of the tree trunk. The third bullet went wild, the fourth shattered the bark of the tree protecting Chris. His hand was shaking violently now.

"MARTY, MARTY, MARTY...." shouted a chorus of mocking female voices, joining the echoes of gunfire off the canyon walls.

Another voice, in the distance, rose above the din; pure and sweet and heartwrenching: "MOM-MY!"

A joyous surge of adrenaline flooded Katya's heart. Instinctively she bolted towards it.

"Hold it, bitch!"

She hesitated, turned reluctantly, saw Marty's gun pointed straight at her head.

Chris stepped out of her hiding place. Marty wavered and Katya saw her stick a quick hand in the pocket of her cargo pants.

"It's all your fault, you cunt," he told Katya, and steadied the gun trained on her.

When his index finger moved on the trigger, she heard a whine before she saw the smooth stone wing his head and bounce off.

Stunned, enraged, like a vicious, wounded animal, he turned on Chris. "Die!" Spittle flew out of his mouth.

Chris seemed frozen in place. Katya's scream blended with a howling gust of wind. She heard the dreaded shot—its thunderous report from cliff to cliff.

Marty DeLeon uttered one small cry before he flew backward over the edge.

Katya stumbled toward the barricade, but couldn't bring herself to look down. Unlike Icarus, Marty never got his moment in the sun. He plunged swiftly down to meet the sharp granite fingers waiting below.

"Sorry I was late for the party, ladies."

Katya turned around as Sheriff Wendell sauntered out of the woods, his gun smoking. It was the closest he would come to "The Duke" in a shoot 'em up flick.

Dazed, Katya could not believe it was finally over. As if guiding a sleepwalker, Sara and Bev led her away. Soon Molly joined them. With the protective circle of women surrounding her, Katya searched their faces for a pair of startling green eyes. And then she saw Chris and Sam in the distance, backlit by the full splendor of the sun. Their faces sharpened as they drew nearer: one small and dimpled; the other, arresting, framed by rebellious short dark hair.

Her chest swelled, flooded with love—filling all the corners of her heart, as she ran to meet the two waiting with open arms.

The End

About the Author

Leslie Grey is a free-lance writer and landscape artist who lives surrounded by the Catskill Mountains in upstate New York. Nurtured by precious forests and streams, she dreams about a feminist utopia where all choices are possible.

When she is not writing, she packs her camping gear and sleeps under the stars, content in a campfire's glow after a good trout dinner, graciously offered by a generous stream. All the little "fishies" she throws back.

Her goal is to use her writing as a statement. And: "Share the awesome journey to the light."

If You Liked This Book...

Authors seldom get to hear what readers like about their work. If you enjoyed reading this novel, why not let the author know? Simply write the author:

Author's name
c/o Rising Tide Press
5 Kivy Street
Huntington Station, NY 11746

MORE EXCITING FICTION FROM
RISING TIDE PRESS

ROMANCING THE DREAM
Heidi Johanna

This imaginative tale begins when Jacqui St. John leaves northern California looking for a new home, and cruises into the seemingly ordinary town of Kulshan, on the Oregon coast. Seeing the lilac bushes in bloom along the roadside, she suddenly remembers the recurring dream that has been tantalizing her for months—a dream of a house full of women, radiating warmth and welcome, and of one special woman, dressed in silk and leather.... But why has Jacqui, like so many other women, been drawn to this place? The answer is simple but wonderful—the women plan to take over the town and make a lesbian haven. A captivating and erotic love story with an unusual plot. A novel that will charm you with its gentle humor and fine writing.

ISBN 0-9628938-0-3; 176 Pages; $8.95

YOU LIGHT THE FIRE
Kristen Garrett

Here's a grown-up *Rubyfruit Jungle*--sexy, spicy, and side-splittingly funny. Garrett, a fresh new voice in lesbian fiction, has created two memorable characters in Mindy Brinson and Cheerio Monroe. Can a gorgeous, sexy, high school math teacher and a raunchy, commitment-shy ex singer, make it last, in mainstream USA? With a little help from their friends, they can. This humorous, erotic and unpredictable love story will keep you laughing, and marveling at the variety of lesbian love.

ISBN 0-9628938-5-4; 176 Pages; $8.95

EDGE OF PASSION
Shelley Smith

The author of **Horizon of the Heart** presents another absorbing and sexy novel! From the moment Angela saw Micki sitting at the end of the smoky bar, she was consumed with desire for this cool and sophisticated woman, and determined to have her...at any cost. Set against the backdrop of colorful Provincetown and Boston, this sizzling novel will draw you into the all-consuming love affair between an older and a younger woman. A gripping love story, which is both fierce and tender. It will keep you breathless until the last page.

ISBN 0-9628938-1-1; 192 Pages; $8.95

RETURN TO ISIS
Jean Stewart

The year is 2093. In this fantasy zone where sword and superstition meet sci-fi adventure, two women make a daring escape to freedom. Whit, a bold warrior from an Amazon nation, rescues Amelia from a dismal world where females are either breeders or drones. Together, they journey over grueling terrain, to the shining world of Artemis, and in their struggle to survive, find themselves unexpectedly drawn to each other. But it is in the safety of Artemis, Whit's home colony, that danger truly lurks. And it is in the ruins of Isis that the secret of how it was mysteriously destroyed waits to be uncovered. Here's adventure, mystery and romance all rolled into one.

ISBN 0-9628938-6-2; 192 Pages; $8.95

FACES OF LOVE
Sharon Gilligan

A wise and sensitive novel which takes us into the lives of Maggie, Karen, Cory, and their community of friends. Maggie Halloran, a prominent women's rights advocate, and Karen Weston, a brilliant attorney, have been together for 10 years in a relationship which is full of love, but is also often stormy. When Maggie's heart is captured by the young and beautiful Cory, she must take stock of her life and make some decisions.

Set against the backdrop of Madison, Wisconsin, and its dynamic women's community, the characters in this engaging novel are bright, involved, '90s women dealing with universal issues of love, commitment and friendship. A wonderful read!

ISBN 0-9628938-4-6 ; 192 Pages; $8.95

LOVE SPELL
Karen Williams

A deliciously erotic and humorous love story with a magical twist. When Kate Gallagher, a reluctantly **single** veterinarian, meets the mysterious and alluring Allegra one enchanted evening, it is instant fireworks. But as Kate gradually discovers, they live in two very different worlds, and Allegra's life is shrouded in mystery which Kate longs to penetrate. A masterful blend of fantasy and reality, this whimsical story will delight your imagination and warm your heart. Here is a writer of style as well as substance.

ISBN 0-9628938-2-X; 192 Pages; $9.95

DANGER IN HIGH PLACES:
An Alix Nicholson Mystery
Sharon Gilligan

Free-lance photographer Alix Nicholson was expecting some great photos of the AIDS Quilt— what she got was a corpse with a story to tell! Set against the backdrop of Washington, DC, the bestselling author of **Faces of Love** delivers a riveting mystery. When Alix accidentally stumbles on a deadly scheme surrounding AIDS funding, she is catapulted into the seamy underbelly of Washington politics. With the help of Mac, lesbian congressional aide, Alix gradually untangles the plot, has a romantic interlude, and learns of the dangers in high places.

ISBN 0-9628938-7-0; 192 Pages; $9.95

ISIS RISING
Jean Stewart

The eagerly awaited sequel to the immensely popular **Return to Isis** is here at last! In this stirring romantic fantasy, Jean Stewart continues the adventures of Whit (every woman's heart-throb), her beloved Kali, and a cast of colorful characters, as they rebuild Isis from the ashes. But all does not go smoothly in this brave new world, and Whit, with the help of her friends, must battle the forces that threaten. A rousing futuristic adventure and an endearing love story all rolled into one. Destined to capture your heart.

ISBN 0-9628938-8-9;192 Pages; $9.95.

SHADOWS AFTER DARK
Ouida Crozier

Wings of death are spreading over the world of Körnagy and Kyril's mission on Earth is to find the cure. Here, she meets the beautiful but lonely Kathryn, who has been yearning for a deep and enduring love with just such a woman as Kyril. But to her horror, Kathryn learns that her darkly exotic new lover has been sent to Earth with a purpose—to save her own dying vampire world. A tender and richly poetic novel. *ISBN 1-883061-50-4; 224 Pages; $9.95*

How To Order:
Rising Tide Press books are available from you local women's bookstore or directly from Rising Tide Press. Send check, money order, or Visa/MC account number, with expiration date and signature to: Rising Tide Press, 5 Kivy St., Huntington Sta., New York 11746. **Credit card** orders must be **over $25. Remember** to include shipping and handling charges: $4.95 for the first book plus $1.00 for each additional book. *Credit Card Orders Call our Toll Free # 1-800-648-5333.* For UPS delivery, provide street address.

Our Publishing Philosophy

Rising Tide Press is a lesbian-owned and operated publishing company committed to publishing books by, for, and about lesbians and their lives. We are not only committed to readers, but also to lesbian writers who need nurturing and support, whether or not their manuscripts are accepted for publication. Through quality writing, the press aims to entertain, educate, and empower readers, whether they are women-loving-women or heterosexual. It is our intention to promote lesbian culture, community, and civil rights, nationwide, through the printed word.

In addition, RTP will seek to provide readers with images of lesbians aspiring to be more than their prescribed roles dictate. The novels selected for publication will aim to portray women from all walks of life, (regardless of class, ethnicity, religion or race), women who are strong, not just victims, women who can and do aspire to be more, and not just settle, women who will fight injustice with courage. Hopefully, our novels will provide new ideas for creating change in a heterosexist and homophobic society. Finally, we hope our books will encourage lesbians to respect and love themselves more, and at the same time, convey this love and respect of self to the society at large. It is our belief that this philosophy can best be actualized through fine writing that entertains, as well as educates the reader. Books, even lesbian books, can be fun, as well as liberating.

WRITERS WANTED!!!

*Rising Tide Press, Publisher of
Lesbian Novels,
is Soliciting Quality Fiction Manuscripts*

Rising Tide Press is interested in publishing quality Lesbian fiction: romance, mystery, and science-fiction/fantasy. Non-fiction is also welcome, but please, no poetry or short stories.

Please send us the following:

- One page synopsis of plot
- The manuscript
- A brief autobiographical sketch
- Large manila envelope with
sufficient return postage

RISING
TIDE
PRESS

5 KIVY ST.
HUNTINGTON STATION,
N.Y. 11746